THE SCHWARZSCHILD
RADIUS

GUSTAVO FLORENTIN

CURIOSITY QUILLS PRESS

A Division of **Whampa, LLC**
P.O. Box 2160
Reston, VA 20195
Tel/Fax: 800-998-2509
http://curiosityquills.com

ISBN 978-1-62007-610-1 (ebook)
ISBN 978-1-62007-611-8 (paperback)
ISBN 978-1-62007-612-5 (hardcover)

Table Of Contents

CHAPTER ONE

ncient Greek philosophers used a face-slapping technique to engrain a point in the student's mind; here, it conveyed the truth that the girl was going to die.

The Webmaster activated the camera, and Olivia Wallen's image traveled across four continents. Her jet-black hair was cut in bangs across the forehead in the classic China-doll style. Her voluptuous American figure was incongruent with her Thai features and was accented by the red Brazilian bikini which offered a triangle of coverage in the crotch.

"Turn around," said the voice. She did so, revealing the flawlessness of her back and legs.

"The skin is like pearl," said the Webmaster, now addressing the others via web cam. "As you like it in the East. She is five-feet six inches tall. Her measurements are 32-24-33."

The clients on the other side of the world were impressed. Men like Masutatsu Nakayama, Vladimir Zeitkin, and Mohammad Qasim.

Vladimir Zeitkin's loyalty to Putin had won him his own oil company and now he spent his time competing with Paul Allen of Microsoft fame by building the biggest yacht in the world. He collected Greek and Roman statuary and Nazi art looted during World War II. But it took time to build mega-yachts, and while the static images of paintings were sublime, the living, breathing art of torture, suffering, and death redefined beauty.

And there was Mohammad Qasim. There was little entertainment in Saudi Arabia despite his oil billions. He had taken pleasure for a while in abusing the Filipina housemaids he brought in for his entertainment and that of his friends, but that grew dull. He sponsored a small jihad organization and followed their exploits as he followed Manchester United, but blowing up anonymous infidels got repetitive.

Now, without leaving his office, he could witness what surpassed even the public beheadings and honor killings he'd seen.

Masutatsu Nakayama was a man for whom all things become tiresome. Now retired from industry with an estimated fortune of two billion dollars, he was on a quest for the few experiences he had left unvisited. And this site gave it to him.

While other sex sites featured photos and videos, the Webmaster's had live captives. He performed whatever the clients requested. And in the end, they always requested death. This left no doubt that the girls weren't actors. The manner of death came from the depths of the subconscious. He had performed hangings, beheadings, electrocutions, tooth extractions, dismemberments. Occasionally they requested a boy, but usually it was a young girl. The clients voted on the type of victim, the race, age, even social standing. For some of these men, it was their first experience in democracy. Payment consisted of a wire transfer to a Cayman Islands bank account. Half due on winning the auction; half after delivery of the product. The clients paid an initial membership fee, then bid on what they wanted done to the victim. The abuse lasted until the clients agreed it was time for execution. This, too, was put up for auction and only the winner received the final product. The winning bidder received the exclusive live stream and download of his request. It was the eBay of agony.

Each girl could produce bids in excess of two-hundred thousand dollars. The longer the pain was drawn out, the more profit was made. The key was to keep replenishing the supply of victims. And the Webmaster had an endless supply.

"Take off your clothes and turn around. Again. Stand against the wall," he instructed. The terrified girl complied and the contrast of her body against the gray of the concrete produced gasps of pleasure from the audience.

"What is your name?"

"Olivia. Olivia Wallen."

"Age?"

"Sixteen."

"Nationality."

"Please let me go."

"Nationality?"

"American."

She was hyperventilating, and this made her lovely chest heave up and down.

"Where are you from originally?"

"Thailand."

"How did you come here?"

Olivia went into her past as far as she could remember.

"Your grades are exceptional. What university did you plan to attend? I said what university?"

"Harvard."

"A Harvard girl, gentlemen. This should appeal to you. What were you going to study at Harvard?"

The tears streamed down her cheeks as the interrogation had its intended effect.

"Medicine."

"You planned to help humanity?"

"Please let—"

"You must answer the questions. I explained that to you. You planned to help humanity?"

"Yes."

"And what do you do in your spare time? Answer the question. Answer the question."

"Reading."

"Reading. What do you read? Who are you favorite authors?"

"Herman Hesse."

"Who else?"

"Hemingway."

"Good, good. So you're well-read. But let's be honest with these gentlemen, there's also another side to you isn't there?"

She said nothing.

"Answer."

"Yes," she said, finally.

"We'll explore that in due course. Well, there you have it, gentlemen. This concludes the introduction. A mysterious and beautiful girl. And we'll find out more about her in each encounter. Bidding for the first torment starts at fifty thousand dollars with increments of five thousand. Gentlemen, what is your pleasure?"

CHAPTER TWO

Rachel Wallen wasn't the first Ivy League kid to enter the homeless shelter. The other was her sister who had disappeared four days earlier. Yet even as she stepped through the door she sensed that this was only a portal into the world that had swallowed Olivia.

She had changed into her runaway outfit—ratty sneakers, ripped jeans, and disheveled hair. Hopefully, that's all she would have to change to find out what happened to her sister.

Transcendence House was a refuge for runaways in downtown Manhattan. It was located next to Tad's Steaks and across from a sex shop. A young Claretion priest was able to snatch the decaying structure from the purveyors of meat, gaining the plaudits of the mayor and newspapers.

Rachel was received by a woman in her early twenties.

"Welcome to Transcendence House. I'm Sister Karen, a crisis counselor. Let's step over here; I need to ask you a few quick questions."

She would have made a beautiful nun if she had really belonged to an order. But Rachel knew from Olivia that everyone here addressed each other as Brother and Sister.

"First, I want you to know that any information we gather will be held in strictest confidence," said Sister Karen. She put a new form in her clipboard.

"Name?"

"Rachel Barino."

"Age?"

"Sixteen." Eighteen was too old to be admitted here.

"Have you been tested for HIV in the last two months?"

"No."

"How long have you been on the streets?"

About an hour and a half, thought Rachel.

"Two months."

"How have you been surviving?"

"The kindness of strangers." She remembered that line from *Streetcar.*

Sister Karen lowered her voice.

"Have you experienced any physical or sexual abuse?"

"No."

"Are you addicted to any drugs?"

"No."

"Do you have any drugs or weapons on you?"

"No."

"Where is your family?"

"Vermont."

"Would you be willing to return home if we gave you a bus ticket?"

"There's nothing for me there."

"Is there anything you need right now?"

"I need to speak to Father Massey."

"Father Massey interviews all our new guests. First, I'll take you upstairs where you can shower and change. You can leave your belongings in those lockers. We don't allow contraband, so I'll ask you to put all your things on this tray."

Rachel emptied her pockets and knapsack. She wondered how the cell phone would go over, but no one questioned it. The modern runaway must be well equipped. Upstairs, Rachel was given her own towel, bar of soap, a T-shirt and sweat pants, a King James Bible, and a journal.

"You're welcome to spend the night," said Sister Karen.

"If it's okay."

"Certainly."

After the requisite shower, Sister Karen led Rachel downstairs to the cafeteria.

"This will hold you till dinner." Rachel was served a bowl of vegetable soup and a ham and Swiss sandwich. She sat diagonally to another girl who had just come in off the streets and watched her devour the food with a desperation that Rachel would have no trouble feigning; she was desperate, too.

Sister Karen returned with a young man of about twenty-one.

"I'm Brother Mark. We all eat together here as a rule. And I'd like to give you the other rules," he said as he handed Rachel a paper with the word *RULES* written in medieval script like an edict.

He struck Rachel as a timid boy who had been given the incongruent task of laying down the law to newcomers.

"No drugs, cigarettes, alcohol, or sex. No entering the boys' dorm without permission from one of the brothers. We have showers, beds, a library, a clinic, a chapel and counseling. We offer classes in computers and GED tutoring and various shop classes. There are phones available to call parents or legal guardians. We rise at six a.m., make our own beds, breakfast, prayer time till seven-thirty, tutoring till eleven, free time until eleven-thirty. We then have lunch, do chores till three, have counseling, study, dinner and one hour of TV between eight and nine. Lights out at ten sharp. Is there anything in those rules that you don't think you'll be able to comply with?"

"No."

"I should tell you that we operate here on the principle of tough love," he continued. "Agápe love is brotherly love, unconditional love. But we temper this with strict discipline."

Rachel sensed that unconditional love was not about to envelope her; it was about to test her.

Father Evan Massey had a lot on his mind. Tomorrow he would be testifying before a Senate subcommittee on runaway children and he needed to get the tone right. He checked the order of his three-by-five cards and stood in front of the mirror where he practiced his delivery. Massey had often seen others as they sat before the microphones reading from sheets, boring the hell out of the world. He liked General David Petraeus' style and, like Petraeus, he would also be wearing a uniform.

Massey was tall, about six one with full, black hair cut in layers. He sported a business suit and looked more like a mergers and acquisitions executive than a cleric. A lawyer's brief with a gold monogram sat on the desk. The office was spacious, but modest, containing a wall of books, two file cabinets, and a metal desk with a banker's lamp. There were photos of Massey with the mayor and governor of New York and some athletes who signed balls and T-shirts at fund-raisers. A large framed Picasso print adorned an otherwise blank wall.

Two weeks earlier, he had been contacted by the office of the First Lady, who was considering him to head up a special office dedicated to addressing the problem of runaways. The post would give him the power and the pulpit to do what he did best—bring attention to an issue. He saw himself thriving in Washington where the powerful want to be seen in the company of a man of impeccable character—a rare and valuable commodity in that town.

At age thirty-seven, his career was in full swing. It seemed that everything he touched succeeded. He had appeared on Oprah and The Daily Show. After he spoke at an MTV AIDS benefit, People Magazine did a story on him entitled, "The Hippest Man of the Cloth." Publishers had approached him about a book deal. He believed that anything he imagined would materialize. He was unstoppable.

His performance tomorrow was crucial—all the more so since it would be covered by C-SPAN. There had already been a touchy moment at the airport when a reporter asked him if he could shed any more light on the disappearance of Olivia Wallen. He had handled it well by replying that it had been his privilege to know and work with Olivia for several months before she vanished, and that she was one of the most special people he had ever known. That made it to print.

There was a knock on the open door.

"Come in." He shook hands with the new girl, introducing himself. "Have a seat." She was petite, had a pony tail, and smelled like Irish Spring soap.

Massey glanced at the information sheet; then set it aside.

"I just want you to know, Rachel, that any data that we gather on you is held in strictest confidence. That said, I would like us to be totally straight with each other. Our guests usually stay for a few days to up to a month. After that, we may be able to arrange transitional housing where you can stay while you train for a job. The object of the program is to make you self-sufficient, not dependent. We've never turned anyone away, although on occasion we've had to ask people to leave for breaking the rules. According to this, you've been told the rules, so there's no need to go over that. Do you know what tough love is, Rachel?"

"I've heard the term."

"Let me give you our take on it. It means that the basic underlying love, which we all deserve and which everyone here receives, doesn't always come across as affection. If an individual breaks the rules, consequences have to be imposed in a way that will be most effective for that person. We don't hit people here—God knows most of our kids have gotten enough of that. Our objective is change, not punishment. And change is what it's all about—evolving. I believe in the infinite power of human transformation." He loosened his tie as if emphasizing this point.

"I don't know if you're going to be with us for a day or a month, but there's one lesson that you're going to come away with—the law of cause and effect. Everything you do while you're here will have consequences, and our job is to make those consequences swift and apparent. Here we address each other as Brother and Sister. Do you have any questions?"

"Yes, Father. I'm looking for Sister Olivia. Olivia Wallen. She volunteered here for a long time and she helped me a lot on the streets. She and I were very close—she was the only person I could talk to."

He rose and tried to soften his expression. "I don't have good news for you, Rachel. Olivia has apparently disappeared. The police are looking for her."

"I know she's disappeared, Father. Will you hear my confession?"

CHAPTER THREE

For penance say ten Our Fathers and ten Hail Marys. Go in peace in the name of the Father, the Son, and the Holy Spirit. I want you to reflect on what you've done. You do seem very troubled, Rachel."

"I am troubled. Did you know Olivia well, Father?"

"I try not to get too close to anyone here on a personal basis, neither the counselors nor the kids. You just can't be effective if you're too emotionally involved. I found her to be very caring and certainly promising."

"Did she ever give any sign that something was wrong?"

"I recall an incident a few months ago—we were at our yearly retreat upstate. I noticed Olivia had been missing for several hours and I found her about a half mile from our lodge, just sitting in the stream in her street clothes. When I called to her, she hesitated, then she came out and fell into my arms sobbing. I asked her what was wrong and she just said she didn't want to talk about it. I didn't insist—looking back, perhaps I should have."

Rachel noticed how smoothly the priest had related that story, which she knew couldn't be true. "You think it was a problem with a boy? He might know something about her whereabouts."

"There's no way of knowing that now. At any rate, these things are best left to the police."

"I'm afraid for her, Father. I fear for the worst. She was like my sister."

His hand reached over now in the role of counselor and rested on hers. "Don't let your heart be troubled. I'll pray for both of you."

Rachel stepped out of the priest's office with more trepidation than ever. Father Massey was lying.

"We'll be watching a short film now," said Sister Karen as Rachel exited the priest's office.

She was led to a room at the end of the hall where other newcomers were already seated in front of a fifty inch TV. The screen came to life with a film entitled, "The Infinite Reservoir."

"I'm Evan Massey," said the narrator, "and this is the record of my mission to India in 1995. I was a twenty-two-year-old graduate with a vague idea that I wanted to do something for the world and I was in a hurry to do it. It's a visual journal, a rough record of the events that occurred over a period of about eighteen months, so there isn't much continuity, but I'll try to tie it together with hindsight. Some of the scenes are hard to watch—they're the kind of images that would require a warning about viewer discretion were they on TV. But look at the problems of these people and then ask yourself honestly if your world is really as bad as you think."

The first scene showed a young Evan Massey, wearing shoulder-length hair, walking side by side with a village elder.

The problem was this:

The people in the village of Krupal in northern India were starving. Every year, the monsoons brought crops and plenty for a short time. Then the dry weather arrived and there was no water for months. They watched their children wither away and die. They saw their own flesh desiccate on their bodies. By tradition, they put their dead on rooftops where the birds picked at the remains, so in dry weather, the roofs were thatched with bones. Every year as the Krupalis starved, the loan sharks came around and lent them money, which was owed for generations and which they had no hope of repaying. The people had lived like this, they said, for two thousand years.

Evan Massey told them that there was a way out, but the work required would be so hard that probably a quarter of them would die from it. But he promised them that if they succeeded, the rest would live. The people were willing to make this sacrifice.

"I'm an engineer," he told them.

"Actually," corrected the voice-over, "I had a two-year degree with an interest in civil engineering and a year of experience doing construction work."

"In those hills," resumed the younger Massey, "there's limestone and iron-rich soil that we'll use to make mortar that's twenty times stronger than concrete. These stones you see all around you—these millions of stones—all these stones will be gone when we've finished." They had five months.

The plan was to build an immense reservoir in the earth, twelve-feet deep and two acres in area, reinforced with stone and mortar. This would catch the monsoon rains and keep the crops alive during the dry season via irrigation ditches scored into the rock-hard soil. For tools, there were shovels, pick axes, baskets, and bare hands.

He chose a site that was in a depression, but still above the fields so that the water could be diverted downward toward the crops. Here the soil was so compacted that it could break a pick ax. Two thousand women, men, and children were organized into teams that mined the limestone, hauled it and gathered the stones that would line the wall of the basin. Another team of women gathered what little food they could. The footage showed Massey taking a soil sample, planting marker stakes, helping an old woman carry a basket of rocks. The people who had started out so dark became white as specters from the limestone they crushed. Where there were no tools; other stones were used to crush stones. Temperatures reached one hundred twenty degrees, but there was no respite. The monsoons wouldn't wait, and if the rains came with the construction unfinished, months would pass before they could try again.

Each day two or three died from heat, thirst, and exhaustion. There was horrific footage of vultures eating the bodies as they awaited burial at the end of the day. Massey forbade them to put their dead on rooftops. He told them that they had learned to dig and from now on would bury their dead in the ground. The idea was simply to change them in any way, to get them to break the mindset of the last two thousand years that had led them to this state of abject misery.

The lens tended to dwell on Massey. Massey surveying, swinging a pick, waving his hand over an expanse of land with drawings under his arm. Massey tending the sick and injured. Massey with the multitude gathered around him as he spoke in Hindi.

Three days before the first rains arrived, the last stone was put in place.

The next scene was shot many months later. The skies were clear as the camera panned across the stoneless landscape. The lens finally turned toward the reservoir and there were men looking across it as people do when they behold the sea for the first time.

The villagers now addressed Evan Massey as Baba, a term of respect meaning "father." Great celebrations were held as, for the first time, crops were harvested in the dry season.

In voice-over, Massey said that the people were able to sell their crops to surrounding villages. They prospered and brought in medicines and vaccinated their children against polio for the first time. The usurers were paid off, then run out of town when they returned. There was shot after shot of smiling faces, children laughing and playing in a small pool of water that had been set aside for just that purpose. Water, which had forever been their brutal master, had become their playmate. Self-esteem and self-empowerment had replaced slavery and death. One couldn't help coming away from the film awed at what one man can do.

The lights came on and the moment was ripe for comment.

"I'm Brother Kenneth," said a young man of nineteen, who had been watching from the back of the room. "You've seen an extraordinary film. What do you think is the point of showing you this—Latisha?"

"Well, he say in the beginning that it's to make us realize that our problems aren't that bad," said a black girl.

"Has it done that for you?"

"It makes you feel good for a few minutes, but when five minutes pass, my life is still fucked up."

"We don't use those words here. I'll let that go this time. What were those people willing to give in order to change their lives? You—Rachel?"

"Their lives."

"That's right. They decided that life wasn't worth living the way they were living it, and that life itself is worth sacrificing in order to regain their dignity and the right to determine their own destiny. My question is, what are you willing to do to solve your problems? You can answer that, go ahead," he said to Rachel.

"I would do anything."

In the rec room, Rachel sat opposite a black boy who had given testimony after dinner. His name was Brother Horace. He was fifteen and his personal mission in life was to go to every major disaster in the country and assist. He was in the Midwest during the great floods, in North Carolina when Edward hit, setting up tents and feeding people. He dug people out of rubble during Katrina. He was eight, then, and it was his own house.

"You didn't say how you ended up in New York," she said to him.

"My family got wiped out. Lost my grandmother and cousins I lived with. After the disaster, people from New Orleans scattered all over the country. I was sent here to stay with a family. But doing a kindness loses its shine like everything else. It cost money to keep people around. I ain't much of a conversationist. I'm workin' on that. That's why I'm talkin' to you. I ended up in foster care and these folks got tired of me, too. I don't like bein' a burden. So I left. Walked the streets for a couple of months and ended up here. I'm a man now. I can take care of myself. I'm training for electronics technician, but I already told them that when disaster strikes, I'm out the door."

"So you sit here waiting for a disaster?"

"And I'm on the road." His eyes shifted back to the pawns on the chessboard.

Rachel considered whether Brother Horace dealt with lesser crises.

"Brother Horace, I need your help."

"Listening."

She sat next to him.

"I had a close friend who used to counsel here—Olivia Wallen. Did you know her?"

"I knew her good. She taught me computers. But what kind of help do you mean—I don't give the holding hands kind." He cut a diagonal across the board with a bishop.

"Did Olivia have a falling out with Father Massey?"

"That I don't know."

"Why did she stop counseling here?"

"She just stopped coming."

"Do you know of anyone who would want to hurt her?"

The boy's brows furrowed again. "Sometimes we find ways of hurting ourselves." He castled for white.

"Was she—hurting herself?"

"I know she was," he said without looking up.

"How?"

18

Now he faced her again. "She had a bad flaw with all she had going for her."

"And what was that?"

"Sometimes you end up becoming the people you're tryin' to help. I mean, she changed while she was here, before our very eyes."

"How?" said Rachel, lowering her voice.

"Not to speak ill of anyone—but she was makin' porn flicks."

"Huh?" Rachel knew she had heard him right and braced herself for Horace's next sentence.

"I ain't lyin' to you. She turned into a stone ho."

CHAPTER FOUR

The next day, Rachel left Transcendence House after morning services and returned home to East Northport. She passed the flyers she and her neighbors had put up, pictures of Olivia with the caption, *MISSING*, with a description of the clothes she was last seen wearing—jeans, cowboy boots, and a plaid shirt. She also had a blue fanny pack with Thermofax insulation which contained her glucose tabs, Sunny Delight orange drink, granola snacks, and insulin and syringe wrapped in a plastic bag full of ice. Olivia had Type I diabetes and needed insulin injections every few hours. She always carried enough with her for one day. That would have run out four days ago.

Rachel's high school graduation present was parked in the driveway. The two-year-old midnight blue Mustang now seemed ostentatious.

Rachel's parents were huddled in the living room listening to the news for anything. This was just a distraction as Detective McKenna had promised to inform them of any breaks in the case before the media got hold of it. But the critical first forty-eight hours had passed with nothing to report.

At forty-four, Elizabeth Wallen had aged beyond her years, despite having more joys than the average parent. It was her nature to worry. She went through life inventing things to keep her awake at night. Since last week, she no longer had to manufacture reasons to worry. Ed Wallen was more positive, and at fifty, was looking forward to a quiet retirement, free of mortgage and college tuitions. Rachel didn't want to repeat the mediocrity of their lives.

"Anything?" Rachel said, knowing the answer.

"They put her in the database for Missing and Exploited Children," her mother said.

That's pathetic, thought Rachel.

"ABC News will be here later," said Ed Wallen. "We have to keep her face on TV."

They didn't ask her about her college orientation, and that was just as well. Rachel was supposed to have spent the night at the Columbia dorm where she would be starting classes this fall.

Since Olivia's disappearance, Rachel's friend, Joules, had created a website called OliviaAlert.org with pictures of Olivia and contact numbers. Rachel had called 48 Hours, Dateline, and Inside Edition, asking them to run a story on Olivia and sent them the press kit she had prepared containing photos of Olivia playing cello and receiving fencing awards. She hoped the media would broadcast it endlessly as they did with Elizabeth Smart playing the harp. So far, only 48 Hours had shown an interest.

The search team had set up its headquarters in the First Methodist Church and Waldbaum's had donated food and paper plates to help feed them. They had combed the area but found nothing. They didn't expect to; Olivia's last phone call was from Manhattan.

Rachel had read about all the other things families of missing children did to get the attention of the public: get bumper stickers printed, buttons made, run/walk events, cake sales. But all this seemed so futile.

Rachel got a glass of water and sat down.

"I heard back from 48 Hours," said Rachel. "They're willing to run a one-minute spot on her on next week's show, but want to wait another couple of days for police to confirm that she's not a runaway. They don't do runaways."

"I was expecting to see her picture nonstop on TV like when the Smart girl vanished," said her father. "There's nothing."

"She was kidnapped from her bed," said Rachel. "That makes a difference. She was also fourteen. The younger, the more coverage—that seems to be the way it works. At sixteen, Olivia is near the cutoff."

"But how can we prove that to anyone—that she didn't run away?" he said. "This isn't right. It isn't right."

"We were lucky to get an Amber Alert out for her, only because she's diabetic," said Rachel.

"I leave the light on for her every night," said her mother. "And make her a toasted cheese sandwich." She put her face in her hands. "We're powerless."

"We're not powerless," said Rachel.

"But what can we do?" the mother sobbed.

"We're not powerless."

Rachel went upstairs and started looking online for the porn video of Olivia. Brother Horace said it was on slutload.com. There were thousands of sex scenes and no index or means of narrowing it down to a particular one, short of looking at them all. Each page consisted of twenty-four thumbnails, and there were over eleven-hundred pages going back two years. This was going to be a first for her. She clicked on a scene and, without ceremony, two people were screwing on a bed. There was a progress indicator on the bottom of the screen which she used to advance the video. No Olivia in this one. Next. So it went for three hours. Why did she believe him? This was sickening. She couldn't believe the things girls did on camera for money. By afternoon, Rachel collapsed in bed and slept.

When Rachel's parents adopted Olivia from an orphanage in Thailand, they took it as a sign that her birthday fell on the same day as Rachel's. She was raised Catholic, though in the last few years, Olivia had started investigating her roots. Her family was Buddhist, and she came from a village so poor that parents often sold their children to feed the rest of the family.

Olivia brought only joy and pride to her new parents. She skipped the third grade, was the salutatorian in middle school, a fencing champion in high school. At sixteen, Harvard had accepted her for the fall. She had always been gregarious and popular, in contrast to Rachel's quiet and reserved demeanor. Rachel had even been a little jealous of the way Olivia could enter a room and immediately become the center of attention. She was beautiful, true, with long black hair and tall figure. She had only to flash that smile and things would begin to gravitate her way. She fended off boys throughout her freshman and sophomore years in high school until the junior prom, which she attended. Rachel didn't get asked.

Olivia could have made a career out of at least four talents. Making friends was another of her gifts. Over the last year, she had acquired forty-seven chat mates in her Yahoo Messenger. Rachel didn't know forty-seven people in this world, let alone forty-seven she'd want to talk to. Before the police took Olivia's PC, Rachel had cloned the hard drive onto the second drive of her own computer in order to comb through her emails for some clue to her whereabouts and state of mind. Several of these friends had struck up online conversations with her over the last four days, and Rachel had had to inform them that Olivia had disappeared.

Olivia's Yahoo Messenger was up and someone was now trying to contact her online.

U there? said the screen.

Rachel was in no mood to get into another conversation. It was three in the morning, and she was tired, but couldn't sleep any more. Over the last few hours, Rachel had chatted with at least twelve friends on Olivia's Messenger list and was tired of being the bearer of bad news. The ID said, *Acharavaypor.*

Hi, Rachel typed.

Sorry late.

OK.

Cam? requested Acharavaypor.

Sorry, no cam, answered Rachel. *Dropped it last night and need a new one.* It was an effort just to type, let alone go looking for the web-cam. Plus, she looked like a mess.

OK. You have news?

No news yet. Rachel couldn't remember if she had already chatted with this one.

What you mean?

Just that, typed Rachel.

What about your promise? What about passport and money?

Now Rachel was wide awake.

You promised me. And now you forget.

I didn't forget. I'm still working on it. Rachel wrote. This was someone new and not a native speaker.

OK.

Cam? asked Rachel.

Let me change PC. This has no cam. BRB.

Ok.

Rachel quickly combed through her sister's emails for some sign of this person. And why did she apologize for being late? Did her sister chat regularly at three in the morning?

23

I'm back.

Acharavaypor@yahoo.com sent Rachel the invite to her webcam. Rachel accepted and waited for the face to materialize.

The image appeared and the person at the other end tousled with the camera to point it.

When it stabilized, Rachel was looking into her sister's face.

CHAPTER FIVE

Rachel was dumbstruck. It looked like Olivia, but with a threadbare T-shirt and an expression of ineffable sadness.

Fix cam for next time, the girl typed. *Your face gives me joy.*

You look beautiful, wrote Rachel.

Terrible. Terrible here. We have to hurry. They plan to take me to new place soon. And more men than ever.

Rachel quickly assessed what she was looking at. This girl thought she was talking to Olivia. Behind the girl was a clock showing the same time as here in New York—3:09 a.m.—but there was daylight streaming in through the window. This girl was on the other side of the world.

More men? asked Rachel.

Now more men. Ten, fifteen men a day. And harder to come to Internet café.

Rachel was slowly constructing the life of the person opposite her. Yet all she could say was, *okay.*

You say it takes four weeks to get passport. Already six weeks pass.

Rachel scrambled to reply. *I'm still waiting. Where is the new place they are taking you to?*

Outside of Chiang Mai. Fifty kilometer I think. I don't know if there is an Internet there. I don't know if I will see you again. Last night one girl try to escape. They beat her, then make her work today. She charge half price now. You have to help me. U r my sister.

I will help you, said Rachel.

Why passport is late?

There are new rules now. Terrorism.

We have much planning and not much time. Tong, he get more drunk now and beat everyone. If he find out my plan, he will kill me.

Don't say that. Let's go over the plan again.

Once I get passport and money, I can get e-ticket, so Tong cannot find plane ticket. He searches everything. I can hide money in my mattress. He makes me go buy beer every day, so I will take cab to airport. I have to find out how much money it need for bribe officials, then I tell you.

What officials do you need to bribe?

Airport security. They need to put entry stamp on passport. You tell me this.

Sure. And anyone else?

Maybe someone at the airport who see me. If Tong follow me, he will bribe, so I have to be ready to bribe same. It's really bad now. You understand?

I won't let you down.

Thank you. U r all I have. Everyone betray. I trust no one. You tell your parents about me? They know I come?

Rachel thought about this one.

Yes, I told them. You are loved and welcome here.

I never forget your help. I have HIV test last week. It come negative today. So glad.

That's great. Great news.

Men don't want condom. Insist no condom.

Rachel didn't write anything.

And ten, fifteen men a day. I don't like to give you my problem.

As God is my witness, I'll get you out of there.

God bless you, sis. We have five minutes. Tell me again about New York.

New York?

How beautiful life in New York.

Rachel put her face in her hands.

It's a beautiful and peaceful place where you can be anything you want to be. And the city is most beautiful at night when you can see millions of lights. When you come here, we'll go shopping in the mall and see the movie stars in Times Square.

That sound heaven. I go back now or they catch me.

When will I see you?

I try come back tomorrow. I love you.

Why would Olivia have hidden this from her? What else was she hiding? Rachel lay in bed unable to get Brother Horace's words out of her mind.

Stone ho.

CHAPTER SIX

The next morning, Rachel confronted her parents.

"How could you have kept it a secret from me all these years?" said Rachel. "It tore me apart when she had to go back to a whorehouse and I stayed here in my warm safe bed. This explains a lot."

"She was already adopted when we found Olivia," said Ed Wallen.

"We would have never separated them," said her mother. "We were told her sister had already been adopted by a rich European family. What were we supposed to do?"

"You could have told me. Did you tell Olivia that she had a twin sister?"

"Why tell her about someone who wasn't part of her life and who she would probably never meet?" said her mother.

"Well, they did meet—how?"

"Online. Bookface, whatever," said her father.

"So this is going on for four months and what—I'm not part of this family?"

"We didn't want to upset you," said her mother.

"You didn't want me to side with Olivia."

"Even if we were willing to take her in..."

"Take her in? Is that how you put it?"

"Calm down," said her father. "It's not as easy as it was when we adopted your sister. Once immigration found out that she's a prostitute, they'd probably deny her entry. I made that phone call to an attorney."

"She's an underage sex slave. People get asylum in this country for a lot less than that. Did you ask that question?"

"Even if we could get her entry—I'm an accountant, not a commando. How was I supposed to get her out of there?"

"Did you even try before giving up? Your sixteen-year-old daughter has more fight than you. Do you know what that poor girl is doing right now?"

"Enough, Rachel! Right now I have to deal with getting my own daughter back—your sister."

"We can't deal with these two things at once," said her mother. "I just want my baby back." She had that bug-eyed look that was beyond reason or persuasion. Rachel left the room before saying something she'd regret.

Rachel slammed the door of her room and had to steady herself on the edge of the bunk bed. She was starting Columbia in four days and her world was collapsing. Anger was now her best friend as it had been so often.

In times of great strife, Rachel found refuge in The Box. She took it down from the top shelf of her closet and removed a key from her drawer to open it. Inside was the sum total of Rachel Amanda Wallen's worldly accomplishments. There was her valedictory speech from Northport Middle School, the medal for writing, the medal for social sciences awarded for her essay on the philosopher kings in modern society. There was a medal given to her by the town of East Northport for saving a seventy-year-old man by administering the Heimlich maneuver in a Burger King when she was twelve. There was the rosary blessed by John Paul II.

Then there was the Intel Award.

The Intel was the Nobel Prize of high school. Each entry had to be an original piece of work in one of the sciences, and students from all over the country vied for one of the top forty slots that sent them to Washington D.C. for the selection of the final ten winners. Anyone who gets into the top forty was guaranteed admission to virtually any college in the United States. The top prize was a hundred thousand dollars.

She unfolded the letter notifying her that she was going to DC. If she ever won a real Nobel Prize, she didn't think it would give her the same transcendent joy.

It is our pleasure to inform you that your entry, "Characterizing Human and Chimpanzee Sera Immune Reactivity Against V1/V2 Regions of the HIV

Envelope Protein" has been selected for the Semifinalist round of the Intel Science Talent Search to be held in Washington DC…

Nothing, not even children, could ever give her this happiness.

She returned from D.C. with thirty thousand dollars—sixth place nationwide. With this money and the fourteen thousand dollar scholarship, Rachel had enough to get her through the first year-and-a-half at Columbia.

But heaven had not yet finished pouring forth its blessings. She had completed her Intel project under the mentorship of Dr. Nandagopal Singh, the Nobel laureate and director of the Memorial Sloan Kettering Cancer Center. She opened the envelope with the recommendation she had sent to every Ivy League university in the country. They all accepted her.

Dear Sir:

For the past eighteen months, Ms. Rachel Wallen has conducted research under my mentorship at Memorial Sloan Kettering Cancer Center. The subject of her research was the characterizing of human and chimpanzee sera immune reactivity against V1/V2 regions of the HIV envelope protein, a subject of formidable complexity. I found her grasp of theory and laboratory technique to be remarkable for an investigator of her age. I was particularly impressed with her ability to think originally in the design of her experiments. She also possesses the one quality I hold above all others in this field: tenacity. She is a consummate scientist in every sense.

Yours truly,

Dr. Nandagopal Singh, Director,

Memorial Sloan-Kettering Cancer Center

It would take more than tenacity to get her two sisters back. And she was going to get them back.

CHAPTER SEVEN

Kirsten Schrodinger's battered image was sent across the world to her admirers. She had entertained them well and they had paid well. She was on her knees chained to a concrete wall. The Webmaster now presented her for the next round of torment.

"We'll begin the bidding."

Twenty-thousand.

Twenty-five.

Thirty-five.

Forty.

"Come gentlemen. This is a blonde, blue-eyed fifteen-year-old. A rare find from Minnesota. Let your imaginations run free. Think of the possibilities. Let me offer a few suggestions…"

The bidding resumed.

"Sold to Client Number One for sixty-three thousand. A fine purchase. Please submit in detail the procedure I am to follow." An email instantly arrived. Client Number One was prepared. The Webmaster decrypted the email and quickly read it. He was impressed with the depravity of the request.

"I'll have to purchase a few items to perform this, sir. Please log in tomorrow at the same time and we'll have a private session. The three of us."

The man entered Home Depot and went to aisle five. He tossed a pair of gauntlet rubber gloves into his cart, then had ten feet of chain cut to length. This was followed by a propane torch, four large D-clamps and fifteen feet of rope. Next was the paint department where he gathered a plastic drop cloth, vinyl floor knife, and telescoping paint handle. In the tool aisle, he found a heavy duty drill. Two huge Rubbermaid storage bins with covers completed the purchase.

Next he had to pick up more insulin for the other kid or she'd croak before she made him any money. The Webmaster was riding high, money was rolling in. He had a trip lined up for Thailand after delivering the final downloads for these two girls. Of course, he had to keep mining for more kids.

When he got back he logged in to his Yahoo Messenger.

Hi, u there? wrote thirteen-year-old Alice.

Waiting for you, wrote the Webmaster.

CHAPTER EIGHT

T hat's a remarkable story," said Detective John McKenna.

"Would you like some coffee, detective?" asked Ed Wallen.

"No thanks, sir. What else can you tell me about Olivia's sister—Achara?"

"She's a stranger to us," said Elizabeth.

"All we know is that she was adopted by a well-to-do family from—Norway, I think," said Ed. "That's what we were told."

McKenna noticed how Ed Wallen had to complete that thought for his wife, who was clearly falling apart.

"And Olivia wanted to bring her to America?"

"First, we would have to get her out of the place where—"

"The brothel," said Rachel, interrupting her mother.

"I'm not a rich man," said Ed Wallen. "We don't even know where she is. In Chiang Mai somewhere. There's a brothel on every street corner in that country. We just couldn't help her."

"How did Olivia plan to help? You mentioned she was waiting for a passport?" asked the detective.

"That's right," said Rachel. "I didn't want to start from scratch or she would know I wasn't Olivia."

"Why did you pretend you were Olivia? Once you realized who she was, why not just tell her you're Olivia's sister? She might know that Olivia had planned to meet someone or go somewhere."

"I didn't know who she was at first, then after, it would have been like I was lying to her. She might have cut me off right there. She's very suspicious, and she doesn't need the news that her twin sister, and only hope in life just disappeared."

"There's nothing new on your end, detective?" asked Ed.

McKenna figured the father was waiting for him to volunteer this. He regretted not bringing it up first. "We've gone through all her emails and know that Olivia was corresponding with several men throughout the country. She was a member of a sort of mail-order bride site. A site where American and European men meet Asian women. Local police have questioned all these men and so far we have no reason to believe any of them were involved in her disappearance."

"And how old are these men?" asked Ed.

"Thirties to mid-forties."

"Isn't it sick for these old guys to be chatting with a sixteen-year-old?"

"In all the correspondence, Olivia was posing as an eighteen-year-old. They might be dirty old men, but it's not illegal."

"Why on earth would she be doing that?"

"Maybe Olivia was trying to get someone to fall in love with her sister by posing as her. Then *he* might get her out."

"Possible," said McKenna. He wrote that one down in his notebook. McKenna was a prolific note-taker. He observed the interior decoration, the CD's people owned, if there was dust in the air vents. Ninety percent of it was useless, but occasionally a valuable clue was buried in things he had written down months before.

One time, he was working a cold case of a murdered woman. The husband was distraught throughout the initial investigation. Cooperated fully with the police, appealed to the public. Inconsolable. Police got nowhere. Two years later, McKenna was reviewing his notes on the case. He had observed that a golf club was found in the garage. The head had been cut off and replaced with a magnet. McKenna figured at the time that it was for picking up metallic parts like screws that had fallen into tight places. Sometime after that, he had watched the Discovery Channel where they called it a meteorite stick, used to test rocks for their magnetic properties. You need three things for meteorite hunting: a metal detector, a meteorite stick, and a pickaxe. The metal detector and meteorite stick were in his notes, but no pickaxe. McKenna figured that was buried in the back yard. Long story short, there it was. The murder weapon. Case closed.

"When did Olivia first tell you that she had found her sister?" asked the detective.

"About four months ago," said Elizabeth, who was staring into empty space.

"How did she react when you were reluctant to bring her here?"

"We argued. It flared up on several occasions," said Ed. "We just couldn't talk about it in a civil way. I tried explaining that getting her out of there was going to be next to impossible. You have to bribe people every step of the way in that country. We'd have to go there and get the local law to help us, the same law that protects the brothels. And even if I could do this without getting killed, we don't have the money for that kind of a fight. I've got two daughters starting college."

"Did she ever threaten to leave?"

He shook his head. "She became distant. I know she was resentful, but my mind was made up. You can't save the whole world."

"Before the issue of her sister came up, did you notice any change in her behavior?"

"I always thought she had too much on her plate. Academics, fencing, cello, volunteering. But she always pulled a victory out of it. Champion fencer—who knew? So I never told her to pull back. I was amazed by how much she could do. It was so much more than I ever did."

"And she never mentioned anything that was bothering her, besides Achara?"

"Olivia was never the kind of girl to express her feelings openly," said Elizabeth. "Opinions, yes. Feelings, no. She would say things like 'I love you,' but she never talked about herself. So you never really knew what was going on inside her."

"Have you gotten any tips from the Amber Alert, Detective?" asked Ed.

"All dead ends so far. It seems she had to be hiding something if she said she was going to attend a lecture when there were no lectures that day. Unless she was mistaken about the date. Is that likely?"

"She never went anywhere without getting online first and doing a MapQuest and finding out everything before setting out," said Rachel. "She hated having her time wasted. Olivia wouldn't have left the house without being certain that there was a lecture. And the lecture she described wasn't even scheduled, so it's not like she was just mistaken about the date. There was no lecture on Atlantis at the Museum of Natural History."

So she was *hiding something,* thought McKenna.

"According to everyone at her school, she was an extremely popular girl. And you're sure she had no boyfriend? Would you know if she did?"

"She never talked about it to me," said Rachel.

McKenna noticed the blank faces on the others. Not a lot of communication in this family, if they didn't know that. He should talk.

"Is it possible she joined a cult of some kind? That's common."

"That doesn't sound like Olivia," said Ed. "She wasn't exactly a regular Catholic, but neither are we. And she was just too sharp for that. She could see through people."

"Mind if I look through her room again?"

The detective went right for the bookcases, scanning the titles. No Hare Krishna material, no Scientology stuff, no Church of the Cosmic Consciousness, etc. Lots of science fiction, SAT practice books, chick lit, The Castles of Europe, Wuthering Heights—he'd seen the movie, never read the book. Photos of her in her fencing outfit and medals were all over the walls.

The pictures reminded him of his own daughter, Brittany. She was seventeen now, and living with her mother, but vanished from his life.

Olivia's cello case leaned against the wall. A complete person. And completely missing. No sign of any dissatisfaction strong enough to make her leave home and abandon a brilliant future. He didn't have a good feeling about this.

"I'll keep you posted," he said on his way out. "It's good that you were on the news yesterday. Every chance you get to appear on TV is valuable in keeping the case before the public and getting Olivia's face out there."

"It worked in the Elizabeth Smart case," said Rachel. The detective didn't add to that.

After McKenna had left, Rachel went to her room and called him on his cell.

"There's something else I didn't want to say in front of my parents, and you can't tell them either. I went to Transcendence House yesterday and spent the night there as a runaway."

"Go on."

"One of the boys there told me that Olivia had been a prostitute. A 'stone ho,' he said."

"Who told you this?"

"His name is Brother Horace. He's a runaway there. And I believe him."

"Rachel, don't do that again. Stay home and give your parents support. Anything else?"

"Yes. The priest who runs that place. Father Massey—he said that when they went on a retreat with the staff of Transcendence House, that Olivia had separated from the group. That he found her a half mile away sitting in a stream with her street clothes on. That can't be. Olivia went camping with us when she was ten and we were playing in a river. She went out too far and got caught in a whirlpool that sucked her under. She was drowning in five feet of water. It took my father and five other men to pull her out, the suction was so strong. From that day on, she never went near water again."

CHAPTER NINE

Rachel was logged into Yahoo Messenger waiting for Achara to appear. While she waited, she looked through the porn site for anyone who looked like her sister.

Three-thirty a.m. and no Achara. Rachel was getting worried. She nodded off.

She awoke from a clouded sleep and reached for the mouse to bring the screen back to life. It was four-twenty in the morning. Achara was calling her online.

Hi. U there?? Please be there.

Hi, Rachel scrambled to type. *Been waiting 4u.*

Sorry late. Hard to get away. Any news about passport???

Rachel's heart sank. *Not yet. As soon as I get it, I'll send it. I promise you.*

I find out how much money I need for bribe officials. It a lot of money.

How much?

I need 2000 USD. You have money for me?

Oh my God, thought Rachel, *it might as well be two million.*

Achara, I don't have that right now. But I'll get it somehow. I promise.

Not much time left. They take me away soon. I don't want them get suspicious to me. They trust me to go buy beer. I save a little money, but only enough for ten minutes of Internet. You have cam?

No cam either.

I like to see your face. When I see your face, I pretend I look in the mirror. U r so beautiful.

Rachel accepted the invite and Achara's face materialized. She seemed to have aged since last time. Her hair was unwashed and she had a bruise under her right eye.

Your eye.

Customer hit me. I fight him back. I always fight back.

Keep fighting, baby, I'll get you out of there. Can you go to a relative or friend's house until I can help you?

No. Tong knows my relative address. He can send men to get me. Nowhere to hide. You still help me?

Of course. I don't want anyone hurting you until I get you out.

Don't worry. I'm very strong. But u r my only hope. I have plan to get out, but just need your help. Passport, money. I hate to ask.

Rachel could see she was losing faith that her own sister would help her.

I promise you, I will get you out. She didn't know how she was going to keep that promise, but she'd keep it if it killed her.

When I see you again?

Day after tomorrow. Rachel hoped that this would be enough time for the passport to arrive—but had Olivia even applied for it?

God bless you.

It was six in the morning when Rachel found it. The blood rushed out of her head as she witnessed Olivia in bed having sex with a forty-year-old man. The scene was uploaded two months ago. And her name was Tia. She watched it all the way through, then she watched it again. She held her cell phone in her hand for a half hour before she could bring herself to hit the speed dial.

"McKenna."

"Detective, this is Rachel Wallen. I found something, but you have to promise me that if it's not necessary to tell my parents, they won't be told."

"I'll have to be the judge of that, Rachel. What is it?"

"I'm sending you a link. It's a scene. A sex scene. With Olivia. There are other people in it."

"You're sure it's her?"

"It's my sister. She's wearing the jade pendant I gave her for her birthday last year."

"I'll look into it right now."

Rachel buried her face in the pillow. In her tangled mind, she tried to fathom how such a transformation could take place. Then Father Massey's words came back to her with new meaning.

The infinite power of human transformation.

CHAPTER TEN

I want to thank you for your support, ladies and gentlemen. Together we'll prevent what happened to Dina Anne Sullivan from ever happening again." Father Massey stepped down from the podium to vigorous applause. The guests had paid three hundred dollars a plate for this fund raiser. Transcendence House was one of the most popular causes in the city, one that brought politicians of both parties into the same room. The murder of Dina Anne Sullivan three years earlier was one of the few things they could agree on.

An eleven-year-old girl runs away from her abusive stepfather and seeks refuge in a convent. Instead of taking her in, she is turned over to a city agency which, after a cursory review of the case, sends her back home. One month later, the stepfather rapes and kills her in a drunken rage. The incident mortified the Church and embarrassed social welfare agencies.

Enter Father Massey, who proposed a bill which would allow the state to underwrite selected religious institutions of all faiths for the specific purpose of taking in, educating, and caring for runaway children under the age of fourteen while their cases are under investigation.

Such a bill would have been subject to the full force of separation of church and state arguments had it not been for the few pints of blood that Dina gave and the tons of ink which followed. Dina's Law had just been signed by the Governor, and it meant that a child could seek refuge in one of these institutions and have the cost of their needs covered by the state.

As Father Massey worked the tables like a bridegroom, the cameras flashed in pursuit. Indeed, to the audience, he was wedded to his unending fight against child abuse. Every politician in New York wanted to be associated in some way with this young, charismatic priest who managed to help illiterate street kids score in the top tenth percentile on their SATs and took hookers off the street and transformed them into IT technicians and computer programmers.

This dinner at a Long Island VFW raised twenty thousand dollars for new computer equipment for the shelter. The new website had donor items ranging from sponsoring a day's worth of medical care in the clinic for ten thousand dollars to buying a tank of gas for the outreach vans and uniforms for the intake staff.

Massey was careful to keep his accounting hound's tooth clean, showing exactly where each and every dollar went. Donors liked that, and city officials did, too, as it was a trick they had never mastered. Every year, Massey brought in independent auditors to go over the books of Transcendence House, Inc. and made the results available on the Internet. This kind of transparency, along with the results made him command the unquestioned respect of all.

The idea was to go national, then world-wide. For this, hundreds of millions would have to be raised, and Father Massey was a born fund-raiser.

As he drove back to Transcendence House in his '99 Honda Civic, Massey thought this had gone well, as had yesterday's trip to Washington. Gabriella had recorded his subcommittee testimony, and he wanted to review that as soon as possible to critique his performance. Then he needed another media event to keep him in the public eye while the Washington job was being decided. That would be tomorrow's project.

In his office at Transcendence House, Massey sat at his laptop inputting his schedule for the next two weeks. Breakfast tomorrow with Cecil Wright, the CEO of Kanga Systems, a microprocessor company. Massey was lobbying for five hundred thousand dollars.

His research had revealed that Wright was a thirty-two-year-old electrical engineer, graduate of MIT and founder, at twenty-three, of Kanga. His firm went on to develop MPP, massively parallel processors used in supercomputers. He was vegetarian and single. Massey hadn't been able to identify any activities outside of fly-fishing that the CEO enjoyed.

What would be appropriate attire? He had located several photos of Wright and he was formally dressed in all of them. In a taped interview, he proved to be a humorless man. Massey debated whether to put on the collar or the Barney's Fifth Avenue. As a general rule, if you were going to ask for money, wear the collar; if you're going to ask for power, wear the suit. The collar it was, then.

After the CEO, it was lunch with Daniel O'Leary, the city comptroller. Just a get-to-know-each-other lunch at Fraunces Tavern. Probably has mayoral aspirations. Massey had to cover himself. He'd use the suit for that one.

His days were sixteen hours long, and he still couldn't get everything done. He wondered how men with families accomplished anything at all.

Someone knocked. It was five minutes after ten. Lights-out.

"Come in."

Gabriella entered and closed the door. She was fifteen, barefoot with thick black hair down to her waist.

"I came as soon as I could."

"Have a seat," said the priest, beaming. "I'll be with you in a minute." He could feel the girl's eyes on him.

She worshipped him. He had rescued her at the age of thirteen from an abusive pimp who happened to be her father. She had come to Transcendence House black-eyed and emaciated from being chained to a basement radiator for three days without food or water. In that time, she had lost enough weight to slip out of her bonds. The first step was to prosecute the father, which they succeeded in doing. She was then handed over to a foster family, where conditions became painfully familiar to her. She reappeared at Father Massey's door five months ago and dedicated herself entirely to him. She looked things up for him, ironed his clothes, tidied his office.

"Writing a letter?" she asked.

"Oh, taking care of a few things."

"I wish I could type like that."

The priest closed his laptop and now was ready to give the girl his full attention.

"I got that book you wanted," said Gabriella, handing him a library copy of *The Elements of Fly-Fishing*.

"Ah, exactly what I need. And plenty of pictures too. I'll dazzle Mr. Wright with my fly-tying."

"You like it?"

"Hey, you're good. What would I do without my administrator-slash-researcher?"

"I went to a couple of libraries, but I remembered you wanted something with a lot of pictures."

"Good choice. I can always count on you, Gabriella. That's a great quality."

He sat next to her on the couch and took her hand.

"How did tonight go?" she asked.

"Outstanding. We raised over twenty thousand dollars and focused media attention on our cause. That's a mighty combination."

"It's great that the law went through."

"Yes. Do you know what it means to make a law? Think of it. You can build a bridge, castle, or cathedral, but nothing changes the course of our lives and of history like creating the laws by which we live. Why are you smiling?"

"I like it when you talk like that. Sometimes I try to quote you, but I can't."

"You don't go quoting everything I say, do you?"

"I mean, no." She gave him her other hand too. "I'm totally discreet, you know that."

"A lot of things go on between us that no one must ever know about."

"I know that."

"I confide a lot of things to you that others might use against me."

"I would never hurt you, Father Evan."

The priest held her face in his hands and kissed her on the mouth. She wrapped her arms around his neck and redoubled the passion. His hand slid up the girl's checkered skirt and she responded by unbuttoning her blouse.

"What do you want me to do for you?" she asked.

He looked at her and brushed her hair away from her face.

"You want me to dance for you?"

He smiled.

"I've got on the new underwear." She got up off the couch.

"I'd like that. No, stand over there. Let me get this out of the way." He removed the print of Guernica from the wall and put it on the floor.

"No distractions," he said.

As the girl began to writhe, the priest's mind became a tangle of guilt, passion, fantasy, and hard consequence.

She showed him a devotion that he was incapable of giving to anyone but himself. Aspirants prayed for this kind of dedication, and here he was, receiving it. Why couldn't he love a woman? Why had it always been children that made him burn? Why was it always thoughts of young girls that accompanied him to bed and awoke him in the morning? And those photos he had collected through the years… He thought they were the most beautiful things in the world, and knowing that it was wrong didn't change it.

She removed her panties now, and every time she was naked before him, he was as paralyzed as though he had been impaled by a stake. In such moments, he would give up all that he had, and could ever hope for, in exchange for those thighs. Others might think that it was he who had power over her, but he knew the truth.

Father Massey's hand groped behind the library shelf and threw a switch. The video camera began to roll.

CHAPTER ELEVEN

C areful getting back to bed," said Massey when they were done. She stood up on her toes and kissed his cheek. She had already turned to leave when he pulled her back for one last kiss.

Father Massey stood looking at the door as though following her beyond the room. He put the poster back on its nail and contemplated the bombardment, the twisted figures, the wailing that was Guernica. It was an image that evoked Dante's Inferno.

He thought about where he had gone wrong.

He had been born into a broken family. His father was an interstate truck driver who was on the road eight months out of the year. His mother had two men on the side. At an early age, he learned to deal with solitude—a gift that would assist him later. With his father away, and his mother entertaining in the next room, young Evan had to care for his three brothers and sisters. A natural organizer, he planned the meals, distributed the household tasks, and scheduled all TV programming. Indeed, his first attraction was to the military, but his nature required immediate results and four years was too long.

He enrolled in Suffolk Community College in Long Island, majoring in pre-engineering. Evan was fascinated by cathedrals and the endurance of the artisans that labored over generations to build them.

After getting his associate's degree, he landed a construction job through a friend making good union scale wages. It would be a good job, he thought, until he could decide on what he was going to do.

Whatever he did, he did well. Massey enjoyed working with mortar and wood, although he hid his aversion to the simple men who did this kind of labor—the sort of men he looked upon with contempt in the trailer park he grew up in.

He had always been drawn to the great mission of helping the downtrodden and became a Claretion.

The Claretions' special emphasis on outreach to youth and social justice appealed to Massey. As a lay volunteer, he could assist in the many worldwide missions without going through the rigors of seminary.

He began by working in a soup kitchen in the inner city in New York. He tired quickly of this and searched for a greater challenge.

After a few months, he saw an ad in the paper for a passage to India via freighter. This was the adventure he was waiting for. He told his superiors that he wished to serve in India and would be in a position to do much good there. They told him that he was free to go, but that the Order couldn't sanction the trip. They wished him luck.

Massey signed up immediately and was off. So it was that he found the village of Krupal in northern India.

Now he contemplated the second half of that story, the half that was not in the video shown to all who come to Transcendence House.

It was all true. Twenty-two-old-year-old Massey had saved a people, had altered the course of thousands of lives for the better. And for this, the villagers were grateful. They addressed him as Baba. They declared May 27th Evan Massey Day, the anniversary of the completion of the reservoir. But it didn't end there.

Massey stayed in the village for twelve more months following the end of the project. He asked that a house be constructed for him, which the villagers gladly did with the finest materials available. There were people to wash his clothes, which now consisted of dhotis made of fine cotton and silk. There was someone to clean his house, to cut his hair, to clean the dirt from under his fingernails. Women were assigned the task of bathing Massey.

No whim of his was too trivial. He needed fresh-cut roses in his living room every morning, and so a boy was given the job of running to another village six kilometers away to fetch them. Massey decided that he wanted satellite TV, and the people spent their hard-earned cash to satisfy him.

He requested a weekly stipend. Small at first, the stipend became a tax, and the tax was raised to support his interminable purchases, which included film and beer.

Playing the role of village counselor, he mediated disputes and imposed judgments which the villagers accepted. And like any bureaucrat, Evan Massey was subject to lobbying. Fathers began to offer the services of their daughters.

Among the villagers, it became a mark of status to have a daughter obtain an "audience" with Baba. Then the daughters started getting younger and younger. Before long, Massey was sleeping with eleven-year-olds. He began filming the girls, then watched the videos incessantly, reliving each conquest.

He still chaired town meetings where he could hold forth, but his audience had changed. While before he was beloved by all, now he was worshipped by some and despised by many.

The end came when accounts of his excesses spread to the surrounding villages and police came looking for him. Massey fled like a common thief.

Returning to America, he found no breathless crowds cheering him. Unemployed with only a two-year degree, he took a job as a waiter in an upscale restaurant. Now he catered to the whims of others. He practiced phrases like, "Will there be anything else, sir?" and "You're right, ma'am. I'm sorry for the inconvenience."

The daily humiliation crushed him, and he couldn't stop yearning for the approval of the crowds chanting his name. That past praise was now a recurring slur that was with him at every turn. He who had given life, who had designed and set things into motion, now scraped bread crumbs off fine linen tablecloths under the glare of a headwaiter.

One night, the news ran a story about a burnt-out church in the South Bronx that was slated for demolition. Many residents were protesting because it was said that several miracles had occurred as a result of the intervention of St. Cecilia, after whom the church was named. St. Cecilia was condemned to death by beheading and had survived three ax blows from her executioner. Whenever there was a critical injury in the violent neighborhood, relatives would pray in the ruins of the church. Like the saint, it had been condemned, but somehow refused to die. It breathed life into the victims for whom prayers were said within its walls.

Massey saw his chance. He contacted neighborhood leaders and offered his services as a "lay missionary," organizer, and civil engineer. The reaction was lukewarm. Massey showed up at a sparse demonstration and took the podium. Spotting a television camera, he played to it with a practiced facility that landed him on the Six O'clock News. The mostly Hispanic protesters at first distrusted this Anglo who had inexplicably taken up their cause, but after Massey created flyers in Spanish and organized a successful postering drive through the local Catholic schools, he gained considerable credibility. The drive gave way to a much bigger rally.

He distributed press kits ordered from Kinko's with his own money. The rally led to a door-to-door fund raiser that financed a one-hundred-dollar-a-plate dinner to which Massey invited politicians in need of the ethnic vote. The politicians pushed for the eighty-year-old church to be granted historic landmark status, a move that would buy time for restoration. When this succeeded, Massey was given full control of the project. He established the St. Cecilia Restoration Fund, and through a series of rallies and appeals to Catholic institutions and lobbying of mob-owned construction companies that were under investigation, the church was rebuilt.

It was a victory that earned him an audience with the Archbishop of New York. Once again, Massey had the admiration he yearned for. So when the young man was told he had a vocation, he was receptive. The thought grew in strength, getting a purchase on his ego, and eventually his will. He enrolled in seminary studies on a trial basis. If nothing else, he could complete his degree and walk away from the priesthood with certainty. The Church had need for men of keen intellect and action, Evan Massey was told.

In the heat of the moment, he enrolled in the St. Bartholomew Seminary in Brooklyn. He completed his studies, all the time maintaining a visible presence in the community. Soon afterwards, he took his vows as a Claretion priest.

Father Massey immediately distinguished himself as a sharp speech writer and fund raiser. At twenty-seven, he established First Step, a place where the homeless could get a bath, haircut and fresh set of clothes, and be pointed in the direction of a job. First Step had only moderate success, and moderation was never his objective. Massey reasoned that the less-than-spectacular results were due to the fact that most of the homeless did not want to be helped. He resolved to focus his efforts almost exclusively on children and young teens that were more receptive to change.

Transcendence House was established on the principle of tough love. Those who resisted change were culled, leaving only those who were truly committed to self-improvement.

This approach led to media-worthy results: former drug addicts and prostitutes scoring 1420 on the SAT's; a fresh-faced sixteen-year-old making forty dollars an hour writing databases for Fortune-500 companies where nine months earlier, he had attempted suicide. A junkie graduates the program and goes on to become a U.S. Marine, returning to give testimony in dress uniform. These stories put Massey back where he needed to be—at the center of attention. He was able to raise enough money to buy forty state-of-the-art computers for the center and invited whiz kids from Stuyvesant High School and the Bronx High School of Science to volunteer their time instructing their less fortunate peers.

He held a weekly forum online to discuss issues affecting youth. Transcendence House sweatshirts and T-shirts, as well as other Catholic supplies, were sold throughout the country, generating still more income for the organization.

Massey himself spent hours every week combing the Internet for anything of value to his organization. Along the way, he stumbled upon electronic bulletin board services.

He began downloading X-rated pictures catering to every sexual preference. Sado-masochism, interracial, teen sex. There was one BBS that promised anything—absolutely anything—but one of the conditions was that members had to contribute pictures of similar caliber. There were several levels of security on the BBS, depending on what sort of photos a member contributed.

Massey couldn't enter the Romper Room Corner without a good submission of his own. He remembered the pictures he had taken in India, images he had not looked at in years.

When he took them out of the box in his closet, he was amazed at the number of photos he had taken. They were in the hundreds. At least three dozen girls under thirteen years of age. These images resurrected all that was good and bad about Krupal. He weighed the photos against the good he had done, the lives saved. In a few days, the scales had settled.

His own submissions got him access to the child porn area. Soon, he lived only for this.

Now the feelings he had so long suppressed about his kids were given full reign again. Massey started to flirt with the young girls who came in off the streets.

The first had been a fifteen-year-old from Alabama. It was hardly her first time, but she was young and he was a priest, so it was a conquest for both of them. Soon she was back on the streets, and he moved on to the next girl.

The thrill he got out of these liaisons was indescribable. In his public life, Massey was the paragon of integrity. Plaudits were heaped on him from both the Church and the public, and his successes kept him from confessing his sins. The sex was drawing him in deeper by the day. Bondage, S&M, humiliation… small, writhing limbs beneath his body were the thoughts he went to sleep with and woke up to.

It made him reckless. He had brought Gabriella to the yearly retreat. They went off into the woods together and, inevitably, made love. The sound of a snapping twig had made him look up and he saw Olivia, not a hundred feet away, watching them.

CHAPTER TWELVE

I want to congratulate you on behalf of the President and myself on the passage of Dina's Law," said the First Lady. "It's a significant step forward and will raise awareness of the plight of abandoned children."

"Thank you, Ma'am. That means a great deal to me, and I'm sure the kids at Transcendence House will be heartened to know that you're in their corner," responded Father Massey, untangling the telephone cord.

"As you probably know, the President is creating a special office that will handle the problem of homeless and abandoned children," continued the First Lady. "This has been a personal crusade of mine for fifteen years. We've finally been able to get the funding for it—not enough to run it the way we want, but as we get results, I feel the funding will increase. Even the political opposition finds it difficult to disagree with this cause. We need someone with extensive experience in this area whose views are in line with the Administration's. I'd like to invite you to come to Washington next Tuesday."

"I'm at your command."

Massey's lunch with the First Lady went superbly. He was offered, and accepted, the position of Director of the Office of Abandoned Children, the brain-child of the First Lady. He wore the suit for that one.

He had been the perfect candidate for the job: experience in the field of runaway children and an impeccable background. This last qualification was a must as so many of the Administration's appointees had lately fallen at the hands of the scandal-mongers. But Father Evan Massey was a Roman Catholic priest with vision. That's how he'd been described in the Washington Post the day before accepting the job.

This would be the radical change he needed in his life. Here, there was power, money, position. Finally, he had come to a place that was big enough for his talents. He envisioned the founding of dozens of centers like Transcendence House all over the country. On this pulpit, he could raise millions.

Of course, he would no longer be able to personally administrate Transcendence House; this task would fall to a priest of his choosing. All this would be hammered out when he returned to New York.

Massey spent the rest of the afternoon looking at townhouses in Georgetown. The rents were nearly Tribeca-league, but this was a lot more to his liking than Manhattan. Here, there was power.

"Step this way, Mr. Massey," said Miriam Bannister, the real estate broker from Henley Group, a prestigious firm that handled the housing needs of secretaries of state and diplomats in the D.C. area. The First Lady herself had recommended her.

"We have here a lovely high-floor five-room with English country house ambiance in a top pre-war building. Exceptional views from a beautifully proportioned living room, refinished hardwood floors, and twelve-foot ceilings. Through here we have a sunny oak-paneled library that looks south. You strike me as the kind of person who has a lot of books—am I right?"

"I'd make good use of that."

"I thought so. Again, high ceilings in the dining room with plenty of windows. A wood burning fireplace in the master bedroom and a walk-in closet. Truly one of a kind."

His new job came with a small paycheck—ninety thousand a year. The job did, however, provide an expense account and a credit card, which was as good as cash. This would enable him to accept the job, and it looked great from the ethics standpoint. The monthly rent for this apartment—$3,200—was within his budget if he included his $1,800 monthly stipend from the Diocese.

"My needs are simple. I'll take it," he said.

He picked up the afternoon paper on the way to his hotel. After a quick shower, he decided to order room service instead of stepping out again to a restaurant. He finished off the lamb's rump and half a bottle of Arrowood Reserve cabernet, then settled down with the paper.

The second story on the front page made him freeze.

The body of a sixteen-year-old girl had been found in the Bronx. She had been brutally murdered.

CHAPTER THIRTEEN

T*he search for Kirsten Schrodinger ended last night when the body of the sixteen-year-old was found brutally mutilated and dismembered. Police stated that judging from the partially healed wounds, the girl had been tortured over a period of days, if not weeks, before being killed...*

... Inside sources have confirmed that an eye-witness saw a man carrying a large duffel bag entering an abandoned tenement the night before the victim's body was discovered there.

Massey dropped the paper into the waste-paper basket, then called the office of New York Representative Richard Smythe to cancel their appointment tomorrow. He threw everything into his garment bag, then got online and tried finding a shuttle to New York in the next couple of hours. Everything was booked. Amtrak then. The five-sixteen would get him into New York by ten-thirty.

While on the train, he cancelled all his meetings and interviews for the next two days. He read every article he could find online on the Schrodinger murder. The police had substantial leads. The Post called it the most brutal murder in recent memory. Pathologists had discovered layers of torture that the victim had endured, just as geologists can read the traumas of the earth in a core sample.

She had been electrocuted as evidenced by the charring at the top of her head and her left foot. The head had caught fire, and the eyeballs had been pushed out, not gouged out. The contractions of the body had been so great that ribs and fingers had broken. She had been violated with a large object such as a baseball bat. This was accompanied by severe beating resulting in the broken radius of her arm, broken hip, ribs and jaw. A number of her teeth had been pulled out.

The article said the FBI had been called in. He stared out the window for twenty minutes. Substantial leads.

He went to the restroom to wash his face and nearly gasped when he saw his reflection. His abundant black hair was wet with perspiration. His eyes looked as if he'd spent the night drinking. He looked like so many bums he'd seen as he walked every day to Transcendence House from the subway station. Massey toweled off and threw his hair back with his hands.

Back in his seat, he googled, *How to erase your hard drive.*

When he arrived at Transcendence House, he had thirty-six messages. Before he could take off his jacket, the phone rang again.

"Joe Sadlis—Daily News."

"Ah, yes. I suppose I have time now," said Massey, collecting himself.

"Kirsten Schrodinger was found dead today. Do you know if she knew Olivia Wallen, who disappeared last week? I understand Olivia volunteered at Transcendence House."

"I'm not aware of any relationship. Kirsten Schrodinger wasn't a guest at Transcendence House, as far as I know."

"As one of the last people to see Olivia Wallen before she disappeared, could you shed some light on her relationship with the kids she worked with, her co-workers, and yourself?"

He had couched that question well and Massey had to handle this guy carefully. The wrong response and he'd print "Despite repeated questioning, Father Massey was unforthcoming."

"As far as I could tell, Olivia had a fine working relationship with her co-workers, and some of the kids had real affection for her. She was a very lovable person. Everyone will tell you that. As for myself, I don't get too close with anyone here, and that's the greatest irony. You just can't function well when you lose your objectivity. My responsibilities are primarily management of our organization, and I don't have the luxury of being able to interact very much with either the kids or the counselors. She had been volunteering here for almost a year, which is an unusually long time. Most kids come here for a summer and that's enough. Not to be cynical about anyone's motives, but that's all you need to put something on your resume. Olivia was different. She had a genuine vocation for this kind of work. Our prayers go out to the family."

"Rumors have been surfacing from multiple sources that she was a call girl. How do you respond to that?"

"I don't, and I hope her parents don't hear this. Please have the decency and professionalism not to print anything, but established facts. I'm afraid I'm out of time. Thank you for calling and good night."

After Massey shredded several dozen documents, he removed the digital camcorder from behind the bookshelf and, with a few strokes, deleted its contents. He overwrote the camcorder's hard drive by placing it on his desk and filming the blank wall of his office.

What else? he thought. He deleted the call log on his cell phone. He went through his emails for anything remotely suspicious. More deletes. Of course, all that could be retrieved by the authorities, but it was a start. There was nothing else in the office that needed to be addressed.

In his house in Bensonhurst, Massey went through every drawer and nook. He found a pair of panties and a condom wrapper. Kirsten Schrodinger had been up here only once, but long hairs have a way of turning up at the wrong moment. He gathered up all his linen and towels and packed them in garbage bags. These went to the curb. He'd need to get new ones right away. The guitar got wiped down, along with everything with a handle on it.

The priest backed up his laptop to the external hard drive. His collection of child pornography had always been his solace, the images that had obsessed him for years, the pictures so beautiful that he could not imagine living without them. He had to see them one last time.

They were boys and girls between eight and thirteen, arching their backs for him, and they never grew old. Like the figures on Keats' urn, they were forever young. They were the first thing he thought of in the morning and the last thing before he closed his eyes at night. They were the most valuable thing he owned, and even he knew there was something wrong with that. And now that he had visited them, he closed the images one by one and was again alone.

Massey now held in his hand the drive which contained all his sensitive files. He knew from all the computer whizzes that taught at Transcendence House that when you delete a file, you are really just deleting a reference to it from a table of contents on the disk. The data is still there and easily recoverable by authorities. One way to permanently delete the data was to overwrite the hard drive using privacy software. He downloaded Window Washer. After highlighting all his porn directories, his finger pressed DELETE, and the children vanished.

Chapter Fourteen

Alexander Hamilton stood magnificent, but unknowing that he would soon cross the Hudson to his death. Rachel walked past the statue and into the Columbia bookstore where she purchased the rest of the books she'd need for Lit-Hum: Julius Caesar, Homer, Aeschylus, Sophocles, Euripides, Herodotus, Thucydides, Aristophanes, Plato, Vergil, Augustine. On the newsstand there was one more reading assignment. Kirsten Schrodinger had been found dead.

"I just heard about the Schrodinger girl," said Rachel on her cell phone. "You know what I'm going to ask."

"There's no evidence they're related, Rachel. At least for now," replied Detective McKenna.

"Did you find out anything about the video?"

"That was just a fragment of a video. It doesn't have the usual disclaimer and records information that all adult videos are required to have at the beginning. So it's going to be hard to locate the source. Still trying."

Rachel had to sit on the steps on hearing this. "So none of the people in the video could be identified? I had high hopes for that."

"So far, no. Sorry you and your family had to read about the Schrodinger murder at a time like this. Don't torture yourself thinking about that. How are your folks holding up?"

"Not well. The worst part is just sitting around waiting for news. Isn't there facial recognition software that you can use to identify the people in the video?"

"Only if they're in a database to start with. Look, Rachel, like I told you last night, just stay in close touch with your parents and give them support. I saw all the posters you and your neighbors put up. That helps. We're getting leads, but nothing's panned out yet."

"Besides putting up posters, is there anything else I can do?"

"You're doing just fine. I understand you're in school. That's good. You need to keep going and not let this take you over."

"It's already taken me over."

"You have to keep functioning, is what I mean. Life can't stop. Rest assured that we're doing everything we possibly can. I hope that gives you the small comfort you might need to keep on going with your life. I'm sure your sister would want that."

When McKenna hung up, he reviewed the platitudes he had just repeated to the girl.

He didn't tell her that he had in his hands at just that moment the Medical Examiner's report on the Schrodinger girl. It was far worse than what the media had described. They weren't even supposed to get that much. You want to keep some information secret, so there's still something that only the perpetrator would know in case you capture him, such as how the body was found and the wounds on it. Damn rookie cop on the scene started yapping to the press.

His eyes panned each photo. The torture was unimaginable and drawn out over a period of days. As he had done many times during his career, McKenna tried to enter the mind of the animal that would do this. It wasn't for money—no ransom had been demanded. It wasn't a political or mob rubout. This was sheer sadism.

Whenever McKenna tried to understand a killer, he had special tools at his command that most police officers lacked: he had been a trained killer himself.

He had been a Marine sniper in Afghanistan nine years ago. He knew what it was like to go after a specific target and kill it, not just in self-defense, but as part of another motive, a greater purpose, he had told himself. He had often contemplated the degrees of separation between himself and the men he now pursued as a lawman. So had his ex-wife.

After returning from Afghanistan, he drank heavily to hold at bay the blown up bodies that kept coming back at night. His marriage, held together by the daughter they both loved, was slipping away fast. When his wife got full custody of Brittany, he just got worse. He was banging in sick once a week when he was told to attend counseling or risk his career. It was a solid year before he stopped drinking. He was learning new concepts like relapse and solitude. At least in war, there was the unwavering loyalty of your comrades. Here, you were on your own. He immersed himself in police work for the next few years, making a few feeble attempts to connect with Brittany. But by the time he had straightened himself out on the job, he had neglected his only daughter. When he spoke with her last Christmas, he could tell she couldn't wait to get off the phone, that she was just talking to him out of politeness or pity. When he hung up, he wished he hadn't called. How do you make up for an eight year gap? You don't.

His eyes dropped back to the photos. These were the sort of images that made it easy to forget his own troubles.

In his gut he knew one thing: The killer who did this to Kirsten Schrodinger also took Olivia Wallen.

Masutatsu Nakayama pulled the Macanudo cigar beneath his nostrils, inhaling its beautiful bouquet. After lighting it and laying it down on the ashtray, he reviewed the scene of the last execution, an auction he had won for $220,000.

She was a blonde girl, about sixteen, with large American breasts. He didn't go through the whole scene, just the foreplay to the death sequence. He didn't want the effect of the final images to wear off like everything else had in his life. The New York papers had confirmed her brutal death and this conferred the final stamp of authenticity to the scene.

He was intrigued by the new Asian girl being offered. Today he had struggled with the other clients, each man trying to steer the torment his own way. Cultures differed even in their taste for torture and abasement. For example, in Japanese bukkake, the girl must be emotionless as the man cums in her face, she must show *gaman*—endurance. Not like the Western girls who are smiling and showing pleasure in that moment. It is a completely different effect. But Nakayama was impressed with the imagination of his competitors. Client Number Two had won today's auction with his request that the girl be raped by a specially trained dog, and the Webmaster was able to comply quickly. Nakayama was feeling new sensations, nuances of thought he believed long dead. He contemplated tomorrow's session.

The first swallow of sake cleansed his mouth of the sickening taste of the bourbon he'd drunk at tonight's dinner party. As he closed the door behind his last guest, he had told himself that he would no longer partake of these functions. But he had been saying this for years.

He stubbed out the cigar. It was bitter, and a glance at the humidor's hygrometer indicated no water. The cigars were ruined. He gazed out the window briefly, then wrote a haiku as he had every night since he was a child.

The feast ends and brings
A silence like no other.
Laugh, then, for stillness.

CHAPTER FIFTEEN

Rachel needed to talk to Brother Horace again. Had he seen the video? Did he know any of the people in it? First, she needed money. She had already raided her coffee can of coins last week, so she took Olivia's Medaglia d'Oro can, which was full. Probably over forty dollars' worth.

TD Bank had a free Penny Arcade. Coinstar would take almost ten percent.

She hit *START* and an animation came up on the screen offering a prize if she could guess how much she was about to put into the machine. Rachel guessed forty-seven dollars and sixty-two cents.

She fed the coins and waited for the final tally and possible prize. The total was sixty-three dollars and seventeen cents. No prize, but more cash than she had expected.

DON'T FORGET TO CHECK THE COIN RETURN BEFORE YOU LEAVE, said the cartoon.

Rachel checked the slot and found three rejects. Two were Canadian coins. The third was an odd coin with PP written over the outline of a naked girl.

"Is Brother Horace here?" she asked back at Transcendence House.

"He's fundraising," said one kid.

"Fundraising for what?"

"For himself. He's hustling the chess tables in Washington Square."

Rachel found Brother Horace in the middle of a King's Indian defense against a hippie throwback. Brother Horace prevailed, then defeated another opponent in seventeen moves—four minutes in blitz chess. He was four dollars richer. Rachel sat down opposite him.

"I know you," he said. "Two dollars a game. I'll give you white."

"I was thinking about what you said, Brother Horace. About Olivia changing. How did you know about the porn movie?"

"Word was going around. Then I saw it."

"Do you know the other girl in the scene—or the guy?"

"I take it you found the video."

"Yes."

"I hear the girl is a graduate of Transcendence House," he said.

"I didn't know they offered job placement for porn."

"I didn't know either."

Rachel lowered her voice. "Was Olivia screwing the priest?"

Brother Horace looked up and his eyes glanced sideways for a moment.

"You gonna play or what?"

Rachel advanced her pawn and hit the clock. Five seconds a move. It was over in twenty-two moves. She collected the two dollars.

"Another. I'll take white," he said.

"You thinking about my question?"

"I don't know the answer to that question."

"Brother Horace, let me tell you something. I knew that girl better than anyone on Earth. We were like sisters. I know she was brilliant, beautiful, going to Harvard, and won more awards than the New York Yankees won pennants. I need to know what made her turn into a whore overnight. Doesn't that interest you in the least, even if she was a stranger to you?"

"Not especially. People can do anything. They can turn in a second. And they can turn on you."

"Did Father Massey know about what she was doing?"

"There isn't much Father Massey doesn't know about the kids."

"So did Olivia get thrown out of Transcendence House for this?"

"Who said she got thrown out?"

This time it took sixteen moves.

"You're distracting me. And cutting into my profits," he said.

"I'll spot you a bishop."

"Hell no. One more. I'll keep white."

"When was the last time you saw her?"

"Four months ago, I guess."

"So she volunteers at this shelter, starts making porn, then leaves on her own. And does what?" Rachel recalled that Olivia's schedule hadn't changed. She claimed, until last week, that she was still volunteering at Transcendence House. That accounted for her hours. So if she wasn't at Transcendence House, where was she?

Rachel defeated him again.

"Damn, woman, that's some fine playin'. You don't mind if a man earns a living, do you?"

"That's Sister Rachel to you. I give lessons if you're interested." She got up and checked her pocket for her Metro Card. She remembered the coin she'd found in Olivia's change can.

"Any idea what this is?" she asked, handing the coin to the boy.

"That's a peep show token. You buy these in the peep shows, then use it to see porn or naked girls in a booth."

Back at her dorm, Rachel did a search on peep shows in New York and got two dozen hits. Her eye scanned the page, then fell on one line: *The Pleasure Palace*, and the logo of the naked girl.

CHAPTER SIXTEEN

I t was on Tenth and Twenty-third among all the other vice dens that were displaced from forty-second Street under Mayor Giuliani. *PLEASURE PALACE* flashed in red neon with a purple nude girl lying down with one leg up. *LIVE GIRLS* flashed up a neon staircase. Buddy booths available. Today's special was two DVDs for seven dollars. In the window, there were love dolls with their latex mouths open in a silent scream.

Detective McKenna flashed his badge at the goon at the door and asked to see the manager.

Zoltan Perlman came downstairs and said some words in Hebrew to his assistant. Another flash of the badge and McKenna asked if the girl called Tia Chan, AKA Olivia Wallen, ever worked here.

The Israeli glanced at the picture and replied, "For a few weeks. She quit months ago."

"I need exact dates. You keep records, I assume."

"Sure we keep them. Give me a minute."

McKenna was standing in front of the sex toy rack. They sold latex cocks the size of salamis in a butcher shop. The owner came back with some papers.

"This is her application and driver's license. She was over eighteen."

"Why'd she quit?"

"She just stopped showing up, so I don't have a termination date. But we hired another girl right after her. I think it was two months ago."

"What about this girl?" McKenna showed him the picture of the other girl in the video.

"She works here."

"She here now?"

"Yeah, I think so." Perlman aimed his booming voice at the top of the stairs. "Ram, is Sonia here?"

"She's with a customer."

"Please get her over here," said the detective to Perlman.

Not once did Perlman ask what this was all about.

The girl came down wearing a bathrobe, to McKenna's relief. She looked way underage with long, dirty blonde hair cut straight across at her waist with Hannah Montana bangs. The detective could see the beautiful body moving beneath the terry cloth white robe.

"NYPD." He flashed his badge. "You know this girl?" He held out the photo.

"We used to work together."

"Not just here, right?"

"What do you mean?"

"I mean you did other work together. You made a video together."

"Yeah. We did." The girl tightened the belt of the bathrobe.

"She disappeared last week."

"I know," she said to the photograph as though talking to Olivia.

"Any idea where she is?"

She shook her head.

"She ever mention anyone she might be staying with? Anyone she had a problem with?"

"No."

McKenna felt funny as the moaning from the porn booths appended itself to his every question.

"Look, you made a porn movie with her, I know you know more than that."

She closed the neck of the bathrobe with her hand and McKenna thought that was pretty ironic considering what she did upstairs.

"I made lots of those movies. I don't even know the names of the guys I worked with."

"Could I see some ID, Miss?"

"I'll have to get my purse."

McKenna could bet money this girl was underage, no matter what that ID said. But that wasn't what he was here for. *Doesn't even know the names of the guys she works with. Christ.*

She came back with a driver's license that was a good fake.

"This says Hannah. He just called you Sonia. Stage name?"

She nodded. He gave it back.

"Who approached you about making the porn flick?"

"A guy came up to me in the street and asked if I'd be interested in doing some modeling. When I got there, he said he'd pay a lot more for adult movies. Then I asked Olivia if she was interested. She was."

"What's his name? The porn producer."

"He just called himself Skip."

Skip. That was about right, thought McKenna.

"When was the last time you saw her or spoke to her?"

"About a month ago."

"Here's my card, Miss. Give me a call if you remember anything that could help us find her. She's been gone over a week. That's usually a bad sign."

McKenna sat in his car and forced down the rest of the Dunkin' Donuts coffee. It was tepid. He was losing sleep in the last few days and wasn't sure if it was the extra coffee or the case. He had a hard time with missing kids. When adults got killed, he could still go home and turn on the football game. Not when he was working a missing kid's case. He was estranged from his own daughter and he missed her, but at least he knew she was alive and safe. But to have a kid vanish on you. To not know if you'd ever see her again—he didn't know how these parents dealt with it. Especially if they blamed themselves.

McKenna blamed himself for losing Brittany. He had always been short-tempered, but the whiskey had made him go ballistic too many times in front of her. She had seen him at his worst. That was the father she knew. She had told her mother that she was afraid of him. That he should go back to Afghanistan and do what he did best. That still hurt.

His one hope in life was to redeem himself in her eyes. He'd be happy to find himself a new wife, but he had to win his daughter back.

He looked at Olivia's picture. The Pleasure Palace was another dead end. It was time to start at the beginning. Father Massey.

CHAPTER SEVENTEEN

From what Detective McKenna said, Sonia had to know more than she was letting on, thought Rachel. There had to be a way to find out. There was always a way. She went to see Brother Horace about getting some new ID.

"I want to see Tarik about getting some paperwork," Brother Horace said to the clerk in the New Amsterdam Smoke Shoppe.

The cashier jerked his head toward the back.

Rachel told him she wanted a driver's license in the name of Lisa Barino, eighteen. Tarik took the order like a civil servant, then snapped a quick picture and collected the fifty dollars.

"Do people ever order a license and then never pick it up?"

"Not usually."

"If Olivia Wallen ordered something here, I'll pay for it and give it to her. Can you please look?"

The Pakistani looked through a leather satchel, then said, "No one by that name."

As they left the smoke shop, Rachel said, "Brother Horace, I'm desperate to find her. You know what it's like to lose someone. Isn't there anything else you can tell me that might help?"

"'Fraid I'm not much help there. But the police are already looking for her. What can you do that the police can't do better? I have an aunt in Georgia. Whenever I needed something really bad I would call her and she would pray and it would happen. She does some powerful prayin'. I know it sounds like bullshit, but some can pray better than others. Some have it down. I'll call her tonight."

"Thank you."

Rachel considered Brother Horace's words. *What can you do that the police can't do better?* The police couldn't spend the night in a youth shelter or mix with runaways on the streets. And there was at least one more thing the police couldn't do.

Rachel stood in the bathroom of a pizzeria next to the Pleasure Palace. She had changed out of her baggy runaway jeans and sneakers into a pair of Olivia's tight black jeans and the black high heels she had bought for the prom, but never got to use. After brushing her hair straight down over her shoulders, she tied off the denim shirt under her breasts. Lots of girls had told her the boys thought she was nice-looking, but had to work on her wardrobe and do something with her hair. It never bothered her. She liked dressing like a librarian or a research scientist, which is what she was. Now, looking at the finished product, she was pleased with what she saw, but anguished over what she was about to do.

CHAPTER EIGHTEEN

T hanks for taking the time, Father," said Detective McKenna, flipping open his notebook.

"Certainly. Have a seat, Detective," said Massey, settling in his office chair.

"Thanks, but I already sit too much. When we initially spoke, you'd mentioned Olivia had worked here for an unusually long time as a counselor. About a year."

"Eleven months."

"And that she had left about four months ago."

The priest said nothing.

"Is that correct, Father?"

"Yes."

"There's been a disturbing development. Olivia seems to have left here and gone to work in a—I guess you'd call it a sex emporium. A kind of strip joint downtown. From counselor to stripper. I see a lot of odd things in my business, but that one stands out." Massey didn't seem disturbed. Not a lot of rapport skills, this one.

"Well, I see a lot of odd things in my business too, Detective. And I know that very young people are extremely malleable. They're still at the age when they can have an epiphany that changes their lives, sometimes for good. Sometimes not." Massey locked eye-contact with McKenna.

"You had a unique chance to observe her in the eleven months before she started stripping. Did anything happen that might have caused her to change like that? Did she confide any problems to you?"

"Detective, it's an effort for me to make time for you, much less our counselors. My job here is to manage Transcendence House and raise money, a lot of it. I rarely get time to chit-chat with anyone here, though I personally interview all the counselors and guests. So I'm afraid I wasn't aware of any issues."

"But during your yearly retreat, you do have more time to interact, am I right?"

The priest didn't miss a beat.

"The purpose of the retreat is reflection and spiritual renewal. I would have *less* time to interact."

"You're a busy man, Father."

"Anything else, Detective?"

"Actually, there is something else." McKenna took his time flipping to the right page in his notebook. He held up a photo. "Recognize this girl?"

Massey's eyes narrowed. "No. No, I don't."

"She was a guest at Transcendence House two years ago. And she stayed for about two months. She goes by Sonia or Hannah, and she works in the same strip club as Olivia. Isn't that odd?"

CHAPTER NINETEEN

Rachel didn't know what she was going to say when she walked through the entrance of the Pleasure Palace.

As she approached the building, her breathing became short and quick. Incense from Nation of Islam street vendors clashed with pork-filled Sabrette hot dogs sold by infidels. Outside a nude bar, a Catholic nun gave out pocket Bibles and spoke in an amplified voice over Sodom.

Rachel walked through the door of the sex emporium unchallenged. There were three platformed cash registers that were reminiscent of guard towers.

At the entrance, one paid for tokens, which allowed entry into one of the forty peep booths on the first floor. The walls were lined with porno DVDs, inflatable dolls, and sex toys. The dolls were packaged in cardboard boxes with cellophane windows. Their mouths were frozen in an extruded yawn that seemed even more artificial as it contrasted with the photo of the beautiful woman on the box.

A neon sign at the bottom of the staircase said, *LIVE GIRLS UPSTAIRS*. The corollary of that, of course, was DEAD GIRLS DOWNSTAIRS.

"Miss, can I see some ID, please," said a big, pony-tailed Hispanic guy who came up behind her.

She took out her new driver's license and held it up.

"Anything I can help you with?"

"Just looking."

"You lookin' for a job, the man's upstairs."

"No. Thanks."

She walked toward the back where there was moaning and groaning coming from the movies in the peep booths that sounded more like human suffering than ecstasy. There was nothing down here but customers. She climbed the stairs.

The girls were dressed in lingerie and standing outside their booths. Some were beautiful enough to beg the question—what were they doing here? The prettier ones wore Brazilian tangas which left little to the imagination. Several could be overweight housewives. None of them fit Detective McKenna's description of Sonia.

Men were in and out in three minutes, often still adjusting their pants as they made their exit. The lunch crowd was coming in—execs, yuppies, construction workers. Rachel hovered in front of a rack of sex toys, inspecting dildos and vibrators in their plastic packaging while watching the girls. It was dimly lit, affording just the right amount of anonymity. She stayed until she saw every girl come out of her booth. No Sonia. She realized she was the only girl in this place who wasn't a sex worker, and all eyes were on her as she made her way down the stairs.

When she fled through the door, the eyes of passing men fell on her as though she were naked.

She needed someplace clean—a holy place—badly.

She put her hair up and changed back into sneakers. The A train took her to 190th and Overlook Terrace. From there, she took the Number Four bus to Fort Tryon Park, The Cloisters.

During a visit here long ago, she had caught a whiff of frankincense that had bonded with the cold, beautiful stones into an other-worldly structure that could exist only in memory. Through the years, she had not wanted to ruin that, and so never returned. The Cloisters were a sum that she kept in reserve for a time of need.

The entire structure of the Cloisters was brought here, stone by stone from Spain and France, yet it looked as native to the landscape as an outcropping of bedrock.

It consisted of architecture and art of several eras, arranged in roughly chronological order. Step through a portal and four-hundred years have elapsed. Gregorian chants played through evenly spaced speakers arranged along the courtyards, giving the effect of walking in a procession of friars.

Rachel entered the sepulchral monument of an ancient family. Adorning the caskets were effigies of knights in full armor, bearing shields pitted by time.

The great oak doors of the Langon Chapel were over twelve feet high and encased in iron strappings that lent them strength. Rachel marveled at the infinite array of cuts and gouges, attesting to the centuries of knife pommels, hammered edicts, and battering rams it had withstood. She raised two fingers, caliper-like, to measure its thickness.

"Excuse me, don't touch."

The guard had been watching her all along as she hovered too closely to the doors. Instantly, the serenity of the place was gone and she felt unclean. Don't touch. The very words implied that the inanimate was exalted above the living. This was, after all, a museum, not a house of worship.

Rachel went on to see the tapestries and the glass-work from the gothic era, but the rebuke stayed with her and nothing was enjoyable after that. But she wasn't quite ready to go home yet.

She called her best friend, Joules Kaplan, catching him before he left the city. He commuted to Cooper Union and usually left the city by three.

When she came up to him in Bryant Park, he was wearing earphones. She could hear the Kyrie of the Bach B-Minor Mass—remote and feeble to her, crystalline and palpable to him, like so many things they tried to share since they were three.

He was refining his paper on the Schwarzschild Radius. Rachel sat opposite him and spun his notes around. She had the unique privilege of free access to his innermost chicken scratches, which she felt would one day make history. She was about to tell him that, once, but in her new-found wisdom, she kept the compliment to herself.

The notes contained diagrams of event horizons and ring singularities. There was some text, but most of it was in tensor calculus and partial differential equations.

She never knew anyone who could do so many things simultaneously so well. As a high school freshman, he had published a paper on game theory in the Review of Mathematics. As a sophomore, he had designed a dexterity experiment that was conducted by an astronaut on a Space Shuttle spacewalk, one of ten experiments selected from the nation's high schools. Then there was his second place in the Intel—a little paper he had put together in four months concerning the Schwarzschild Radius. He could take up, contribute to, and discard entire fields at will.

Joules removed the earphones.

"Any news?" he asked.

"Nothing. It's bad. Really bad. I'm desperate, Joules."

Joules extended his hand across the table. It fell short of Rachel's. "You went to class?" he asked. She nodded.

"Good. You have to keep going. How many credits?"

"Eighteen. You?"

"Twenty-one. What are you taking?" he asked.

"Intro to Biomedical Engineering, Contemporary Civilization, Physics, Chem, Advanced Calc and Literature Humanities—LitHum. When I was looking through all those courses I wished I could have two more lives to take them all. And you?"

"Chem, Physics, Astronomy, Linear Algebra, Advanced Calc, Computer Design, Art History."

"That's a heavy load."

"I want to get out in three years."

"You're a masochist. Cooper's free, so what will that extra year buy you?"

"Not exactly free. Free tuition. Fees are on me."

The breeze moved his blond forelock, dramatically, and Rachel thought of all the things she would like to say to him, but couldn't. She took the easy way out.

"So explain to me for the eighth time what the Schwarzschild Radius is."

Joules leaned forward as though only the sharing of abstractions could bring him closer to people.

"When a star about two or three times the size of our sun dies, it collapses until the entire mass of the star is concentrated at one point—a singularity—a black hole. As it's collapsing, it becomes denser and its gravitational attraction increases until nothing can escape its surface. In the case of the Earth, the escape velocity is seventeen-thousand miles an hour. But when the gravitational attraction is billions of times greater, the escape velocity exceeds the speed of light. Nothing can travel faster than light, so nothing can escape the surface of such an object. When the collapsing star reaches that size where its gravitational attraction is so great that nothing, not even light can escape, it's reached its Schwarzschild Radius.

"This has a number of consequences. A distance away from the center of the collapsed star, there's a region called the photon sphere where gravity isn't strong enough to pull light into the black hole, but strong enough to prevent it from escaping. Here, light orbits forever around the black hole.

"It also gives rise to the possibility of parallel universes where there could be other versions of ourselves living different versions of our lives. The mathematics of all this is sublime. That's what I'm investigating. But you didn't come here to fathom black holes."

"It's taken me over—Olivia. Do you know what I mean?"

"I know all about that."

"Were you ever so obsessed with something that you knew was hurting you, but you stayed with it anyway?"

"Yes."

"How did it hurt you, if you don't mind me asking?"

Joules brushed his hair away from his face. "Regret. It's probably the worst kind of hurt, aside from a crippling physical trauma. My mother was in the hospital for an emergency gall bladder surgery, and I didn't want to take the time to go there because I was working on the math paper that I was submitting for publication. I ended up going after my father said a few things to me from which our relationship never really recovered. I regret that. The paper could have waited."

"Did you ever do something knowing that it would hurt you?"

"I do it constantly by being alone all the time. But in my case, it's as though I'm missing the nerve endings that are connected to loneliness. I just don't feel bothered by being alone—the way you don't feel your legs when you're freezing to death. How can this not hurt you? What began as a preference for my own company became an overpowering desire to be alone. So much so that sometimes I walk along the halls at school and refuse to look anyone in the face for fear of having to make conversation.

"And I think it's a special dispensation, this power to be alone. Think of all the things you could accomplish if you didn't waste time with people, parties, marriage, kids. I don't desire these things and I think that I'm blessed. I can go weeks without talking to anyone. I know this can't be right."

"Then why do you do it? Why don't you try to socialize more?"

"The effort for me is exhausting. I know I do such a poor job of being a pal that I like myself more when I'm alone. I'm good at that."

"You do a great job of being a pal."

Joules' torso edged away. They were no longer discussing the stars above.

"And what if we enter one of these parallel lives—back to the Schwarzschild Radius—can we ever come back?" said Rachel.

"I sense you're at a crossroads."

Rachel was taken aback by Joules' perceptiveness. Though he wasn't much of a participant in human affairs, he was a keen observer.

"What's on your mind?" he continued.

"I can't say right now, I may not go through with it. And if I do, it would be best if no one ever knew."

CHAPTER TWENTY

It was the third time Rachel approached the Pleasure Palace.
She could do it. It would only be for one day. She told herself she
could do this for one day and still be a good, decent person
afterwards. But didn't every girl in this place say that when they
hesitated outside this entrance?

"Honey, do you mind?" a voice said behind her.

Rachel got out of her way. The Puerto Rican girl in a red miniskirt
entered the Pleasure Palace as men nearby gave her a momentary glance.

Rachel walked to the street vendor and bought a Coke. She never drank
soda, so she just stood there, holding the open can as though doing something.

Indecision was an unnatural state for her. What she was considering
was bizarre beyond anything she had ever contemplated doing. Did
Olivia pace along these same streets before changing herself forever?
She'd been looking for something, too. Inside Rachel, opposing forces
of equal strength vied for her judgment. If she walked away this instant,
what would she do when she got home? If she walked in that door,
would she be the same person tonight, or would she leave some part of
herself behind? Would it be enough to tell herself that it was for a
righteous cause?

Rachel walked in the door.

She was dressed in low-cut blue jeans from Olivia's closet, a tube top,
and red heels. Her thick dark hair framed the large O-shaped onyx earrings
along the sides of her face. As she approached, the big, black bouncer

behind the counter knew why she was there. When they were face to face, he turned away to listen to the rest of a story, making her wait.

"The old geezer walks in here three times a week to buy videos," said the cashier. "He's dyin' of cancer and wants to see all the oriental action I got before he dies. 'Magine that goal?"

"He better have it on fast forward," said the other guy. Both men laughed. When the bouncer turned once again toward Rachel, his face was implacable.

"Who do I see about a job?" she said.

"Upstairs. Second door to your left. Mister Perlman."

Rachel walked up the single flight of stairs and heard the unmistakable sound of human teeth snapping shut behind her.

Two girls in Danskins body suits were offering soft drinks to the arriving men while other girls stood outside their booths inviting customers in for a private show.

Rachel was the only one who had no role here. The girls entertained; the men gawked. They stared at Rachel, waiting for her to change into her costume.

Huge men, disproportionate to their menial task, stood with small pouches of tokens for the customers.

The second door to the right was closed. Now was the time to turn back. This was a sign that she wasn't supposed to do this, that she had done enough and should go back to her dorm room and prepare for tomorrow's lectures.

Nausea attacked her. How long had she been doing nothing in this place where everyone had a clear purpose? She almost asked one of the girls tending bar if the boss was in, in the hope that he wasn't.

On Mr. Perlman's door was a sign that said, *DO NOT ENTER.*

Rachel knocked.

There was no answer at first. The music was loud and could drown out a knock, a heartbeat, even a small scream. She knocked again.

Someone yelled something that couldn't be understood.

When he opened the door, Rachel could see a black girl pulling up her body suit.

"Who do I see about a job?"

"Doing?" said Zoltan Perlman.

"Doing this. Out there."

He asked his companion to turn down the stereo.

When he turned again to Rachel, the smile collapsed. This was his game face. "And you've done this before?" he asked.

"I did something like this."

"Something like this. What's something like this?"

Rachel hadn't expected an audience at this interview.

"I used to dance."

"Okay. That's valuable experience. Before we go any further, I need ID that says you're eighteen."

Rachel gave it to him. He glanced at it, then pulled a sheet of paper out of a drawer.

"Fill this out and wait for me in the room at the end of the hall."

When she entered the room, she put her back to a wall. It was stark with a desk, a camera on a tripod, a place for processing.

She filled out the fields in the application. Name, social security number, age, preferred hours, references. She left that blank. Rachel already felt she was revealing too much information. But this was just the beginning. She sat there for twenty minutes, then Perlman and an Indian assistant came in the room and closed the door behind them.

"Let me have that ID again." He made a photocopy of the driver's license with no attempt at small talk while she waited. Perlman's ample black hair was combed straight back with the strong smell of Vitalis to hold it in place. His long-sleeved shirt stretched over his muscular torso with the tension of angled tent stakes. It bore the Bugle Boy emblem and his trousers displayed the B.U.M. label. Without much inspection, one could see the Gucci logo on his leather shoes.

He put the ID on the desk and sat behind it. His assistant took a position behind the camera. There was nowhere for her to sit.

"Could you look into the camera and stand against the wall, Miss," said the cameraman.

Rachel did so.

He took two pictures of her full face and two more profile shots. Rachel felt she was being booked for a crime she was about to commit.

"You know anything about this business? You know how it works?" said the owner. He lit a cigarette.

"Pretty much," she said.

"Pretty much isn't good enough. I want you to know exactly how I run my place. It's a buck a day, plus you gotta tip the boys. I want payment at the end of every shift. No excuses."

"You mean I have to pay *you?*"

"Correct. The house provides a safe and clean place for you to do business. In exchange, you pay rent for the booth you work. I can't tell you how important it is to get that straight."

"Understood."

He glanced at the application. "Okay. Let's see what you've got." He made a downward motion with the cigarette that was self-explanatory.

Rachel had steeled herself for this moment. The assistant parked himself in the corner and wasn't going anywhere. She didn't think there would be anyone else in the room.

She slipped off her shoes, making herself shorter and instantly more vulnerable. As she pulled off her top, Rachel stole a look at the man through the weave of the clothing as it passed before her eyes. It was the only way she could face him. The bra stayed on.

"Miss—" He looked at the ID. "Lisa, I just want to see your body. How you get there isn't important right now. In other words…" He tapped his watch.

She removed her pants and folded them neatly, but there was no place to hang them. She made a small pile on the floor.

"That bra come off?"

"It comes off."

"You're not going to cry on me are you?"

She shook her head, no longer trusting her voice. The bra came off.

He smoked.

Rachel fixed her hair.

"If you can't do it here, you won't do it in the booth. You've got a nice body, is that what you want to hear?"

Rachel took off her panties and held them in her fist.

"Turn around a couple of times, up on your toes. That's good. You're hired. I see you need the four to nine shift, Monday to Wednesday. Okay. You get forty-five minutes for dinner and a fifteen minute break. I got a booth sitting idle right now. You ready to start?"

Rachel wished he would avert his eyes for just a moment, so she could put her underwear back on. She found herself having to talk while dressing.

"Do you have a ladies' room?"

"Sure thing."

Rachel sat on the toilet with her face in her hands, sobbing. When that was over, she washed her face and, inevitably, had to look in the mirror. She didn't look much different than when she had cried about bad test scores.

"Somebody suppose to be workin' number twelve," said a black girl, sticking her head in the door. "You—you workin' number twelve?"

"Number twelve?" asked Rachel.

"That your booth, is what I'm askin'. Boss wants you in it ASAP."

As she brushed her hair, the strokes grew harder as did her stare into the mirror. She had put herself here for a reason, a good one. She wasn't going to let herself down.

CHAPTER TWENTY-ONE

The girls stood outside the booths, which consisted of a small compartment for the paying customer and a larger one for the girl with enough room for her to lie down in. It was furnished with a plastic chair. Separating them was a three-eighths-inch Plexiglas window. The customer bought tokens for five dollars each, good for one minute. During this time, the two talked via telephone. He gave her instructions, she obliged.

An opaque partition descended when the time was up and the viewing and the conversation, if any, was over. There was a tip slot at the top of the booth. For ten dollars a girl took off all her clothes. Other requests were negotiated for additional tips and tokens.

The house rules were posted in front of the booths. *NO CONTACT BETWEEN THE CUSTOMER AND THE MODEL. NO CAMERAS ALLOWED INSIDE THE BOOTHS.*

It was late afternoon, and the first stragglers from work were stopping in for a little voyeurism. The men spanned all classes. There were businessmen in three piece suits, bikers, old men who dug into their social security checks to come here.

Rachel had to have a hundred dollars for Perlman by the end of the shift. Plus another forty to pay for the red body suit she had to buy. As she stood outside booth twelve, her life was unrecognizable from what it had been a half hour ago. Worse, there was no sign of Sonia. None of the girls fit her description. And did she go by Sonia or an alias like Candy or Kat or Sugar or whatever?

A black girl in a gold bikini who had been dancing nearby finally spoke to her.

"Sweetheart, you can loosen up. You ain't guardin' Buckingham Palace."

Rachel forced a smile. As she turned away, a middle-aged CEO type thought the smile was for him and approached.

He entered his side of the booth.

"Well, go on, baby, he's a good tipper," said the black girl.

The door of the booth opened. "You coming?" said the customer.

Rachel closed the door behind her.

When he put in the token, the opaque screen came up, leaving Plexiglas between them. He looked like a warden peering into a gas chamber.

The customer put a bill into the tip slot. "Aren't you going to take it?"

"I was going to take it after." Her hand went up and fumbled for the money. It was a twenty.

The customer told her what he wanted her to do.

"I'm sorry, I can't do that. You better have this back."

She thought she could stall long enough for the session to end, but time itself was distorted in this place.

"What *can* you do?"

She took off the body suit as slowly as she could.

The customer asked her to sit in the chair and do some things with her legs. She complied.

"You didn't earn that," were his last words as the partition came down.

Another one like that and she'd get fired.

Another suit walked in.

"And, what's your name?"

"Lisa."

"This is for you, Lisa. Haven't seen you here before." He slipped a twenty-dollar bill through the slot.

"I just started today."

"What are you going to do for me, Lisa?" She was hoping they could continue the conversation.

"I didn't catch your name."

"Okay. I'll give you a name. Phil. Phil Ashio."

"That's pretty clever."

"Tell you what, why don't you undress while we talk?"

She forced a smile and began the ritual. First the straps of the body suit, then turning her back as she pulled it down over her shoulders.

"You're not stalling me, are you? That's the second time you've looked at your watch. Here goes another token. Why don't you try facing me, so I can see something?"

Think of it as a medical exam.

She began to slowly work the body suit over her hips while she faced him.

"I don't mean to rush, but I have a meeting across town in thirty minutes."

"You know what I do for a living, what do you do?" she asked.

"Risk Management. That's very nice. Let's lose the bottom."

She removed the bottom.

"Open your legs. Open yourself up."

The customer quickly undressed. Rachel couldn't believe what she was seeing. Beneath his Barney's suit, he wore black fishnet stockings, a garter belt, and a matching bra. When he was done doing what he was doing, he left without a word to go to his meeting.

She rushed to the ladies' room. She had gone this far. It couldn't get any worse. She might as well try to get what she had come for. Stay. Stay a little longer.

Over the next three hours, seven men gave her their business cards along with forty-dollar tips. They wanted dates and some came right out and offered money for sex. Time had never passed so slowly, and nine o'clock seemed like it would never come.

After every customer, Rachel had to call in Bob, the mop-up man. He walked around with his bottle of Windex and a roll of paper towels. Did he grow up wanting to do this? Was there no bottom to human depravity?

During her fifteen-minute break, Rachel was called in to Perlman's office. She immediately began to perspire.

He stared at her.

"I just want to tell you that if you lose your looks, you're out. I give my girls drug tests every so often. On another subject, I can introduce you to a friend of mine who makes adult videos. He's looking for girls."

"I'm not interested."

"That's very decisive. The offer stands. A young girl like you can make a lot of money in the business. Much more than by taking your clothes off."

For the first time in her life, she wished she was a man. She wished she could grab Perlman, throw him up against a wall and get information out of him. Squeeze the truth from his thorax, make *him* pay. Never had she entertained such thoughts of hate.

She spent the rest of her break in the bathroom. Rachel knew she had to get to know other women in this place if she was to succeed in getting anywhere. At the same time, she would have to set a time limit for herself: if she didn't find Sonia and a substantial lead in the next four days, she was quitting. She could feel herself falling, sinking, and at some point, she would be lost.

CHAPTER TWENTY-TWO

When the partition came up, Rachel picked up the phone as she had thirty-two times before. A smooth baritone voice came over the line, and Rachel now waited for the demands he had just paid for.

"It's late in the day," said the young man in a blue suit.

"Yeah. Been a long day."

"I noticed you as soon as I reached the top of the stairs. You're new, aren't you?"

"First day."

"You have a fresh face."

"Thank you."

"I'm just making an observation. What's your name?"

"Lisa."

"I'm Michael. Pleased to meet you. I know you must be tired, so I won't take up too much of your time. I know you hear this twelve times a day, but I was wondering if you'd like to have lunch with me tomorrow. I'm single, thirty-six, and solvent. And I'm told I have a nice smile."

"I appreciate the offer, but I have a boyfriend." Now she waited for the humiliating requests.

"It's just that I'm a big concert and theater goer and I'm looking for someone to share that with."

"I'm going to ask an obvious question. Why would you come here looking for a concert-lover?"

"It's one of the few places you can ask a woman that question without her walking away two seconds later. Are you a concert-lover, Lisa?"

Talking beats stripping, thought Rachel.

"It so happens I love classical music, especially sacred music as ironic as that may sound. As for theater, I guess you'd say I'm involved in the performing arts."

That made them both laugh and the partition came down at precisely that moment as if it were the end of act one. It came up again.

"I'm back," said Michael.

"Good to see you again."

"Where were we? So do you go to shows like Jersey Boys?"

"I love Jersey Boys, but I don't do much of that. It's pretty expensive."

"Ticketron sells those half-price tickets, but you have to go on the same day you buy them. And there are clubs you can join that get you pretty good discounts. Or you can go with me next week and it won't cost you a thing."

She laughed.

"I find you not only attractive, but interesting, Lisa."

"I appreciate that, but really, I can't."

"Well, I don't want to be insistent. In case you change your mind, here's my card. And this is for you. Good night."

It was fifty dollars.

Rachel opened her purse and stared at all the money. She couldn't bring herself to count it, but it had to be at least four-hundred dollars. She killed another fifteen minutes in the booth and went to the ladies' room. By the time she emerged, she just had to stand outside her booth for another ten minutes before quitting.

"I see you got the customer-of-the-month," said a Puerto Rican girl in the dressing room. "I think he splits his time between here and Lincoln Center."

"Ever go out with him?"

"Never asked me. I guess I don't strike him as a Mozart-lover."

"I'm Lisa."

The other girl didn't mention her name, but Rachel had heard her called Tanya. She had small scars all over her face covered with heavy makeup.

"You just starting?" asked Rachel.

"My shift or this career?"

"Your shift."

"Yeah. Eight to midnight. That's a sorry-ass shift. Not too many Wall

Street types at that hour. More like the Hospital/White Castle types. But I'm not a day person anyway."

"And when did the career start?"

"Probably the day I came into this world. But I remember walking in here two years ago and actually filling out the application, fulfilling destiny."

"You don't believe this is destiny, do you?"

"What then?"

"I kind of think we put ourselves here."

"Like hell we do. This shit's the wheel of karma running over my face."

Rachel was too drained to pursue this. She finished dressing and tied her hair back.

"How much do I tip the bouncer?" asked Rachel.

"Twenty'll do. You can pay that in various coins, if you know what I mean."

"I'll pick greenbacks."

"And don't forget the jizzmeister."

"I feel for him. What does he get?"

"Ten will do."

Tanya went off to her booth before Rachel could ask anything else. It was just as well; she was spent.

It was going to be a long ride back and an even longer night. She felt like she had a tumor in her stomach. She took the express at Penn Station, then transferred at Ninety-Sixth Street to the Number One Local to One hundred and Sixteenth Street, the Columbia stop.

In her room, she looked around for a place to hide the cash and settled on the battery compartments of her PC speakers. Grabbing a towel and a change of clothes, she slipped into the bathroom at the end of the hall, praying she didn't run into anyone who would want to engage in conversation. After soaping herself twice in the shower, she knelt down and let the water pour over her as she cried.

Over the years, she had acquired the skill of putting things out of her mind. To what extent was it justified to abase yourself when you're trying to do something good? She could inform Joules that the parallel dimension was no paradise. Somewhere out there, the real Rachel Wallen was still untouched. She wanted that Rachel back, and yet she knew that tomorrow she would go through it all again.

Men's needs were horrible. Perfectly normal and accomplished men harbored unspeakable desires. Now she was being pulled into these desires as Olivia was. Rachel was retracing her sister's steps all too well. What was at the end of that road?

She called her mother to tell her everything was okay. There was no news, of course. These calls had always been awkward. Hers was not an affectionate family. Her father had a great sense of responsibility toward Rachel and Olivia, and her mother was dutiful, but it just didn't work the way she'd seen in other families. When she had gone to summer camp one year, she often heard her friends end a call with, "Love you, Mom." With her it was always, "Okay, glad everything's okay. Bye now." It was different with Olivia. She gave more love to her parents than Rachel, and Rachel knew that they loved her more. How could it be otherwise?

Rachel lay in bed reviewing the day.

Day one: She had thirty-three customers. That's nothing to be proud of, but it was more than any of the other girls and it probably generated some jealousy. That's the last thing Rachel wanted. She wanted to blend in and disarm them all, so they would open up to her.

Sonia had better show up soon. She had to get Sonia to like her and get her to confide. She *had* to know something more about Olivia. Why would she confide in the police? They had to be close to make porn movies together. It was still hard for Rachel to believe that Olivia did all those things, but then Rachel was on the same path. You give someone the right reasons and they'll do anything. Anyone can be blown off course. Olivia had to have been doing it for Achara. None of this would have happened if her parents had tried to get her out of that brothel. Everything would be like before.

And what was Rachel going to do about Achara? She promised to help, and she had to keep that promise. Did Olivia really request a passport for her? What if she didn't get around to it before she disappeared? What would it cost to get a fake one? That's much harder because of all the security now, the holograms and such. Achara had it much worse. Rachel could walk away anytime she wanted. She had to keep that in mind when things got bad.

In the meantime, she'd gotten to know two girls, somewhat, but was getting strange looks from Mr. P. *Looks like he's got a whole career path planned out for me*, she thought. He must know more than he was letting on, too.

Rachel didn't want to be a hero. She just wanted her sister back. She thought of that middle-aged man in the plane that plunged into the Potomac years ago. When the rescue helicopter arrived, he kept passing the rescue line to the next person and the next until he was the last, and then he drowned.

CHAPTER TWENTY-THREE

McKenna had gotten nowhere with Sonia. Today, he had called the Pleasure Palace to get her phone number. What he really wanted was her phone records to see if she and the priest were in contact. But she used disposable cell phones, according to her. Great. So there was no way to confirm if Massey was lying about knowing her. None of the kids at the shelter were much help either. They all just said they loved Olivia. She was good to them.

Two girls from Transcendence House end up stripping in the same joint. Coincidence? McKenna didn't believe in coincidence. When the National Guard was ordered to stand down in Dallas on the morning of November 22, 1963, that was no coincidence.

He had put that to Father Massey and the priest just dismissed it, saying that recidivism was the norm, not the exception. There weren't many sex emporiums left in New York, so it didn't strike him as unusual that two people who were connected with the same organization at different times might end up working in the same place.

The detective continued combing through the Transcendence House records Massey had turned over when he was first questioned about Olivia. They were pretty thorough. All the counselors and all the kids were there, going back five years, even if they just stayed for one night. Lots of notes on each kid, too. Kirsten Schrodinger wasn't on the TH list, so no connection there.

McKenna had no suspects at this point, but anyone who had prolonged contact with a murder victim or a vanished child was a person of interest in his book. Rachel seemed convinced that Massey was lying about Olivia being in the stream at the retreat. McKenna didn't want to bring that up yet. He had no comeback if the priest just dismissed it.

He wondered if other youth shelters kept records as detailed as Massey's. He googled "youth shelters in NYC" and got about a half dozen hits. Covenant House, Trinity Place Shelter, Safe Horizon, MCCNY, and others.

That afternoon he made the rounds and collected soft copies of personnel records from all these shelters. They had a right to ask for a warrant, but they cooperated, given that it was a missing child case.

McKenna entered his two-bedroom apartment in Kew Village, Queens. In the three years since he had moved here, he had yet to have a guest sleep in the other bedroom. For that matter, he had yet to have anyone stay in his bedroom either.

He threw a packet of macaroni and cheese in the microwave and sat down with his laptop. He had a database of all the children who had disappeared or had been murdered in New York City in the last year and was cross-checking it against the list of kids who had stayed at all the shelters.

The macaroni and cheese was hot, so he put it aside. Pretty soon it was cold, and McKenna was still cross-checking. After two hours and the third reheat of the noodles, he noticed something.

Belinda Knights was a thirteen-year-old who had disappeared for about two weeks six months ago. She was then found under a bridge, slaughtered, tortured and missing her hands, eyelids, and lips. The photos taken at the scene made McKenna throw his dinner in the trash.

She had stayed for two weeks at the Metropolitan Community Church of New York Youth Shelter. In her profile, it stated that she had previously stayed at other shelters, including Trinity Place Shelter and Transcendence House. McKenna went down the list of kids in the TH records.

Belinda wasn't there.

CHAPTER TWENTY-FOUR

One experience had taught Rachel that she could become inured to almost anything: witnessing a human dissection at Albert Einstein College of Medicine where she had done a summer internship in her freshman year. It was the body of a homeless man. That smell—a mixture of formaldehyde and rotting flesh. If abandonment had a smell, that was it. Half the interns had to excuse themselves to vomit, even the boys. Rachel decided that she was going to stay no matter how her mind and body rebelled against her will. Her blood pressure tumbled at the sight of the thorax being split open by a saw; her back pressed against the wall for support as the chest cavity was exposed by the retractor. The next day, she reviewed the notes she had taken. They were fragmented and undisciplined. One day she would go through that again and take notes that were calm, coherent, and rigorous. That's what she had to be now, even if it was she who was being dissected.

She sat in her booth for a moment before going out into the loud music again.

It was the third day of her new profession and sadness competed with anger. Anger at having failed, at having to leave this place empty-handed after all the sacrifices she'd made. What was there to lose now? She wanted to feel disgust, shame, embarrassment, revulsion. These were the vital signs of decency. Anything less was to embrace this. One more day.

During her dinner break, she went to the ladies' room.

"That your money layin' there?" asked a voice. Rachel didn't know there was any one else in the bathroom. The stranger jerked her chin toward a wad of crushed bills sitting on the sink. "Well, you better stick that in your shoe or some other crevice. You a cherry, ain't you?"

"If that means am I new, then yeah, I'm a cherry."

"Tishy."

"Lisa."

"You look like you in trauma, Lisa. Nothing you don't do for free at home. Half the time, they as nude-ass as you."

"So I've seen. How long have you worked here?"

"Six weeks. Up from Atlanta. You?"

"New York."

"Not too friendly here. Not much esprit de corps, you know what I'm sayin'?"

"How about a friendly bite to eat?" asked Rachel.

"Sure. Lot of the girls just call it in, but I like to get out. Cross the street, a Tex-Mex place, or passes for one. 'Cept you can't tell what's in these urban fajitas. Italiano at the other corner. Some New-Age, holistic, spirit-of-the-Andes burger place over yonder."

"That's sounds about right." They stepped into the street. "I never thought I'd call this fresh air, but that's what I think now," said Rachel.

"I see ya'll want to put some distance between you and your job, but slow down and smell the roses," said Tishy.

Rachel perused the menu at Quantum Leap. The BLT with soy bacon sounded interesting.

"Next time we'll go Italiano," said Tishy, still looking at the menu. "This is some rarefied shit to me."

"You live far from here?" asked Rachel.

"Two blocks thataway."

"Well, the commute's good."

"It would be if this was a job. The shit you see, you don't get on any other job. Like the guy—I call him Trenches—he comes in my booth twice a week and cuts farts that violate the Geneva Conventions—it comes through the tip slot and I'm overcome. The only redemption is that he gives me fifty bucks for my troubles—I'll have the soy burger with lots of onions."

"Ever meet anyone dangerous?"

"They're out there, but they don't act that way in the place. They wouldn't last a minute. Isaac, the black bouncer? He's real irritable, especially when he's hungry. I heard once he crushed a man's balls for giving him confusing directions to a pizzeria."

"Perlman is creepy," said Rachel.

"They say he was in Israeli intelligence," said Tishy. "Was one of the guys who went around the world killing the Arabs who killed the Jews in the Olympics back in seventy-two. Sword of Gideon or some shit."

"Nice guy. Fits him to a T."

"Yeah, I heard he did some heavy shit. One mean motherfucker."

"He ever hurt any of the girls?"

"He don't do shit himself. He retired from the heavy lifting if you know what I mean. Just follow the rules and you be fine. Rule One: never date a customer. Never even give them your real name."

"I'm already on to that. I'm really Rachel, by the way."

"Savannah."

When they returned to the Pleasure Palace, a girl called from across the room. "Tish, have you seen Julia? I have a client lined up and promised him two girls. Dayna just had her period, so I need a sub."

"She's out today. Family issues."

Rachel glanced in the direction of the voice. It was Sonia.

CHAPTER TWENTY-FIVE

Sonia was already approaching two other girls and Rachel had to make a decision fast. Where would the show be? What would it involve? When would they return? By the time Rachel walked over to the girl, she had decided.

"Hi, I'm Rachel, you mentioned there's a job."

"You new?"

"I started this week."

"Ever do a private show?"

"No, but I could use the cash. But just dancing, right?"

"That's it. "

"'Cause I don't do anything else."

"It's two bills for two hours. Eleven tonight."

"I'm available if it's not too far."

"Brooklyn."

"That's okay. I could really use the money."

"Okay, but don't get shy on me. You gotta get balls-ass naked." She got on her cell phone.

"Jack, this is Sonia. We still on? Dayna can't make it, but I've got someone else. No, just dancing. Don't worry about it. Okay. See you later."

"We go after my shift ends. You got any Victoria's Secret?" said Sonia.

"Ah, not with me," said Rachel.

"Get some. He likes that and he tips good."

At break time, Rachel tallied up her earnings. Three-hundred-ten dollars cash. No wonder girls did this.

A couple of blocks away, she bought a Sexy Little Things black lace thong and Sexy Satin Kitten thigh high stockings with a push up Miracle Bra. Sixty-seven dollars. These were somberly paid for at the register, trying to feign a smile at the overly friendly sales lady. And then the lady said precisely what Rachel was dreading she'd say.

"Oh, he's going to love you in these."

At nine, they took the L to Brooklyn.

Sonia quickly braided her hair in pigtails and brushed her bangs out. She had washed off the heavy makeup at the Pleasure Palace and now looked a lot younger.

"You look good with the straight hair," observed Rachel.

"Our client is partial to the wholesome little girl look."

"What do I need to know about this client—besides his taste in lingerie?" asked Rachel.

"He's loaded."

"What does he do?"

"He does real estate now, but he made his money stealing from ATM machines a few years back. Was making like forty grand a day before he got caught. He did some jail time, but he never gave back the money."

"How old is he?"

"Forties, I guess."

"Anyone else going to be there? This isn't like a bachelor party is it?"

"Just him. I don't do bachelor parties. Just clients I know or come highly recommended."

"So is he a highly recommended or do you know him?"

"Recommended a few months ago. What are you worried about?"

"I'm nervous."

"Just do your job, you'll be fine. How old are you?"

"Eighteen."

"You're fourteen."

"Huh?"

Sonia put Rachel's hair in pigtails and held them with scrunchies. She brushed out the bangs and fluffed out each tail. "Perfect. Fourteen."

"And what's with fourteen?"

"Our client's a pedophile. They all are."

The Red Hook townhouse had a lovely view of Manhattan.

Sonia pressed the buzzer.

"Jack, it's Sonia."

He buzzed them in.

He was about five-foot eight with a pony tail and the physique of a bodybuilder whose goal was cut, not bulk. Rachel always made note of what job a man had if he wore a pony tail and had so far logged a car mechanic, bicycle messenger, a record store employee, and hair dresser.

"Jack, this is my friend, Lisa."

"How you doin', Lisa?" He took Rachel's hand. She returned a smile and was grateful when Sonia removed her shoes, so she could do the same and break the eye contact.

He led them to the living room which was lined with walls of CDs and housed a powerful Bang & Olufson stereo system with speakers mounted on stands that towered over the girls. The place was beautifully decorated with glass coffee tables, white torch lamps, and matching sconces. A Persian carpet covered the bamboo floor. There was no dust to be seen, and even the coffee table books were arranged in perfect order on the corner of the table.

"Let's get some more light in here." He turned the dimmer switch, then smoothed out the carpet where the girls' steps had altered the grain. "Let's get business over with," he said, handing each girl two hundred dollars. "So what are you guys drinkin'? Heineken for you. How 'bout you, Lisa?"

"Um, just a Coke for me. I'm underage."

That brought a smile to Jack's face. "Soda it is."

He tapped the remote and summoned Brazilian jazz.

"Yous eat? I got menus. Szechuan, Cantonese, Rick's Italian Place. Pick what you want and I'll fax it in."

The girls pored over the menus like research assistants. Rachel could feel the man's eyes on her, inspecting her, pawing at her with his imagination. Then the music changed to New Age, something with Gregorian chants and heavy breathing.

They ordered fried rice, ribs, and General Tsao's chicken.

"I'm going to use the ladies' room," said Sonia.

"You have a beautiful place," said Rachel.

"Thanks. I wanted to give it an international flavor. Each room has artifacts from different places. Over there I got fans and Buddhas from the Far East. I'm starting an Africa room," he said in a Brooklyn accent that he didn't try to hide. He reminded Rachel of a low-budget production of Romeo and Juliet she'd once seen in the Village. The actors wore street clothes and spoke the beautiful lines in unfiltered New York accents.

"Ever traveled?" he said, sitting next to her.

"Just to a few states, that's all."

"You on your own now?"

"Pretty much." She sipped on the can, conscious of his eyes falling all over her body. The body he would soon be seeing.

"Life on the road can get rough. It pays to make a few good friends. You got a good start with Sonia."

"She's really cool. Have you met many of her friends?"

"None as nice as you, I gotta say." His hand touched her knee, lightly. "Can I get you another soda?"

"I'm okay. It's bad for your teeth." She felt like rubbing the spot he had just touched.

"You got a nice smile. I'm sure I'm not the first guy to tell you that."

"I guess you sort of are." No man had ever been this close to her.

"No way." He put his hand under her chin. "How old are you?"

"Fourteen." She went for another sip, so he'd withdraw the hand.

"You have a boyfriend?"

"Not yet."

"You're a really cute girl, Lisa. You could go far just on your looks alone."

"What do you mean?"

"I think that's pretty clear. What do you want out of life?"

"To be at peace."

"That's one I didn't expect. Money, security, a home—they can give you peace of mind. It's all attainable."

"How?"

"Take an inventory of all your assets. Ask yourself what you have to offer. You have two huge assets—looks and youth. The world is very looks and youth oriented. I think you're also smart enough to know what I'm saying to you, so I'll stop there. Do you know what I'm saying?"

"I think so."

"Do you or don't you?"

"Yeah, I do."

"Give it some thought." He rose to change the music even though the remote was next to him. Andean flutes filled the air. Rachel could sense what he was going to do next. He sat down next to her and put his arm around her.

"You nervous, Lisa?"

"A little."

"Why?"

"I've never been in a guy's house before."

"Sonia'll tell you I'm a good friend to people who are good to me. So relax. You like this music?"

"Sure, I like New Age."

"What do you listen to?" he asked.

"Believe it or not, I like classical."

"Who in particular?"

"Yo Yo Ma on cello playing Bach." His hand rubbed her shoulder and she knew where it was going next.

"I have to pick up a copy, so I can impress my friends the way you're impressing me."

"Am I?"

"You know you are." His hand slid down around her waist. Next stop—her left breast.

"Um, I guess I could use another soda," she said.

"Hey, relax. I'm cool." He got her another can. "How do you like these speakers? Get up, I want to show you something." Rachel did so, relieved at the distance.

"Press against the speaker, embrace it. Now feel this." He turned the dial and the sound pounded against Rachel's heart. It beat against her thighs. Her hands finally rose up to her ears.

"Four-hundred watts. It could double as a defibrillator. Feel it going through your body? Some girls tell me they can orgasm like that."

"Do you give all your guests that little demo?" she asked, ignoring the last remark.

"I don't get many guests here. I'm selective about my company. I can tell you that I already like your company." He sat down on the couch, but now with some distance between them.

"Same here. Thanks for the soda."

"How long have you been on your own?"

"About three months."

"If you don't mind me askin', how've you been getting by?"

"The kindness of strangers."

"Well, I hope you and me don't stay strangers after tonight. I'd like to be your friend. I liked you as soon as I saw you, and I want you to know that you're welcome to come here any time you want, no strings. I don't make that offer to everyone."

"I really appreciate it, Jack. That's very sweet of you." No way she'd spend time alone with this creep.

The meal went easily. The host was a good talker and created the illusion of an uncle lunching with his favorite nieces.

"That was a great meal. Well, I'm ready for a little entertainment, ladies."

"As you wish," said Sonia. "I'm going to jump in the shower."

Rachel, fearing being left alone again said, "I—I guess I'll go too."

"You can use the other shower in the guest room. Straight down and to the left."

As Rachel let the water run over her, she began to hyperventilate. There would be no Plexiglas screen between her and the client this time. No three-hundred pound bouncer. She would be naked in his house locked behind a steel door. And what did she believe she could accomplish by this? How far would she go to get a scrap of information? *For a smart girl, look what you've gotten yourself into.*

CHAPTER TWENTY-SIX

When Rachel walked out of the shower, Sonia was already dressed in a black garter belt, black stockings, a bustier, and stiletto heels. Rachel put on her black lace thong, thigh-high stockings, and bra.

"When does the clock start ticking?" asked Rachel.

"When we walked in the door," said the other girl. "We have to look like we really like his company, okay? He tips good. Ready?"

"I… I don't think…"

"You're not bitching up on me now, are you? You've done this at the Palace. Look, I'm doing the heavy lifting tonight, so chill."

"What do you mean?"

"I mean you don't have to sleep with him. I've got that taken care of."

"You said just dancing."

"You just dance. I'm gonna fuck. Now let's go."

When they got back to the living room, Franco was smoking a joint. He extended the clip and Sonia took a hit. Rachel declined.

"It'll relax you," said Franco. She shook her head and appended a smile to the gesture.

He pressed the remote and some Lee Ritenour played. Sonia began to writhe and Rachel followed. She wasn't much of a dancer. It wasn't required in the booth.

"Sonia, your friend can't dance worth a shit," said Franco, now loosening up. "We're a little behind schedule, so let's say we start taking some clothes off."

Sonia took off her bustier and tossed it on the floor. Rachel was breathing so hard she knew her breasts were going to be heaving up and down when she took off the bra. She turned her back to Franco and swayed her butt back and forth while watching him in a wall mirror. Sonia took off her shoes and the stockings went next. Rachel resisted the temptation of looking at the grandfather clock and took off the bra. She had to balance herself against the coffee table to take off the stockings.

She kept her back to Franco a tad too long.

"That wall's not a paying customer, Lisa. Over here."

"Sorry."

Sonia pulled down her panties and now it was Rachel's turn.

She slipped it off and faced Franco.

"Lisa, you might want to trim the kitten for next time. I like a nice triangle on top with the rest shaved."

Rachel looked at Sonia whose pubes were cut in precisely that manner.

Franco requested floor work, requiring them to get on their backs and perform acts with their legs and hands.

The ordeal ended forty minutes later when the man looked at Sonia and jerked his head toward the bedroom.

"We're going to hang in the next room," said Sonia.

"Make yourself at home, Lisa," said the host. "You know how to work the disk player, right?"

"Can I just get my clothes out of the bedroom?" said Rachel, passing him in the narrow hallway naked, his arm brushing up against her breast. Then she had to pass him again.

"Join us," he said.

"No, really. Thanks." She clutched her clothes to her body. Sonia tugged at his arm and closed the door behind them.

Rachel sat, fully clothed on the couch, staring at the wall. She couldn't believe what she had just done. Where she was. Had Olivia done the same thing and ended up walking into the wrong apartment? Did Franco know her sister? Rachel had paid dearly for entry into this place and she was going to make it worth the price of admission.

In the bathroom, she was able to lock the door while inspecting the medicine cabinet. Some cold caplets, eye drops, Band-Aid kit, deodorant. No prescription medicine. Rachel wasn't sure what exactly she was looking for.

There were two book cases with about a hundred volumes. Rachel always thought she could tell a great deal about a person by the books, or absence of same, in their home. Let's see. Science fiction, science fiction, a book on the Tri-lateral Commission, The Further Prophesies of Nostradamus, a few MAD Magazines.

The entertainment center contained rows of video tapes, DVDs, and a fifty-six-inch plasma TV. Terminator—One and Two, Rambo, The Magnificent Seven as well as an extensive collection of hard-core porn. Issues of The Minuteman going back years.

She scanned the walls for security cameras. None. Next, the drawers of the end tables. A clean ashtray and matches from the Algonquin Hotel. The study. There was a Dell PC.

She stood by the door motionless and listened to the muffled sound of Sonia moaning. Rachel had to think of an excuse for snooping around in case he walked in on her.

The PC was running and the screen saver created moving star patterns as though one were looking through the portal of a space ship. She might as well be in another world. A push of the mouse and the monitor came alive. The screen lock was on, prompting for a password. Rachel made a few stabs at it: FRANCO, ADMIN, PASSWORD, JETS, YANKEES, METS, NEWYORK, RANGERS. No luck. She made note of the model of the machine. There had to be a way of getting in. It might take five or ten or fifteen minutes for the screen saver to kick in again. If Jack showed up before that, he'd know she was poking around.

She moved quickly to the kitchen and opened the refrigerator to keep herself busy. Rachel's heart was racing and she wasn't even doing anything suspicious now. Her eye fell on a vial in the butter compartment. Steroids. Roid heads had explosive tempers. She recalled one incident in school where a boy who had acquired massive muscles in the span of six weeks suddenly exited through the window upon receiving his board scores.

"What are you looking for?" said a voice behind her. Franco stood at the entrance of the kitchen wearing only his boxer shorts. His torso was brutal.

"Just looking for some orange juice. The chicken was salty. Do you mind?"

"You shouldn't keep the refrigerator open so long. Take out the juice."

As she opened the container, he said, "What were you doin' on the computer?"

"I—I just thought you might have some video games, but it asked for a password." She felt him running his eyes all over her.

"When you're done with the juice, put it back." Then he disappeared into the bedroom.

Her pulse raced as she retreated to the living room. He could go from gentle to threatening in a heartbeat. She selected a CD.

There was nothing here to indicate that Jack killed anything besides childhood. Nothing that would give the police the right to break in and investigate. He was committing statutory rape, but that couldn't be pursued without Sonia's testimony.

When Sonia and Jack Franco were done, the couple exited the room with a neutral demeanor. Sonia was still adjusting her pants.

"You ready?" she said to Rachel.

"This is for you, Lisa," he said, handing her two fifty dollar bills. "Remember what I said about being welcome here any time."

"Thank you, Jack. It was a real pleasure meeting you."

Outside, Sonia called a cab.

"I thought we might spend the night," said Sonia. "But he had plans."

"I didn't know you were going to sleep with him," said Rachel.

"You think he's going to pay four-hundred bucks to watch two girls strip, then jerk off? Stop questioning so much. Look at you. Three-hundred bucks for two hours' work, not even." Rachel didn't ask how much Sonia had earned.

"I have another gig tomorrow." She looked at her cell phone. "This guy's a doctor, so if you feel sick like tonight, he can help. You down?"

"I am. But I don't do sex, Sonia."

"Did I take care of you tonight? Same deal."

Franco watched them as they crossed the street, watched the beautiful arch of Rachel's back, the way her buttocks moved as she hurried to keep up with her friend. He would definitely be seeing her again.

Chapter Twenty-Seven

R achel figured out a way to get into these perverts' PCs. She had programmed a flash drive, so that as soon as it was inserted, it would upload a Remote Administration Tool, or RAT, that would enable her to take control of the machine remotely.

She and Joules used to play around with hacking into each other's computers back in the day, but three years is a long time in that field. Firewalls had become more robust, Internet security software was more aware of attempts to penetrate their host computers. There was no time to start figuring all this out from scratch. The Web offered an abundance of RATs.

Rachel chose SubSeven. It was a Trojan horse, a program that installed a server on the victim's PC, neutralized the firewall, and opened a port, allowing access from outside. Rachel's laptop had the client version of the software and could connect with any of the computers she had infected. SubSeven could take full control of the target machine as well as allow her to access files, determine the size of the hard disk, version of Windows running, and cached passwords. Another crucial feature was that it could activate any camera connected to the PC and record video images without the target knowing it. With this, she would be able to see what was going on in a room and possibly the face of the remote user. The program was open source, which meant that it was not only free, but that some of the greatest hackers in the world were constantly perfecting it over the years. The user's manual was thirty-seven pages long, and Rachel figured she could read it before Chem class.

After returning from class, Rachel went to the computer room in her dorm and inserted the flash drive into the USB port of a machine. She had to find out how long it would take to gather the information—crucial to know when stealing data in someone else's home. After repeated tries, it appeared that it took two minutes to complete the operation.

Once she had the information on the drive, she pulled it out and went back to her room. After retrieving the target's IP address from the flash drive, she input that address into the SubSeven client program. Five minutes later, she had control of the remote PC and was accessing all its data. Now she was ready.

When classes were over for the day, Rachel set out for the Pleasure Palace. She recalled that there was a PC in Perlman's office. How would she get access to it? At Forty-Second Street, she got off the train and walked to the library. She needed to download a death certificate.

Just as Rachel started up the steps to the entrance, her phone rang. It was Sonia.

"Rachel, listen, my client tonight wants a threesome with us—four-hundred each—you down?"

"Oh, God, no."

"Did you hear me—four bills for doing what you do at home? What's wrong? I had to bargain hard to get that rate."

"You said just a show."

"He changed his mind when he heard I had a new girl. I usually go with Dayna. If you say no, that might blow the whole thing."

"No. I don't do that. Sorry."

"Jeez. What am I going to tell him? If he insists, I may have to find another girl."

"You'll definitely have to find another girl."

"Whoa. Okay. I'll call you back."

Rachel was aware that homeless girls don't refuse four-hundred dollars lightly. The phone rang again.

"He agreed you would just do a show, no sex. Two-hundred for you."

"Okay. But that's all."

"Mr. Perlman, can I ask you a favor? I need to make a copy. Can I use the machine in your office?"

"There's a Staples or something not far from here."

"It's just one sheet." She held it up. "It's a death certificate."

The side of Perlman's face twitched.

"Ram, the lady needs to make a copy in the office." He held up a heavy chain of keys that could have been a jailer's.

Ram—Perlman's assistant—led her upstairs. He swung the door open and Rachel's eyes fell on the USB port of the PC. Ram followed her inside. As she raised the copier lid and positioned her paper with one hand, she pressed the configuration buttons with the other, setting it to seventy copies, legal size. When she pressed the start button, it began to spit out sheets in quick succession.

"Oh no," she said, hitting the stop button. Guaranteed paper jam. "Ram, can you help me? I really need to make a copy of this. It's a death certificate." He couldn't conceal his annoyance and said something under his breath.

"Put it back on the scanner," he said, as if not wanting to touch the dead.

"I'll get rid of these," said Rachel, removing the printouts from the tray and ripping them up. Ram was now engrossed in reading the LCD instructions. Rachel walked to the waste paper basket. As she passed the PC, she stuck the flash drive into it. Now she needed two minutes.

"I think the jam is in the second tray," she said.

"I took the paper out, but it still says paper jam," he said.

"I always power off and power it back on. Then it resets." That would take two minutes.

Ram did this and they waited as the power-on self-tests completed.

Now she just had to get that drive back out.

"It has to be letter-sized. Just one copy." Rachel stepped back toward the PC, blocking the flash drive with her body and pulled it out.

"That's it. That's what I needed," she said, holding Ram's work in her hand. "Thank you, Ram. I just can't do anything right today."

She changed into a black teddy and started the evening's work. After three customers in quick succession, Rachel got a breather. As she was standing in front of her booth, her eye fell on a familiar figure on the other side of the room. It was Detective McKenna.

CHAPTER TWENTY-EIGHT

S he instantly bowed her head, so her hair obscured her face and went straight for the ladies' room.

Rachel sat on the toilet shaking. If he saw her—if her parents ever found out—she'd rather die than that.

Savannah walked in. "What's going on out there?" Rachel asked.

"Cops are asking questions 'bout a girl who worked here. The one who vanished."

"Did you know her?" asked Rachel.

"Some. We had different hours. She was tight with Sonia. I think she was doing some sidelines that got her into trouble."

"What kind of sidelines?"

"She was doin' outcalls for rich johns. She was underage and the freaks pay big time for that. God knows we got freaks comin' in here."

"Listen, I know that detective out there. I had a problem with him. Can you let me know when he's gone?"

"Sure thing."

Rachel was losing her nerve. The insanity of the last week was starting to settle in. She was supposed to be attending engineering classes at Columbia; the police were supposed to be chasing pedophiles. What if something happened to her too? Her parents could never go on. It was all so obvious. Achara's life had fallen into a chasm; Olivia went in after her, and now Rachel after her.

Perlman banged on the door. "Lisa, I need you out there. Customers waiting."

"Not feeling well. Something I ate for lunch," she yelled back.

"Do I have to come in and get you?"

"If you come in here, I'll throw up all over you."

Fifteen minutes later, Rachel poked her head out the door. Jesus, McKenna was still there with another detective, talking to Sonia. Rachel put her head down and made her way to her booth where she stood with her back to McKenna. *Don't come over here.* She could see the detective in a mirror. He finished with Sonia, but didn't leave. The other detective was scanning the area as though looking for someone they hadn't yet questioned. A construction worker walked toward her from the other side of the floor. When he got within ten feet, Rachel turned and smiled at him. He smiled back and said, "How 'bout a show?"

Rachel never thought she would love hearing those words. She darted into her booth.

When she came out, McKenna was gone. Thank God. That was close. Rachel followed Sonia to the ladies' room.

"What did the cops want?" Rachel asked.

"They were here before asking about Olivia—the girl who vanished last week. She used to work here. We were friends."

"What happened to her—Olivia?"

"We fell out of touch a couple of months ago. She was trying to get her twin sister out of a whorehouse in Thailand. I remember wishing I had someone who cared enough to reach over and pull me out. Someone who would go to the ends of the earth for me. She said she needed a lot of money to get her out. So I said she could go on gigs with me."

"And did she? Go on gigs with you?"

"We couldn't keep up with demand."

"Did she ever make the money she needed to get her sister out?"

"She made that ten times over."

"So why didn't she quit?"

"She loved it, and the guys loved her. One customer became obsessed with her. Started following her all over the place. He used to watch her come out of her house in Northport and follow her all the way to the city and back."

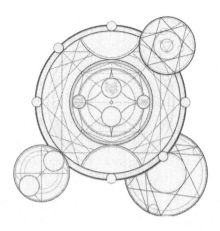

CHAPTER TWENTY-NINE

A ntonio Beltran was going to be a good boy and not stop by his favorite strip club until the job was done. Those mulatas were phenomenal. You don't see butts like that in Mexico. And they liked him too.

The rental hit a pothole that made his duffle bag jump in the trunk. He had packed everything securely for the long ride. The Glock nine mm and a Smith & Wesson .357 magnum. He also carried a Taser in case he got into some unexpected close up action. His ID was specially made in Virginia. Cost him plenty. Al-Qaida used these guys.

It was going to be a straightforward job. His business was on overdrive since the drug wars in Mexico increased the demand for assassins on the Mexican side and he started using online advertising to get clients. He had fiddled with the ad until he got it right and business started rolling in.

Assassin ex-military professional and discreet. Work guaranteed in 10 days or less. Have worked in Spain. $8,000. Serious requests only, and a hotmail address as a contact.

He had a Spanish ad, too, for the Mexican market, but he could only ask one thousand.

The client had checked out okay. Beltran prided himself on not taking payment in advance. Once the job was completed, the client had all the motivation in the world to pay. The dead were his bill collectors, he always said.

He had no problem paying his bills these days. At thirty-two, he drove a new Mustang and bought himself a house in Nuevo Laredo. He had come a long way from the days he roamed the streets of Nogales offering himself as a tour guide to gringo tourists.

The tour always ended up in a motel room where he would suck dick. One guy fell in love with him when he was ten and was able to smuggle him back to Arizona in the trunk of his car. He lived with the man for three years, attending school in Tucson and perfecting his English. Finally, Child Protective Services got wind of what was going on and sent his benefactor to prison for twelve years. Beltran went to stay in foster care and, although he wasn't sexually abused, he got beaten left and right. He finally ran away and got back to Mexico. By then, he was thirteen and ready to work for one of the cartels as a smuggler or lookout. They exploited his ability to speak English and kept sending him over the border with a backpack full of drugs. After four years of crossing the Sonoran Desert and getting chased and shot at by Border Patrol, he joined the Mexican Army.

Once Beltran had left the military, there were few prospects. There was some small-time dope dealing at the border, then he saw some Chicano high school boys driving seventy thousand dollar cars and found out they killed for money. Antonio made friends with these buttonboys and asked them to subcontract some work to him. Being generous, they had assigned him the job of wiping out a distributor who had insulted their boss across the border. Antonio capped the man in a workman-like manner as he pulled into his driveway. He had to kill the woman who was with him, too, but he didn't get more money. If he had been a Zeta, he would have commanded nine or ten times the fee. They were specially trained by U.S. Special Forces and Israelis. But he was working his way up the ladder of respectability.

The car slowed as it passed a state trooper. Beltran had to start lining up multiple jobs to make these trips cost-effective. After this job, he might stay and sightsee.

He'd never been to New York.

CHAPTER THIRTY

Rachel had two assignments: the first three chapters of Plato's Republic and stripping for Dr. Sartorius.

On the train to Long Island, fear overwhelmed Rachel as she sensed the thing she was pursuing drawing closer. She was horrified at the thought that one of these perverts had been watching her house, obsessed with Olivia. He might have also observed Rachel. He would know her, but she wouldn't know him.

Sonia flipped through the messages on her phone. She had about three dozen steady clients who were forever texting their love to her.

"Did you know that more people are killed annually by donkeys than in air crashes?" She pressed the advance button on the cell phone. "A pig's orgasm lasts thirty minutes. Christ, can you imagine? This is how I got most of my education. I only made it to seventh grade."

"Why's that?"

"Where I come from, no one gets past eighth grade. I'm Amish."

"Get outta town."

"No, really."

"With the buggies and baking? Where?"

"Intercourse, Pennsylvania. Go ahead. Laugh."

"So what brought you here?"

"We were a big family. Fourteen of us living in one house. A big house with a barn. I had an uncle who would take me into a room every day and rape me."

"Did you say anything to anyone?"

"You have to understand that things are very strict in an Old Order Amish household. You just don't go accusing someone of rape and sodomy, especially if you're nine years old. So this went on for four years until one day I told my mother. She told me to shush. Women don't have a lot to say in that society. I finally got up enough nerve to tell my father, and he whipped me for lying."

"Don't they have elders or something?"

"When I was thirteen, I went to the bishop after a prayer meeting and told him. He told me to wait where I was and I saw him conference with the elders. Well, the conclusion of all this was that they told my father and he whipped me again. Pretty soon people were avoiding me and stopped talking to me. Even under my own roof. This was more fucked up than getting raped every day. And this uncle, Lemuel, wouldn't even look at me at meals like he was building up for all the attention he was going to give me later. Then, no matter how hard I tried to stay in a room with people, he'd call me away for chores. This is in a place where if you wear your hat crooked, you get disciplined. If you use an electric saw instead of a hand saw, the course of your life can be changed. Once a boy was going to marry his girl and someone brought up the matter that he was seen using a neighbor's electric saw, and the bishop wouldn't let them marry."

"So what did you do?"

"So I made up my mind that I wanted Lemuel dead. I prayed for this, but it wasn't answered. Every Saturday morning a Mennonite friend would come over and cut wood for the family. He could use a chainsaw since he was Mennonite. But I knew that Uncle Lemuel secretly loved to operate that saw. The only time I saw him grin was when he made that sawdust fly. It was to the point where my uncle was doing all the work.

"In a grocery store, I had once heard a radio story that some tree-rights activists were driving spikes into redwoods to keep the loggers from cutting them down. What happens is that when the logs are processed and cut, the saw blade hits the steel spike and shatters. Sometimes it kills. I found some rusted ten-penny nails and banged them into four or five logs that were in the next day's stack of firewood.

"Sure enough, when the chainsaw arrived the next day, Uncle Lemuel started cutting. I heard the scream because the saw stopped and I could see him running around the yard trying to hold the two halves of his face together. The Mennonite friend put him in his truck and drove him to a hospital where they managed to save his life. He was out a week later with a mark across his face that looked like something God had made. He couldn't work for a long time and others had to do his planting. But even though he couldn't plant corn, he had a hatred growing in him. They had taken the nails out of the fire wood and concluded that because they were rusted, they were probably there for a long time. But he knew it was me, and I knew that it was only a matter of time before he was going to do something to me. I wasn't going to let him rape me with that face of his. The face I had given him. And he was getting better and better. I took fifty dollars out of the jar and went to the train station. The teller thought it was strange to see a fourteen-year-old Amish girl traveling alone, but he had no way of confirming my story. Amish people don't have phones. I've been on the streets ever since."

"And these clients don't scare you? A lot of the men at the Palace scare me."

"They don't pretend to be something to me that they're not. I can handle a transaction—I get that."

"What about this doctor? He's a pedophile too?" asked Rachel.

The other girl nodded. "Lost his wife three years ago. He did the daddy/daughter role playing with her all the time. Now he doesn't have to role play."

"You've slept with him?"

"I sleep with all my clients."

"And—you don't mind me asking…"

"Ask."

"You play his daughter?"

"He loves it. I drive him crazy and that gets me off—the power I have over them."

"Did you start out just dancing for them?"

"Everyone starts out like that. Then you give head. Then sex. It's a natural progression."

"So I guess I'm on my way."

"No one forces you. You just wake up one morning and decide to go all the way. It's a lot more money; why give it away to some jerk whose going to have a good time for a few months, then stop calling? You've got to look out for yourself."

"You're not scared going to the homes of these men? I am."

"My clients are all pillars of society with a lot to lose if they got in trouble with the law. They're businessmen and doctors, not killers."

Dr. Willard Sartorius opened the back door and ushered them inside before any greetings were exchanged.

"There's a bucket of wings on the table. Potato salad and corn. Help yourselves," he said without asking Rachel's name.

He was a large man, over six-foot-three with massive shoulders and legs and a Buddha's belly. Rachel had always been intrigued by the dignity which the title medical doctor conferred. She saw this point played out in the movie *One Flew Over the Cuckoo's Nest* when several escaped mental patients are, one by one, introduced as doctors. As the camera pans to each, their blank stares and disheveled hair exude learning. Here again, Rachel saw this phenomenon at work as the surgeon's inelegant paunch and bald head evoked power, not plainness.

"Excuse me," he said and exited the kitchen.

"This is some house, huh?" said Sonia. "It could be on MTV Cribs. It's got fireplaces in the bedrooms and a game room downstairs."

The doctor was elusive. When he wanted Sonia, he poked his head into the kitchen and said, "See you for a moment?" He knew beforehand that Sonia was bringing a friend, so there could be no surprises here. He seemed extremely self-conscious about what he was doing.

After dinner, the girls took showers. Rachel was instructed to use the guest bathroom in the basement. It was large and lined with white Italian marble, yet there wasn't a bar of soap or bottle of shampoo in sight. Rachel closed the door, but it wouldn't lock. She hung her knapsack on the door hook, then let the water run. As the mirror began to mist, she undressed.

Fortunately, she had brought her own soap. The hot water felt so good on her back as she massaged her feet and legs. After putting on a change of clothes, she went in search of a blow-dryer. She checked some linen closets and shelves. There was a constant droning sound that had been there all the while, and she finally located its source. It was the water pump of a huge aquarium. The two-hundred-fifty gallon tank was populated with exotic fish that Rachel had never seen, and she felt even farther from home as she shared these depths.

She opened the closets one by one. The musty smell of old possessions enveloped her. Here was a gift graveyard, a place where all the unwanted and unusable Christmas presents and birthday notions of the last twenty years had gathered. Everything here was new, but old. She inspected the cheap ashtrays and picture frames doled out at weddings that never saw their intended use.

She found old notebooks, meticulously arranged in boxes from Sartorius's medical school days. Rachel went through them and came to know a twenty-four-year old med student better than she wanted to.

He had been a prolific margin writer. Alongside the lectures on anomalous pulmonary venous return and ischemic heart disease was exhaustive commentary on the breasts of female students and the examinations he would like to conduct on them.

As the semesters went by, the comments became more graphic, more self-revelatory. Sartorius related the autopsy of a young girl in what began as clinical observation. Suddenly he wrote of the girl's beautiful white, untanned skin and firm breasts that he so loved. He wrote of his excitement even as her body was being cut open, of her undiminished attractiveness. The words now spilled beyond the narrow column alongside the page. It was as though the thin blue margin that had separated the sane from the psychotic had given way. Then, in the darkest sentences of all, he described how he had returned to the body later that evening and had done things to it.

CHAPTER THIRTY-ONE

Rachel wanted to vomit.

She wanted to run out of here, to rid herself of these men, to end the pursuit and get back to her life. As she darted to the top of the stairs, she ran into Sartorius.

"Find everything?"

"Yeah," she said.

"What were you doing down there so long? The shower stopped thirty minutes ago."

"I was looking for a blow dryer."

"Are you all right?"

"Where's Sonia?"

"Upstairs in the shower," said the doctor, not yielding the way.

"I—I need a blow-dryer. Do you have one?"

"My ex-wife had one. Come with me." He led her upstairs to his bedroom. Rachel could hear the shower going.

"Rachel is such a Biblical name," he said in the bedroom. Already Rachel felt violated. Why had Sonia given him her real name? Rachel couldn't think of anything to tie in with that, so she kept working on her hair with the towel.

He appeared to be looking for the dryer, but Rachel believed that there was nothing in this immense house that was beyond his cognizance.

"Here we are," he said, pulling it out of its original box. Rather than hand it to Rachel, he plugged it in for her.

"Low heat or high?" he asked, blowing her hair for her.

"Low is fine. I can manage." She took the blower from his hand and stroked it the length of her long hair while Sartorius sat not four feet away watching.

"Do you like it out here in the open country?" he asked.

"I've been out here before. Nice fish tank. Doesn't look like there would be anyone here to take care of them."

"Oh, I have cleaning people here regularly. They handle it. So tell me about yourself, Rachel."

"There isn't much to tell. I work with Sonia in the city."

"The Pleasure Palace?"

"Uh huh. I just started this week."

"And what were you doing before that?"

"I was staying at a shelter in the city. Transcendence House."

"I see. So did you bring any fancy underwear for your show tonight?"

Not exactly an Albert Schweitzer segue, thought Rachel. "I have some stuff." She was hiding her face behind her hair as she dried it, hoping he would get the message that she'd like to do this in private.

"You know, I'm sure I have some outfits I can give you. My wife bought a lot of things she never wore. I didn't have the heart to throw them out. You must be a size two."

"That's right," she said, creeped out at the thought of wearing a dead woman's lingerie.

"I have a keen eye for these things. Relax, Rachel. You seem really nervous."

"I am really nervous. I'm not used to working in other people's homes. Just the booth."

"Well, you have nothing to concern yourself with. Let me take your pulse."

He reached over and put his fingers on her wrist while looking at his watch. She still held the brush.

"Your heart is racing. Calm down. You're among friends." He no longer measured her heart, just held her hand.

"You seem pretty young to be working at the Pleasure Palace."

"I have ID."

"And how old are you really?"

"Is that a problem?"

"Oh, it's no problem whatsoever with me. I just need to know how old you are."

"Fourteen." Rachel pulled her hand away. "I better dry this hair or it'll frizz up."

He seemed pleased with the answer, but his brow furrowed at the rebuff. At that moment, Rachel realized the power of her sexuality. She had something indescribably desirable to this man, something alluring enough that it crushed this doctor's power to heal, leaving intact only his cold, accurate talent to observe.

Sonia entered the bedroom wrapped in a towel.

"Just what I'm looking for. You done with that?" she said.

"In a bit."

"Well, girls, let's get on with the performance. I'd like you to come out one at a time. You first, Sonia," instructed the doctor. "I'll get some music going. Descend the stairs slowly, but make sure your hair is completely dry."

Rachel looked at Sonia and her face said everything.

"It's two-hundred bucks. Just remember that," whispered Sonia once the doctor was gone.

"Why did you give him my real name?"

"Oh, shit. I slipped up. No big deal."

"It is a big deal. That's my name. I don't want him to have it. That makes me feel like dirt, that he said my name."

The girls prepared in silence.

Sonia looked in the mirror. "I'm worth a thousand. This outfit is hot." She pulled down the dragon print tapestry bustier to reveal more breast. The matching red thong was tiny. She took a pair of spike heels out of her bag and put them on.

"See you," said Sonia and left.

Rachel sat on the bed and listened to the performance downstairs as she tried to calm herself down.

A medley of seventies love songs played.

"Tell me what to do, Daddy. I don't know what to do," she heard Sonia say.

Sartorius gave her precise instructions. Which hand to use, which finger, how fast. Point your toes, sweetheart. Excellent. Good girl. Rachel felt sick. She sat there, hugging herself as she waited for her turn. Now Sartorius was asking Sonia about Rachel. She couldn't hear what.

Footsteps echoed on the stairs. She dreaded this moment.

"You're on, kid," said Sonia. "You look hot in that."

Rachel was trying to tuck her pubes behind the tiny thong. She gave the other girl a look of desperation.

"Hey, take it easy. It's the same as the Palace, only nicer. Go on, he's waiting."

Rachel came down the spiral staircase, the kind she had seen in her dreams where she was dressed as a bride. Not this.

"Sonia's a tough act to follow, but give it your best," said the client.

Rachel pushed a smile to the surface. The saxophone demanded more than that. She started.

She decided to get it over with. She took off the bra and twirled it around a few times, then tossed it at Sartorius.

Now the doctor's face lit up. "Good," he said.

She slipped off the bottom and threw it on the couch.

"Could you lie down, please," said the doctor. It sounded like he was about to take out a speculum. She complied.

"Do you know what floor work is, Rachel?" She nodded with her head against the carpet.

"I'm going to give you some instructions and I need you to follow them precisely. Your tip depends on it. Understood?"

"Okay."

"Say 'yes, sir.'"

"Yes, sir."

The requests gradually became orders. He had to correct her repeatedly, like a music teacher, and she repeated the moves again and again until done to his satisfaction.

"Very good. You need some work, but you have a lot of potential."

"Thank you, sir."

"Come here and sit next to me. No, don't dress."

Rachel noticed that she had lost her self-consciousness. It had become a source of power.

"You're really pretty, Rachel. Why are you forcing a smile? You haven't had a real smile since you got here."

"I guess I'm just nervous."

"Why? You have nothing to be afraid of."

"I'm just new to all this, people's homes and all."

"I understand. I'd like you to come back, but I need you to relax and be more playful. We're all here to have fun, after all. Do you mind if I kiss you? On the forehead?" His lips traveled down her neck and it was all she could take. She craned her neck upward as if trying to break the surface of a pool.

"Do you want to get dressed?"

"Yes, sir. I do." That seemed to take Sartorius to another level.

She struggled free and picked up the clothes.

"Wait," he said. "This is yours. You did well." He handed her three hundred dollar bills.

"Thank you, sir," she said. "I appreciate that."

"Now you can get dressed."

She paused at the top of the stairs to put on the panties before entering the room.

"How'd it go?" asked Sonia.

Rachel said nothing.

Sartorius appeared at the door. "Sonia."

"I'll see you later, kid," said Sonia.

"And what are you going to do now?" he asked Rachel.

"Would you mind if I read one of your books downstairs?"

"Read. Just don't touch anything."

Even in a rich man's house the walls could be painfully thin. Rachel sat in Dr. Sartorius's living room which was directly below the bedroom and could hear every grunt and blasphemy going on upstairs. The contempt in the man's voice when he said 'don't touch anything' killed her—the arrogance that denied others the right to touch, yet gave him license to fondle everything. Rachel hoped she didn't hate all men before she learned to love one.

Yesterday, she was at the Forty Second Street Library and stroked Patience and Fortitude—the lions which guard the entrance. Those were precisely the qualities she was running out of as this charade went on. At what point would she tell Sonia that she's not really on the streets? Was that a betrayal? She'd never betrayed anyone. Rachel had to remember what she was really here for: to find Olivia.

There was plenty to touch. Aside from medical books, there were many others about fly-fishing and skeet shooting and sporting clays. There was a catalog of rare shotguns from Sotheby's. The man was eclectic all right. Rachel searched through every drawer and cabinet. In one she found cognac that was dated 1921, never opened. Proceeding to the closets, she went through every pocket of every piece of clothing.

The doctor was a meticulous man. Everything was neat and categorized.

National Geographics with National Geographics. American Journals of Medicine with American Journals of Medicine. The grass and shrubbery outside were maintained with clinical attention. The house spotless. The fish, colorful and happy. It was as if this exaggerated outer order was needed to counterbalance an unseen derailment.

The house was immense. Rachel proceeded from one room to the next, rifling through drawers, opening coffee tables, sticking her hand down sofa seats. There had to be an office and she prayed it was downstairs. She wandered barefoot until she found the study. There was a PC under the desk, powered on. She quickly reached into her pocket and removed the flash drive.

It was dark back there. Damn, she should have brought a flashlight. In order to be sure she was plugging the drive into an active port, she followed the mouse cord to the chassis and pulled it out. After some work, the flash drive went in. She stopped breathing and listened to the sounds on the second floor. There was nothing. One minute. God, hurry. Kneeling in the darkness, she would have no excuse if he walked in on her. Two minutes finally passed and she pulled out the flash drive and held her finger on the USB port in order to guide the mouse cable back in. Done. She put the plastic cap back on the flash drive and slipped it in her pocket. Silently, she padded out the study, then downstairs to the guest bedroom.

She locked the door of the bedroom and put the drive back in her knapsack, tying it to an inside loop by its lanyard. Back to those college notebooks. There were twelve of them with every page dated and the subject of each lecture underlined. Everything organized and ordered.

Around the beginning of his third year, she noticed a change. Subtle at first, then more marked. He was seeing a girl called Layla. At first, the remarks were filled with the joys of incipient love. Her gestures when she used a fork in a restaurant, the loveliness of her skin, the joy of her company. A few weeks later, the comments became more clinical. Her body parts were described in precise detail, every mole and dimple. He devoted two pages to describing her private parts and the sounds she made during intercourse. Her oral technique was analyzed. There was mention of photos taken of her in bed. Her last name never came up. It was just Layla. Petite brunette with narrow hips and upturned nose. No mention of whether she was a fellow student or where they had met.

After a while, her name was no longer mentioned; she was "the specimen." The foreplay now consisted of clinical examinations conducted with Sartorius fully dressed and the specimen lying on a table, not a bed. There were detailed descriptions and drawings of her body cavities, the inside of her mouth, the strength of her PC muscles. It began to resemble Da Vinci's notebooks, the writer's voice detached and objective.

Then one note marked the end of the relationship and Layla was not seen again: *Layla is gone.*

CHAPTER THIRTY-TWO

S artorius dropped them off at the train station later that evening. Rachel rode in the back and saw him constantly looking at her in the rear view mirror. *What would he be writing in the margins tonight?*

"Thanks," said Sonia. Sartorius just nodded to them and they were out of the car.

Before Rachel could comment on the night, Sonia said, "I have another stop, but this one doesn't pay any money."

"You do charity work?"

"Sort of. You may not want to come along. I have to visit a friend of mine. She's got AIDS. She's in a hospice and I may not see her again."

"I'll go. If you don't mind."

Christa House was a twelve-bed hospice for patients in the last stages of AIDS.

"You can wait here if you want," said Sonia, outside the building. "I won't be long."

"I'm okay."

Outside every room was a box of disposable latex gloves. Rachel considered the tons of literature she had studied about this disease during her research. She knew she couldn't contract it through casual contact, but she wanted to put on the gloves, mask, and gown, and breathe different air than they breathed.

The room was suffused with the light of a red bulb.

There were three women with advanced AIDS. They were all young, under twenty-five, clinging to life. The air reeked of vaginal infection and diarrhea. Rachel wanted to vomit.

"Maureen, it's me. It's Sonia." The woman extended her arms to embrace the visitor. "This is my friend, Rachel." The patient nodded at Rachel.

"Would you like to sit down?" asked Maureen, showing that what was killing her had not taken away her manners.

"Sure, I'll sit down," said Rachel.

"You can bring that chair over here. And this is Adele and Louise." They waved from their beds and Rachel waved back from her chair.

"Why is the room red?" asked Rachel.

"Chromatherapy," answered Louise. "An hour of red, two hours of indigo. I researched that."

"Louise is our miracle researcher," said Maureen. "She looks for cases of spontaneous remission."

"Alexander Solzhenitsyn was terminal with pancreatic cancer—he was even put aside into the death room. Then he recovered," said Louise. "There are lots of cases like that."

"How's things?" asked Sonia. "You look like you've gained weight."

"Thanks for lying. I've lost three more pounds."

"They're going to close us down," said Adele.

"What's this?" asked Sonia.

"They have no funding, so we only have four more months and they close the doors. We're the last hospice in Long Island."

"Is that so?" asked Sonia.

"That's what we heard," answered Maureen. "We can't focus on that. We have to focus on ourselves. And you? You look good."

"I am good." Maureen glanced at Rachel just long enough for Rachel to realize that Sonia was HIV positive.

"Well, maybe some good guy will step forward and make a donation," said Sonia. "Look, we brought you guys some strawberries, just picked right here in Melville."

"Oh, that's great. Could you wash them over there?"

They all ate some strawberries.

"I look for passages in the Bible and the Upanishads that have power," said Adele. "For inspiration I find hopeless battles in history that were won by the underdog. Agincourt. Five-thousand English defeated twenty-thousand French. At Thermopylae three-hundred Spartans held off a million Persians for days before they were overcome."

"Adele, it's time for the whales," said Maureen. The other woman slid a tape into a cassette by her bed.

There was the moaning of whales and the surf.

"We're investigating every avenue to save ourselves," resumed Maureen.

"I'm sorry, what's your name?" asked the searcher of battles.

"Rachel."

"Rachel, could you do something for me? Could you turn my sheet around so the butterflies are flying toward me?"

She was so thin that her outline beneath the covers looked like the bas-relief of a person. Rachel and Sonia spun it around, altering the flight of butterflies, but that would be the only miracle today.

"In the battle of Midway," said Adele as though that conversation hadn't ended, "we were against overwhelming odds. Eighty-six Japanese ships to our twenty-seven. Two-hundred-seventy-two planes against our hundred-eighty.

"At 4:30 a.m., a squadron of Japanese bombers hit Midway Island, wiping out two-thirds of the U.S. planes on the ground, and returned to their carriers without losses. By 9:36 nearly all of our torpedo bombers had been shot down. All our fighter escorts ran out of fuel and fell into the sea. Then the Yorktown sent up torpedo bombers and seven out of ten were shot down by Jap zeros—"

"Adele," said Maureen.

"This is the moment of hopelessness. This was the darkest hour. When our entire fleet was at the brink of destruction. Then—"

"Adele."

"Then one of the Enterprise's dive bomber groups, which was lost, finally found their way and got to the Japanese fleet. Then a miracle happened. Within five minutes, this small squad of planes sunk four Japanese carriers. The enemy fleet was destroyed in the most decisive battle in naval history."

The room was silent for a moment. Rachel thought of another battle she hoped Adele would never know about—Masada.

"Can I have the nurse bring you anything, anyone?" said Rachel.

There was silence, but for the droning of the whales.

"Sorry for making you feel sorry for us. We just like to talk," said Maureen.

"No, please don't apologize to me. Is there—"

"There's nothing. Nothing at all. But thanks for staying longer than you had to."

"We're gonna be going," said Sonia. "You guys get some rest."

"Good to see you again, kid. It really is." Sonia kissed her good bye.

"I'll be on the other side soon. Rachel, is there a message you'd like me to give a friend?"

Rachel looked into the eyes of the doomed woman.

"I have a message," said Sonia. "Tell Kirsten Schrodinger that I loved her."

CHAPTER THIRTY-THREE

McKenna had turned over the photo of Belinda Knights to the Cyber Crimes Unit to check if she had appeared in any child porn seized over the last twelve months.

Steve Stultz of CCU reported back that the photo had been passed to the NCVIP. Using facial recognition utilities, they located a ten minute video of Belinda dancing nude. The National Child Victim Identification Program had the largest database of child porn in the world, confiscated from suspects on and off the Web.

"So where do we go from here?" asked McKenna. "How do I see this video?"

"You don't. Not even cops are allowed to look at them. I've got contact info for an FBI agent who has clearance. He can answer questions."

McKenna got in touch with the agent, who was very polite, like the CIA guys McKenna had known in Afghanistan.

"What are you looking for, Detective?"

"I'm trying to determine where the video was made and who might have made it."

"I'm afraid there isn't much in this video. It consists of the girl dancing naked against a blank wall. There's a Christmas tree that comes into view a couple of times, but that's it. No one else appears in the shoot."

McKenna had no patience for this.

"I'm working the Olivia Wallen case. She disappeared here last week. She and Belinda have a shelter in common—Transcendence House. One was a guest and the other counseled there. I'm dead in the water. Is there any way you can PhotoShop the girl out of the video or something so I can see the rest?"

"We could. That'll take time. Again, it's just a nude underage girl against a beige blank wall. No doors or distinctive markings are visible. There's only a Christmas tree that comes into view on two occasions for about two to three seconds each time. That's it."

"Is it one of those small artificial trees or a large one?"

"It's a large one."

"Can you cut out the girl?" McKenna could hear the guy swallowing.

"I'll arrange it."

McKenna received the email later that night. It could be sent over the Internet since now it contained nothing criminal. It was eerie. The sanitizing process removed graphic material, leaving intact the background and the children's faces. In this case, Belinda Knights' head floated in space as she danced from side to side, foreshadowing the disembodied ghost she would soon be.

The FBI guy was right. Just a blank beige wall. The camera didn't move much to the left or right. That would have shown more of the room. The Christmas tree came into view for about two seconds and again near the end of the video for about four seconds. Another dead end.

CHAPTER THIRTY-FOUR

The Webmaster had been waiting online for two hours for his next prospect and now she arrived.

I'm here, he typed.

Sorry I'm late, replied cindy2di4.

That's OK. You're worth waiting for. I didn't know if you'd show up.

Sure I would.

I have a photo of me I'd like to send you, he typed.

OK.

He sent a picture of a young man, early twenties, handsome and dressed in a plaid shirt.

That you?

Yup.

U R really handsome.

Thx. How about a pic of you?

I scanned it at the library today, said the girl. *Gimme a sec to send.*

As the photo began to resolve on his screen, he became aroused as he always did. She was about thirteen with brown hair and beautiful legs. She was sitting on a basketball, wearing shorts and a pink halter top.

WOW! he typed. *All the guys must stare at you in the street.*

No. I don't have a lot of friends. I'm new in town and there are a lot of clicks in school.

Cliques.

Right.

He "listened" with infinite patience to her discussing her day, her thoughts, her anxieties. He listened and took notes.

I really like talking to you, she wrote.

I love talking to you, Cindy. You are a really interesting girl.

I hope I don't bore you with my day. It's pretty ordinary, I guess.

It's not boring to me. I like listening to you.

It's just that I don't have a lot of friends. I'm sort of lonely.

I want to be your friend. I don't have many friends either.

But u r so handsome, she wrote.

That has nothing to do with it. There aren't a lot of good people out there. And I'm very busy these days with my business. So I don't get out much, he said.

What's your business?

I'm setting up a website where I can sell imported stuff from South America.

That sounds so neat. What's the link to your site?

It's still under construction, so you can't get to it. I'll let you know when it's finished.

k

Let's get online again tomorrow. Same time?

Sure.

Bye ☺

Bye ☺

After closing the chat session, he launched the intruder program. The file he had sent Cindy contained a Trojan horse which enabled him to take over the PC and inspect its contents.

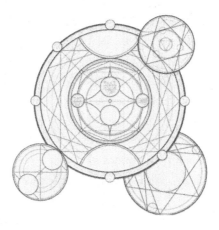

CHAPTER THIRTY-FIVE

W hat am I bid?"

Only one bidder raised his paddle this time and it wasn't Armand Greyson. The Guston was overpriced at $2.6 million and the buyer's premium would push it way over his budget.

And budget was important these days. Sales were declining at his gallery and he had a nasty divorce on his hands. But his dictum in life was "for every problem, there is a solution."

And Armand Greyson had a problem.

Since the discovery of Kirsten Schrodinger's body, he was just going through the motions of his daily routine. Get up, shave, shower, coffee, dress, get down to the gallery.

At least a dozen times a day he got online to follow the Olivia Wallen disappearance. *No Clues about Honor Student Disappearance*, was the Yahoo headline this morning. Police were baffled. There were now rumors that she had been prostituting herself to pay for college. If they knew that, they might know a lot more.

Greyson looked at his watch—he had an appointment he had been looking forward to all week. He left Sotheby's and returned to his apartment on Eightieth and Fifth to assess his options. Brazil had no extradition agreement with the US. He would have to liquidate all his assets here first, and that wouldn't be easy. He couldn't put the co-op in the name of an LLC; the association wouldn't permit it. He had a home in

Greenwich, Connecticut—the wife would probably get that anyway. Last summer, he had spent two weeks in Fortaleza, Brazil, and in between romps with fourteen-year-old girls, he checked out some beachfront property. It would be a good place to disappear to. Living was cheap and peaceful. Not many art galleries, but you couldn't have everything.

His phone rang.

"Yes, please," he said. Minutes later, there was a knock on the door.

"Hi, Armand. This is my friend, Lisa."

"Welcome, Lisa. Come in. How's my favorite niece?" said Greyson.

"Right," said Sonia.

"You have a beautiful apartment," said the other girl, scanning the massive stone fireplace, twelve-foot ceilings, fine art, sculptures, and antiques from all over the world.

"Let me show you around," he said. "You can put your jackets in here. Sonia's seen all this before, but maybe you'll be more interested, Lisa."

"Yeah, I'll sit this one out," said Sonia.

"These are things I've collected during my travels over many years. These are masks from the Akan tribe in Ghana. Those are Balinese theatrical masks. This hallway—after you—has some of my favorite pieces." As she walked in front of him in the narrow hall, he was inspecting her thoroughly. His pulse raced when she had taken off the denim jacket, displaying her beautiful breasts in a white tube top. The cut-off jeans revealed lovely, creamy white legs. She would have no tan lines. He was torn between a genuine passion for the articulation of art and his addiction. The addiction won every time.

"Very beautiful," said Lisa. "Your whole apartment is beautiful."

"You have good taste. It was built in 1931 and designed by Rosario Candela, New York's most celebrated luxury residential architect."

"How many rooms is it?"

"Fifteen rooms total. Five bedrooms, four and a half baths, two maid's quarters, five fireplaces, eighteenth century oak floors. It was love at first sight. Do you believe in love at first sight, Lisa?"

"I guess."

"Have you ever been in love?"

She shook her head.

"And how old are you?"

"Fourteen."

"Are you new in town?"

"Sort of. A few weeks. I've been hanging with Sonia for about a week."

"She's a doll. Well, fourteen's a great age."

When the tour was over, Greyson poured himself a drink and flipped through his vast collection of music for some ambiance.

"It's dinner time. What would you girls like?"

"Menus?" said Sonia.

"I have them memorized." Armand began rattling off the specials from Josie's, The Center Room, and Café Lalo with the speed of a head waiter.

"I'll have the cheddar burger, onions, mushrooms and that Italian cheese cake from Lalo's," said Sonia.

"Done—Lisa."

"Same here."

"I love symmetry," said the art dealer. "I'll balance that with the angel hair pasta and garden vegetables."

As they ate in the formal dining room, it was evident that Greyson was a practitioner of the lost art of conversation, which often strayed into his love of the Old Masters.

His appearance belied his accomplishments. He was tall and skinny with a comb-over, red notches along the sides of his nose from the glasses he wore during the day, but was likely too vain to wear now, a college ring on one hand and a signet ring on the other. The suit was tailored, but with telltale dandruff along the shoulders. He looked like a salesman at Men's Warehouse. Rachel wondered if the doorman really believed that Sonia was his niece. *It's amazing what money can do*, she thought.

He told them how he had started out as a warehouse worker in Long Island City. It was a company that sold art supplies and instructional books. He bought some supplies with his employee discount and started what he thought would be a great career as a painter. He ended up getting a scholarship to the Parson's School of Design. That led to a job at Christie's and, years later, his own gallery.

"I really worked at the painting, but the competition in that field is beyond brutal," he said.

"What sort of art did you paint?" asked Rachel.

"Nudies," answered Sonia.

"Sonia has a talent for over-simplification. I painted what's known as Fantasy Art. I'll show you some afterward. It hearkens back to mythology with super muscular men, women and animals. It demands a lot of imagination—you create your own monsters."

When dinner was over, he was true to his word. "This way to my studio. By the way, here's carfare." He handed them each two hundred in cash. The host led them into a great room that would have been well-lit during the day. The curtains were drawn now. On the walls were paintings of voluptuous women wielding battle axes and Scottish Claymore swords. They rode on the backs of tigers and two-headed steeds. Rachel had to admit, it was impressive and powerful.

"She look familiar?" asked Sonia, pointing to a scene of a girl in a silver thong holding a spear in one hand and a mace and chain in the other while facing a bison-like figure emerging from a cave. It was Sonia.

"He laid it on with the tits and ass, but a pretty good facsimile, right?"

"It looks exactly like you," said Rachel. "You're really good. These must sell for a fortune."

"These don't sell at all," said Armand. "Strictly my private collection. I make a living now selling other people's work."

"Well, I'm going to take a shower," said Sonia.

Rachel turned to follow when Armand said, "Oh, Lisa, could you stay a moment?"

Rachel could see this one coming.

"I would love to paint you nude. I know you're here for a show, but I'd rather we spend the time creating something more meaningful and lasting. You would look beautiful in a painting."

"Won't that take a long time?"

"Oh, I take photos and work from those. I'm quite a skilled photographer. I can tell you it would be something really special because you're so special. And next time you come here, you'll see yourself transformed into one of these."

"You gonna take pictures of me?"

"Yes, of course. No one would ever see them, so no need to worry about that."

"Well—I guess so. I was gonna ask. I don't have a place for tonight. You mind if I stay till the morning?"

"Of course you're welcome to spend the night."

"Okay," said Rachel.

"Fine. Well, let me get my equipment. Why don't you get undressed and stand over here."

Rachel was having a hard time keeping up the facade of the fourteen-year-old homeless kid. *Just get it over with and spend the night rifling through his house.*

The art dealer stood motionless as Rachel took off her clothes. She watched him scanning her body. He didn't make eye-contact.

"No tan lines or tattoos. Good," he said almost to himself. He set up the camera and tripod without taking his eyes off Rachel's body. It was as though he was in the thrall of something so powerful that it directed his movements.

"Stand against that white background. I need to take a shot from all four angles. That's good, Lisa. Now sit in that chair and put one leg under you. Look up at where the wall hits the ceiling. I'd like a serious expression." The camera flashed. Stand. Turn around. Shake your hair. Lie down on the bed. Open your legs. The poses were barked out with increasing hostility. He was now videotaping her as well as taking still shots.

Rachel could see his erection through his pants and knew she was one step away from getting raped. *Sonia, where are you?* The fear, the humiliation was breaking her down. She swore this wouldn't happen, but she couldn't help it.

"What are you doing?" he asked.

"Nothing."

"I need you to stop crying."

She turned her back, not wanting to give him the satisfaction of making her cry. He photographed her pain. Her revulsion. And finally her hatred.

"I think that will do," he said. "You still owe me an hour and twenty minutes before you earn that two-hundred. Step into the living room."

CHAPTER THIRTY-SIX

Greyson poured himself a scotch and sat back in a leather wing chair. "Let's lose the TV and get on with our own show, shall we?"

A commercial break came and the newscaster said, "New details about the honor student disappearance at eleven."

This seemed to break the host's concentration. He took a sip of his drink and stared into space for a moment.

"How about some music, maestro," said Sonia. "Or you want mime?"

"Yes, put something on," he said vacantly. "And turn that off."

They danced to salsa.

Greyson's eyes were on this new girl. He looked at her as a sculptor looks at a block of marble and all the possibilities, all the outcomes that lie within it. If only the artist could bring it out. He imagined her living here permanently as his niece. His sex slave. He could tutor her in art and history, so she would be educated and make intelligent conversation. He would teach her the art of sex, the art of submission. When she pulled off her panties, a rush came over him that only this could produce. Greyson desired her with an overpowering force that compelled him to put everything he had at risk. He knew he was reckless, but that didn't sway him. He could only yield to this power, not defeat it.

Then his revelry was broken by the stark truth that he would soon leave this country. Could he take her with him? The fantasy wouldn't let go. No, he couldn't, was the answer.

"That's good. I'm ready to turn in," he said.

"I'm sorry I cried before," said the girl.

He ignored the remark. "You can sleep in the maid's quarters. Unless you want to join us in the bedroom."

"The maid's room is fine."

"Well then, this is yours. I enjoyed the show. I hope you come back, Lisa."

"Thanks, Mr. Greyson," she said, taking the hundred dollar tip.

When they were gone, Rachel put her clothes back on and went to the bathroom.

You've got to do this, she told herself. You've got to hang in there. She washed her face and hands. She felt like taking a shower, but she didn't want to take her clothes off again. In her hand, she held the flash drive. Please let this work out, she prayed. Please don't let this be for nothing. Please watch over me.

She locked the room to one of the maid's quarters and lay still on the bed for half an hour until they were settled in. Then barefoot, she walked soundlessly throughout the carpeted apartment. She began with the studio. Always have a reason for being in a room, she told herself. She could say she wanted to see the paintings again. There was a file cabinet. Locked. She opened the drawers of a desk. In it were the usual office things: paper clips, stapler. The place smelled of paint and thinner and brought back memories of the Long Island Institute of the Arts where she studied piano for a year. The first target was the camera that held her own naked pictures. That memory stick came out. Then the camcorder.

Two big busted Amazons stood like sentries over three camera cases sitting on a shelf. She pulled a chair over and hopped on top to reach the cameras. She took one down and looked at the case. The flap was held closed with Velcro. She began to tug on it and it sounded as loud to her as a flatbed emptying a load of gravel. She put it under the covers of the bed and opened it. Once the camera was freed, she quickly flipped open the memory compartment and pulled out the memory stick. Replacing that camera, she proceeded in the same way with the other two.

After putting the chair in its original position, she rifled through his bookshelf, which contained more papers than books. Something occurred to her. She went back to the desk. There was a key. It opened the file cabinet.

The tabs said, *PARIS, NEW YORK, LONDON, ROME.* There were photos of paintings and sculptures. Notes on the provenance of various pieces. She was looking for pictures of kids. She was looking for Olivia. She went through all three drawers, but no luck. This guy *had* to have pictures of kids around. Rachel had seen how his eyes had lit up when she said she was fourteen. The man was sick. There had to be evidence of his sickness here somewhere.

Rachel pushed aside a pocket door to a study. There was a burgundy leather recliner and a brass lamp. Everywhere, fine books—Alexander Pope, Will Durant's *The Story of Civilization,* all thirteen volumes, leather-bound Harvard Library volumes of *The Iliad, Ivanhoe,* Churchill's *A History of the English-Speaking Peoples.* Not the reading list she would have expected of a pedophile.

There was a laptop case leaning against the recliner. Rachel stood perfectly still and listened. The walls were thick in this 1930's building, and it seemed to filter the passion out of Sonia's sounds until only a distant homing signal arrived.

Rachel picked out a book which she'd grab in case she was interrupted. It was entitled, *The City of Florence.*

She made note of the position of the zippers before opening the case. After lifting out the Dell, she placed it on the chair and opened it. She pressed the power button and turned the screen away from the door. Now her own breathing was the only sound.

The machine began to boot and what a long time that took now that she was in a hurry. She plugged in the flash drive. Two minutes—another interminable age. The laptop booted all the way, displaying a Rembrandt-adorned wallpaper. She pulled out the drive and shut down the machine. Now to swiftly and deftly replace… suddenly the Windows logoff sound played. It pierced the silence like an alarm. Someone stirred in the next room. Footsteps came her way. It was too late. The light came on.

"What do you think you're doing?" Greyson had a towel around his waist.

Rachel was breathless and excuseless.

"I thought I might play some video games. I didn't think you'd mind. I'm sorry." He pushed her against the wall.

Shoving the laptop into the case he said, "Don't EVER touch anything without permission. Now get out of here."

"Hey, chill," said Sonia, standing by the door naked. "She didn't break anything. Let's go back to bed."

"She leaves."

"I'll go. It's okay."

"No, wait. You can't just throw her into the streets now, it's late."

"Can't I?"

"She was gonna play some fuckin' video games. What's wrong with you?"

"I don't need someone lurking around my house like a cockroach."

"You're fucked up. I'm outta here," said Sonia.

"Where do you think you're going?" he asked her.

"I go with her."

"Enough. Both of you. Out."

"Damn straight." The girls scrambled, gathering their jackets, knapsacks, and were out the door.

Greyson spent the next fifteen minutes checking to see if anything was missing. Then he found something that wasn't supposed to be there. On the carpet, near the laptop, was the plastic cap of a flash drive.

CHAPTER THIRTY-SEVEN

S orry I wrecked the night," said Rachel outside.

"Don't sweat it. There's more where he came from. The world is full of asshole guys willing to pay for us. And by the way, that's why you get paid up front."

"Listen, yesterday when we went to see your friends—"

"Yeah."

"Can I ask you something?"

"The answer is yes."

"Huh?"

"Yes, I'm HIV positive."

"I'm…"

"Skip the condolences. I'm going to beat this."

"What about the men you sleep with. Do they—"

"Some of them know."

"And it makes no difference to them?"

"For some of them, it increases the thrill. What can I tell you? Kirsten was positive, too. We were going to beat this together. But everyone I love leaves."

Rachel looked behind them to make sure they weren't being followed.

"How did you two meet?" asked Rachel.

"I was in the Mid-Manhattan Library one day last year. I was feeling pretty lonely and I went on Facebook. I looked through a bunch of guys' profiles, then I told myself I really needed a friend, not a lay, so I looked through the girls' profiles. She was from Minnesota, blonde, really pretty, and fifteen. She was on the streets over there, and we started corresponding, and a funny thing happened. It became something to look forward to. That I had someone. We started talking on the phone, and I told her, since she was already on the streets, why not come to New York and stay with me. It's better than the streets. I have an apartment, sort of. I remember the day I was waiting for her at Port Authority. I was waiting for her with all my heart, and when she got off that bus we just fell into each other's arms.

"We started doing outcalls, but I wouldn't let her fuck any of the guys. She just danced. I wanted to keep something clean in this world and she was clean. And she was mine. But they started offering her a lot of cash and she gave in. She told everyone she was twelve and she looked it. Eventually, she moved in with a boyfriend and we drifted apart. And now she's dead." The wind blew her hair away from her face, but there were no tears.

"Let's not talk about that. Look, we're doing good. Let's head back to my place."

Rachel was torn between getting into the memory sticks and keeping Sonia company. They both needed a friend tonight.

"Sure. Where's your place?"

"We'll take the D uptown."

The apartment was on Tremont Avenue in the South Bronx, not a place you'd want to be at two in the morning. It was a fifth floor walkup.

"Mi casa es su casa," said Sonia.

"Thanks." There was a couch that looked like it came in off the street, a TV set and in the bedroom, a mattress on the floor. No pictures on the wall.

"As you can see, my money doesn't go into interior decorating. I invest in HIV cocktails."

"What are you taking?"

"I started this new drug called Atripla. It takes the place of three other drugs. You only take one pill a night instead of twenty pills a day. Twelve-hundred a month. It's been okay, except for the depression. Fifth floor may not be the best place when you're taking that. Well, make yourself at home. Bathroom's over there."

After brushing her teeth, Rachel was trying to decide on where to lie down. The couch didn't do it for her. The mattress was a twin.

"I need to get a cover for that couch," said Sonia. "You can share the bed, if you don't mind."

"Sure. Hey, thanks for sticking up for me back there."

"Forget it. We have to stick together. We'll be fine." She took her pill and threw back a glass of water.

Rachel laid down on the mattress with her jeans on, not knowing whether to take them off.

Sonia stripped down to her panties, flipped off the light, and slid under the covers. Rachel took off her jeans and left her tube top on. She was oddly bashful now in the dark with this girl. She'd never been in bed with anyone.

"You mind if I hug you?" asked Sonia.

"Sure." The girl's arms wrapped around Rachel and their breasts were touching. Rachel didn't mind. She couldn't see Sonia's face in the dark, but it was right next to hers. Sonia's breath brushed her neck. She knew she couldn't get to sleep in this position, but didn't want to do anything to change it. They held each other like that for three minutes, then Sonia's lips brushed against hers. Rachel kissed her back, then put her head next to Sonia's neck and they went to sleep.

The next morning Rachel had to excuse herself and rushed back to the dorm. She hated having to leave Sonia so abruptly, but she didn't have any time to lose. After digging her digital camera out of one of the boxes, she sat down at the desk and inserted the first memory stick into it.

There were pictures of what looked like Amsterdam with canals and tour boats and bicycles chained to the railing. There were some shots of Greyson in a hotel room dressed elegantly. Then the venue changed and it looked like a third world country, somewhere in Asia. The shots were taken from an open taxi of some kind. Shots taken inside a strip club. Naked dancers, bright, gaudy lights, and bored-looking Westerners. Greyson seemed interested enough to take over thirty photos of various angles of the girls' bodies. The scene switched to the inside of a hotel room. A nude young girl. Another one coming out of the bathroom. Then there were close-ups of the girls performing oral sex on him, she guessed, since his face wasn't in the frame.

Next stick. Back in New York. There was a picture of an Egyptian obelisk in Central Park. Rachel had seen that once. Next, his apartment studio. A naked model on the same bed Rachel had posed on. Rachel could still hear the orders being shouted out like a military drill. The photos had an artistic look to them, Rachel grudgingly admitted. He had control of the light, the angle, contrast, brightness. He had control of everything except himself.

The next photos were of Rachel herself. She could hardly look at them. The humiliation. The fight against tears. She could barely believe that was her. It seemed like someone else. At least he would never get the satisfaction of looking at them and doing God knows what while he looked at them.

Next stick. This was a boy, about thirteen, also naked on the bed, also posing for Greyson. He was smiling, almost enjoying what he was doing.

The next image was of Olivia.

CHAPTER THIRTY-EIGHT

Rachel held her sister in her hands and dreaded advancing the frame for fear that she would be gone forever. Olivia was posing naked on the same bed and was smiling. *What could possess her*, thought Rachel? Why had she chosen this? Rachel had never seen her more beautiful, her long Asian hair that Rachel had always envied falling across her breasts. Did Greyson enhance that beauty with his manipulation of light and shadow to magnify the horror of its destruction? Rachel pressed the advance button.

Olivia was giving someone—presumably Greyson—oral sex. She looked straight into the lens. He abandoned any pretense of artistry when he attempted to shoot himself having sex. There were off-kilter snaps of Olivia kneeling over him; he over her with the shadow of the camera on Olivia's chest. There were other, pensive shots when they had finished. In one frame, Olivia was wearing the Bali theatrical mask Rachel had seen in his house.

The final memory stick presented the same images with a different model. A young blonde girl with a dazzling smile. Greyson posed with her on the couch fully clothed, over the remains of a meal. There was something familiar about this girl. It was Kirsten Schrodinger.

There was a shot of her naked, holding a spear and wearing a tiara. Posing for one of his paintings, no doubt. There were several of these poses—with her foot up on the bed, wearing armbands and thrusting a Claymore sword. She looked like a warrior.

If she handed these over to McKenna, how would she explain how she got them? What she couldn't do is tell him she was going to the homes of pedophiles. She downloaded all the pictures to her laptop, then deleted the pictures of herself from the memory sticks. Now what? Someone could have given her the pictures, but the police would insist on knowing who. If Rachel made any mention of Sonia and sent the police back to her, the relationship would be over and all this would end. She decided to email the pictures anonymously with a note containing the art dealer's name and address. Joules had shown her once how to chain two remailers together and send an untraceable email. Every instinct told her she was getting closer to a killer.

What's your favorite movie? typed the Webmaster.

Oh, it's an old one. My mom rented it last year. Ninja Turtles, replied cindy2di4.

I liked that one too.

I like the second one.

Yeah. You watch it with your parents? asked the man.

My dad passed away last year, she wrote.

I'm so sorry to hear that. It must be lonely.

It really is.

Did you get the file I sent you? he asked.

Yeah.

What did you think of it?

Kinda weird. What they were doing.

They really loved each other. That's how it's expressed. Nothing wrong with it, he wrote.

I don't know.

I just wanted to share that with you. I hope you don't think any different about me now, wrote the Webmaster.

No. No.

Does it change anything between us?

No. I just never saw anything like that before. Forget it.

Do you want to forget it, or are you curious to see more? said the man.

I guess I'm kinda curious.

Well, I have another.

OK.

Should I send it now? asked the Webmaster.

Sure.

Done.

Wow. This one's a movie, right? wrote the girl.

Yeah. Shows more.

She's beautiful.

Sure she is. What he's doing to her is beautiful too. See how she likes it? said the Webmaster, getting aroused.

Yeah

So how's your Mom? Still working late?

Yeah. I just sit here and surf till she comes home.

That's lonely.

Yeah. I like talking to you.

Me too. You promised me another picture of you, he wrote.

I know. I need to scan it at school.

What kind of a picture is it?

Me at Disney World 2 years ago. On the water slide. And I think I'll be able to borrow my friend's cam tomorrow.

That would be great. I really want to see you, Cindy. You already know what I look like.

OK. Well, it's late. We've been chatting for like 2 hours. I gotta get to bed.

When can we chat again?

Tomorrow night. Same time.

The Webmaster had downloaded the last piece of information that he needed from Cindy's PC. Now he was ready.

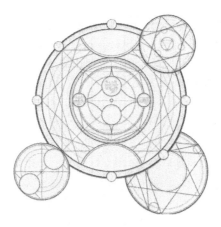

CHAPTER THIRTY-NINE

Massey introduced himself as Ian Bride and entered the house in Richmond Hill, Queens.

"Irina," said the realtor.

"Shall I take off my shoes? I know that's a growing custom," said the priest, now disguised in blond hair, mustache, and glasses.

"Oh don't worry about it. Well, this is it, three bedroom, one and a half bath. It's a nice neighborhood."

"And you said the garage can be entered from inside the house?"

"Yes," she opened a door off of the living room and turned on the light. The steps descended directly to the garage.

"That's great on cold winter days," he said.

"It definitely is. What part of Ireland are you from?"

"County Cork," said Massey in the accent he recalled from his father.

She nodded vacantly and said, "Is this what you had in mind?"

"I believe so. It's close to Manhattan." It had what he was looking for. A quiet street, a foyer, and direct-entry garage where he could enter and leave without being seen.

"And you mentioned you could pay six month's rent in advance."

"Yes, that's not a problem," said Massey, looking up and down the street through the window.

"Well, the owner is amenable to that in lieu of a credit report. There is this water damage over the bay window, but they'll repair it before you move in."

"That won't be necessary," said Massey, already defending his privacy. "I'm a bit of a handyman back home. So it's eighteen-hundred a month and one month's security? Good. I'd like to close the deal then if there are no issues."

"I have all the paperwork here."

"Oh, is there garbage pickup, or is that extra?" he said, once again peering out the window.

"The city takes care of that. That's where our taxes go. You can make out the check to Joanna Federman. And you say you're moving in when?"

"I have cash, and I had planned on moving in immediately, if that's alright."

"Yes, of course. Let me give you a receipt."

I'm so glad you were able to make it tonight, typed the Webmaster.

Me too. I miss you. So you liked my picture? typed cindy2di4.

I loved it. You are gorgeous, baby. I'm really excited about meeting you tomorrow.

Me too. I hope you like me.

Of course I will.

You might think I look different than in the picture.

I would love you even if you were ugly. I can see you are a beautiful person, he wrote.

I have a cam today. You want to see me? she said.

Sure. She sent the invite. He accepted and her face materialized. It was more than he had hoped for. She was a little older than her picture, still, fourteen with dark pigtails and a beautiful Italian face.

Is that really you? he typed.

Who else is it going to be?

Stick your tongue out.

Huh?

Just let me see you stick your tongue out. She did so. It wasn't just a video of a young girl. This was a live girl and she was gorgeous.

What do you want me to wear? The outfit in the picture? she asked.

No, in fact don't dress any differently than usual. If you're telling your mother you'll be at the library there's no reason to get all dressed up.

Yeah. But I have to be back by 9:20. The library closes at nine on weekdays.

Not a problem. I'll leave you off a couple of blocks from your house. Is that OK?

That would be great. I've never been in a guy's car. I'm kinda embarrassed to say.

You'll like my car. But I hope you like me more.

Your Camaro? wow ☺

It's fast, so I'll get you home on time.

Gerard, can I ask you something?

Ask away.

Are you chatting like this with any other girls?

Are you kidding? This takes time, and I'm a busy guy. What do I need more girls for when I have the best one? Just relax. This feels so right.

It feels right to me too. But my Mom can't find out or I'm dead.

Part of being an adult is being able to keep a secret. Can you keep a secret, Cindy?

Sure I can.

Then we have nothing to worry about.

God, I can't wait to see you this Tuesday. So we'll meet at 322 Clancy Street in Richmond Hill? said the girl.

I'll see you then.

CHAPTER FORTY

The police had been tailing Armand Greyson for the last two days—ever since they received the anonymous photos. McKenna sat in the long-term parking garage at Kennedy Airport with Detective Aldo Marchese, waiting for Greyson to return from Boston. He had flown there yesterday for some kind of art dealer's thing and was scheduled to return on the six-thirty shuttle. Their unmarked car was three-hundred feet diagonal to Greyson's, so they couldn't miss him when he arrived. If he had scheduled an international flight, they would have moved in.

"I say bring him in for questioning," said Marchese, lowering the sun visor, cutting off the top of his thick head to the outside world.

"All we have now is photos of nude underage girls which we didn't find on him."

"They were taken in his apartment."

"By who? Maybe the person who sent them to us. We still can't connect Greyson with the photos," said McKenna. "All we have of him is the base of his cock in the kid's mouth. We would need a couple of more inches for a conviction. Found out today that Greyson's not his real name. Legally changed it from Ira Shickelgruber twenty years ago. Wasn't that Hitler's real name too?"

"Ira?"

"Schickelgruber."

Marchese adjusted the seat. "I hate waiting. Never good at waiting."

McKenna was used to it. Used to waiting in the brush for hours, sometimes days for his target. That's what snipers do. You play games in your mind to stave off boredom. And you have to remain alert at all times. It was the toughest part of the job. Shooting was the easiest. He wished the shooting part had been harder.

In Afghanistan, he had waited once for two days. They were on a mountain ridge waiting for a Taliban commander and his men who were making incursions behind coalition lines, scoring high casualties using IEDs and snipers. He recalled how bad the mosquitoes were, but they couldn't use repellant. Snipers weren't allowed to smoke, use aftershave, or even soap to prevent the enemy from smelling them. You just stand still and take it. If you had to take a shit, you shit in your pants. You endure.

He and his spotter thought they were well-hidden in the shadows. Then, in the early afternoon, two figures passed a hundred meters below them and spotted them. A month earlier, a four-man SEAL team had encountered the same situation. They were discovered by a father and son as they waited to snatch a Taliban commander. They let them go and the civilians alerted the Taliban who returned with a hundred warriors. The four men fought valiantly down the sheer mountain. Three were killed, then a U.S. rescue helicopter was shot down, killing all sixteen aboard. McKenna wasn't going to repeat that mistake. With a single glance at his spotter, the agreement was sealed. They dropped both targets. Four hours later, the Taliban arrived.

They waited until the group was out in the open, then the commander was dropped first. John McKenna pulled the trigger twelve more times and twelve more bodies littered the landscape. After dark, they descended the ridge. Something in him compelled him to check the two civilians he had shot, a decision he would live to regret. He turned over the first one and pulled off his head scarf. It was a boy of fourteen. The second was probably his brother. Maybe thirteen.

He came home to his wife and seven-year-old Brittany and thought that would help. Two years later, he got divorced. McKenna had given Brittany his email address last year, but never got a message. He checked every night when he got home.

"Yeah, waiting is the toughest part," said Marchese.

Greyson removed his five-hundred dollar shoes at airport security. He used to enjoy travel, but now with all these security checks, it had become tedious. He had taken a quick jaunt to Boston for the opening of a friend's gallery. It was a good opportunity to network and there were several Brazilian dealers attending. He had wanted to get an idea of what it was like to operate out of Brazil. Grabbing his carry-on, he headed for a newsstand to pick up the Post.

There was nothing on the front page about any of the disappearances. Good. He flipped through the paper quickly and found a small story on page six about the missing Asian girl.

Police still have no solid leads in the disappearance of Olivia Wallen, the honor student who vanished last week in Manhattan. Teams of volunteers scoured the woods near her house in East Northport while NYPD conducted interviews with everyone known to have interacted with her. Olivia was a volunteer at Transcendence House in Manhattan, a shelter for runaway and abused teens. Police and family are becoming more concerned as the days pass with no clue as to the girl's whereabouts. She did not leave any notes behind and had never run away before. A sense of desperation has set in, according to one source, after the discovery of Kirsten Schrodinger's mutilated body this week. Police are as yet unwilling to conclude that the two disappearances are related. In the meantime, a prayer vigil will be held...

It looked like a dead end. He tossed the paper and headed straight for the long-term parking.

He powered up his Blackberry and scrolled through his messages as he walked. His divorce attorney had advised him to get rid of the uptown apartment and rent a modest place to look like he was just making ends meet. So he rented a dump in Brooklyn that reminded him of the way he used to live and was putting his Fifth Avenue place up for sale next week. It was time to start liquidating assets. It had taken a lifetime to gather all the artwork in that place. He couldn't take it all with him. Ninety percent would have to be auctioned off. He thought of putting it in storage, but it would be too easy for the government to seize. He couldn't leave any assets behind, just as he had left no trace of Ira Schickelgruber twenty years ago.

Greyson's green 1966 Jaguar was faithfully waiting for him. This was one luxury he wasn't going to give up. A quick walk around showed no scratches. If he relocated to Brazil, the Jag was coming with him.

When Greyson turned the key, a large bomb exploded beneath his seat, splattering the remains of his body into the concrete ceiling of the garage.

CHAPTER FORTY-ONE

A ntonio Beltran had decided on the method of execution. This was a favorite of the cartel for urban assassination. For three days, he had tailed his prey, following him from Queens to Long Beach, back to malls and the Bronx. The schedule was irregular and the routine varied. The target used the same vehicle every time. That would be his coffin.

Beltran sat in a motel in Queens downloading the rest of the information he needed. On the bed were the tools of his trade: Glock, AR-15, garrote, binoculars, commando knife. He had killed with each of the weapons at close range and long. There was no escaping death. The AR-15 rifle with the Zeiss 12X scope was his favorite for long distance jobs. But most of his work involved the motorcycle helmet he'd brought with him from Mexico. A veteran of several jobs, it was with him when he had ended the re-election campaign of the mayor of Ciudad Juarez. He used it to terminate two rivals of his client in the Gulf cartel.

Wearing rubber gloves, he carefully wiped off enough ammunition to fill the clip of the AR-15 and the Glock. He checked the silencers he had hand made before leaving for this job. He always made his own silencers. These were disposable and caught most of the powder residue in the silencer chamber. Simple device, it was made of a ten-inch section of a brake line, perforated with holes. Then the brake line was encased in PVC tubing, capped at both ends and drilled to accommodate the barrel. The space between the PVC pipe and the brake line was filled with steel wool, then small holes were drilled around the cap to allow gases to escape. Once the target was dead, the silencer was thrown away. Untraceable.

He entered an address into Google Earth and zoomed in on the target. The whole neighborhood could be seen. He traced out his avenue of escape. Now he was ready.

Through binoculars, he observed his victim exit the building and walk half a block to his car. On previous days, Beltran had followed him in a rental, but this morning he was on a stolen motorcycle in Long Beach. The Kawasaki was fast and provided the perfect means of escape once the job was done. Then he would dump the bike, the gun, and the helmet.

The target headed east on Beech street toward the Atlantic Beach Bridge—one of only two ways out of Long Beach where it attached to the mainland of Long Island. Beltran calmly put it in gear and eased in the throttle. He went directly toward the bridge and waited for the target. There wasn't much traffic today and he had checked the reports for any major bottlenecks on Long Island. There were none.

The silenced Glock was cocked and ready in his shoulder holster. The car appeared in the distance and Beltran watched it approach in his rear view mirror. It made the right onto the bridge and the chase was on.

Beltran kept his distance along the span. He couldn't move on him until they were on the Nassau Expressway, but he had to strike before they got to the Van Wyck Expressway, which always had traffic jams due to Kennedy Airport. The target sped by the toll booth without stopping. That lane had the barcode reader. Beltran reached into his pocket and grabbed the two dollars and two quarters he had prepared. By the time he exited the cash lane, he was ten cars behind the target. The Kawasaki could easily close that gap with a twist of the throttle.

They got onto the Nassau Expressway. There were several cars in front and behind him and that wasn't necessarily a problem, but Beltran preferred as few witnesses as possible. He never knew when he was going to run into a hero in a fast car.

What he liked about this road was that it was straight, not winding, so he could see ahead for several hundred yards in order to make an escape.

He closed the gap to five cars. There were now only two cars behind him, a mini-Cooper and an old Mazda—too slow to catch up to him. Up ahead, there were four cars, no motorcycles. The target got onto the fast lane. Beltran could kill with either hand, but he preferred to be on the left of the target because the driver's side was closer to the barrel of his gun. If the attack came from the right and the victim dove to his right, he'd be protected by the passenger door.

They'd be hitting Rockaway Boulevard soon with slower traffic leading up to the crawling Van Wyck. The target passed the four cars up ahead, then drifted back into the right lane. It was clear sailing. Perfect. Beltran would be in the passing lane as he shot him. Riding four cars behind him, the hitman glanced in his mirrors to gauge his isolation from the other traffic. The car picked up speed. Beltran held his position; he didn't want to shadow his target move for move.

This was like a chess game. Beltran had to wait for a moment when he could pass the intervening traffic, take out his mark, then have enough clear road ahead to make an escape. He searched the horizon and mirrors for police cars. His keen eyesight could spot an unmarked car two-hundred yards away.

The moment arrived. He dropped the visor of the full-face helmet. There was only one car between Beltran and the van. His right hand cranked the throttle; his left reached into his jacket. Here, he had the singular advantage of being left-handed. Not only could he maintain control of the throttle while shooting, but he could hide the gun with his body from rear onlookers. As he pulled up to the van, his hand came out of the jacket with the Glock. He turned his head momentarily to locate the target and fired three rounds into the window. The glass turned white from the impact, and Antonio Beltran knew at once that he had a problem. It was bullet-proof glass.

He had to take evasive action. The van veered violently to the left, nearly striking his rear wheel. Beltran nailed it and sped off. The van receded quickly in Beltran's rear-view mirror. There was no way it could catch up. Ahead of him was clear road that would enable him to vanish. Then a shot rang out and the Mexican's right shoulder blade was shattered. Now he couldn't control the throttle.

Beltran lay across the gas tank, making himself a smaller target to both the wind and his pursuer, but the van was catching up. He held the gun behind his back and fired at the pursuer. No good. The van loomed in his mirror.

He changed lanes, hoping the enemy would come alongside for a shootout. He didn't take the bait, but swung directly behind the motorcycle with a clear shot to his back. Desperate, Beltran nailed the throttle, barely able to control it at over one-hundred-fifty miles an hour. The van momentarily receded from view, but in the split second it took him to glance at the mirror, the motorcycle veered out of control, taking ten-foot swings on the highway.

His right hand dropped off the throttle. It hung uselessly at his side now. His left hand swung across to take over, but in that instant, the pursuer pulled up behind him and slammed into the rear tire. He was heading for the edge of the road. He put the bike down on its side and slid forty yards on the gravel. The van stopped behind him, blocking the view from oncoming cars. Unhurried footsteps approached Beltran, but instead of a gun swinging up, a foot came down on his head.

That was the last thing he remembered until he woke up in the dungeon.

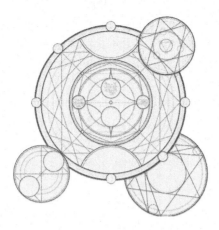

CHAPTER FORTY-TWO

H e was naked, spread-eagled and tied to U-bolts on a wall. His shoulder had a dressing on it, but it was agonizing. The figure in front of him sat in a chair.

"It seems you've come a long way to kill me and I don't even know you," said the voice. "So we must have a mutual friend. But we'll get to that later. First, your name? I'm a stickler for formal introductions." He gripped the man's penis with a pair of pliers. The scream died quickly in this place.

"Oh, come on, your name can't be 'AAHHHHHHHHH!' It's got to be something else like John or Gregorio or something like that. Let's try again."

"Antonio—Beltran."

"Antonio Beltran, it looks like you have some basic assassination skills. Did you take the home study course?"

Beltran grimaced and glanced at his shoulder.

"Don't worry about that wound. The bullet went clear through. That's not what's going to kill you. Now, back to your skills. Where did you learn to do drive-by killings? Let me guess—you're an amateur button boy who works south of the border and you wanted to expand your business. I admire ambition in a young man. Did your mother teach you ambition? I said, *did your mother teach you ambition?*"

"Yes."

"And which shit hole border town were you born in? Nuevo Laredo? Tijuana, Rosario?"

A bright light shone on Beltran's face, so he couldn't see the features of his captor, but he could see something dark come out of that light toward him. The gloved fist landed flush on his beautiful white teeth, knocking them out of his mouth.

"Have some pride and tell me what town you're from."

"Nuevo Laredo."

"So you're Antonio Beltran from Nuevo Laredo and you are ambitious and in New York to kill me. Well, I've got to tell you, you arouse my curiosity. Do I know you?"

"No."

"Then on to our mutual friend. And who might that be?"

"There are people who know I'm here. They know who you are, and when I don't return, they'll come after you."

"So I should just cut my losses now and let you go, is that what you're saying?"

"You figure it out."

"You know something, Antonio Beltran? I'm looking at you right now with your balls hanging out and a bullet through the shoulder in a place no one will ever find you and you don't strike me as a man with a lot of bargaining chips."

"They'll find you."

"Did they send you to kill me?" No answer.

The Webmaster switched on the camera to record what followed.

"Not much in this life is guaranteed. But I guarantee that you will tell me what I want to know. You can tell me now or after you're missing your balls and some limbs. Now once again: who paid you to kill me?"

Still no answer.

The figure connected jumper cables to the victim's testicles. Though Beltran's screams were deafening, there was no chance of anyone hearing him, not down here.

"This is only the beginning, my friend. In a moment this is going to get much worse. When I connect the other end of the cables to this car battery, you're going to see the world very differently. Last chance to tell me who paid you to kill me."

The jaws of the jumper cables were released on the battery terminals and they devoured the life out of Beltran. The tormentor varied the path of the electricity by attaching the clamps to the assassin's penis and anus, his lips and his toes, his eyelid and his penis, his tongue and his toes. Each time the current slashed through his body with the ferocity of a Samurai sword.

In seven minutes, he was ready to talk.

"… Greyson … Armand Greyson…"

"Who else?"

"No one. No one else, I swear."

"Why?"

"No one ever tells me why."

"But that's the most important question in life."

Three hours later, Beltran's torso was dumped in a landfill next to the Hefty Bag containing his arms and legs.

Chapter Forty-Three

O livia didn't know how many days had passed since the nightmare began. Her tormentor arrived each day to feed her, to give her the insulin, to check on her vital signs and prolong her life. Later, he would return to torture her. Each time he came as the provider, she hoped she could move him to spare her, to free her. As the provider, he could be considerate, soft-spoken, even caring. Yesterday as he was wiping her forehead with a wet towel, he had asked how she was feeling. She said that the last session of torture was all she could bear. That she was at her limit. He nodded and said, "I understand." She hoped that message would reach his other self—the man who suspended her from the ceiling and screamed obscenities as he raped her endlessly. But it hadn't.

"We've entered the last stage of the bidding process, gentlemen."

Olivia's spent image was transmitted all over the world with a flick of a button. She hadn't bathed in days. Her face bore the marks of countless blows as she lay naked on a bed. Her once flawless white skin was covered in welts. Her vagina and anus had been ripped by the objects inserted into them over the last week. A specially trained German shepherd had mounted her as the camera recorded every abuse, every scream and grunt, all the pleading for her life.

The host had challenged the imagination of the clients to conjure some new abuse, a novel act of degradation to subject her to. They had risen to the occasion. She was raped a dozen different ways—chained, suspended from the ceiling, forced to role play and speak lines from a prepared script. She had performed well, and this is what had kept her alive.

But now the imagination of her tormentors was exhausted. Now it was time for the final act.

"In keeping with tradition, I will now show the condemned videos of all the past executions and you can see her react." He ordered Olivia to sit on a table opposite a laptop that began to play the images. The camera panned back and forth between the screen and Olivia's face. She turned away and her abductor grabbed her by the hair, pointing her back to the screen.

"You have to watch," said the Webmaster.

When the Schrodinger murder was played, Olivia vomited on herself. She fell to her knees and begged to be spared. She promised sex for life. She promised to love him forever. Faint applause came over the speaker as the audience approved. Then she appealed to the men who weren't present that she might be spared as some bulls are spared in the ring.

"She's asking for your mercy, gentlemen. We've never had a reprieve, but cast your votes."

One by one the votes came in.

"It's almost unanimous. Death."

CHAPTER FORTY-FOUR

Sonia was still in bed with another client—Hector—while Rachel sat on the couch reading. Where did Sonia find all these guys? They all had tons of money. Some of them were pretty good looking, yet they risked jail, disgrace, or a gunshot from an outraged father to have sex with an underage kid.

Last night, Hector wanted each of them to come out separately as Dr. Sartorius had. At least his music was better—Latin. He smoked a joint while she stripped and that made her even more uncomfortable. What would it take for him to just reach over and put her down on the carpet? But he just sat there, a bright smile on his face with his legs crossed. Didn't ask for floor work. After she took it all off, he had complimented her on her body and lovely hair. Then asked her to get dressed and sit with him for a few minutes. They talked. He owned a bar, had been a U.N. peacekeeper, traveled the world. She declined the joint and made him laugh when she said it caused lung cancer. He asked about her circumstances and she gave him the stock answers. Ran away from Vermont. Staying at a shelter. Working at a peep palace downtown. Rachel wondered why each man needed to hear this as if their voyeurism extended beyond a girl's body to her whole messed up life.

Hector was originally from Mexico, and Rachel wowed him with her high school Spanish.

"*Tu eres muy linda,*" he said.

"*Gracias, señor. Y usted es muy caballero.*"

He took her hand and kissed it, something Rachel had always wanted from a man, but not in these exact circumstances. She liked those old world customs. She wished everyone spoke with English accents and had the command of language that the characters in Jane Austen's novels had.

"You can tell Sonia that her audience is waiting." She took that as a dismissal and got up. He tipped her a hundred dollars. Spanish class had paid off.

Rachel rifled through his house during the night, but no PC. It hadn't been a total waste—she had brought her copy of English Romantic Poetry and curled up on the couch to read for a few hours before getting some sporadic sleep.

What a mess Percy Shelley's life was. Married a sixteen-year-old, got her pregnant, abandoned her, married a seventeen-year-old, first wife commits suicide, writes gorgeous poetry, then drowns at twenty-nine.

Thy brother Death came and cried,

Wouldst thou me?

Thy sweet child Sleep, the filmy-eyed,

Murmured like a noontide bee,

Shall I nestle near thy side?!

Wouldst thou me?—And I replied,

No, not thee!

Death will come when thou art dead,

Soon, too soon…

Hector and Sonia came downstairs. Rachel shut the book and slid it in her knapsack—homeless kids aren't supposed to read lyric poetry.

"I hope you slept okay," said the host.

"The couch was fine."

"I guess we should make like a shepherd and get the flock out of here," said Sonia.

"Cool."

"It was a pleasure meeting you, Lisa. Here's my number. If there's anything I can do for you, give me a call. You're welcome to come back."

"Thanks, I really appreciate that, Hector."

He watched them from the window. Great girl, that Lisa. Fourteen, alone and cute. Too bad there wasn't any of that when he was a U.N. peacekeeper in the People's Republic of the Congo. There were young girls, but the Africans just didn't do it for him. Like a lot of other soldiers, he had traded food for sex with the twelve-year-olds. No problem getting college girls to come over with a promise of free beer and weed. But getting the young ones, that was another story. There were plenty of middle-school girls willing to put out for money or thrills, but the risk was too great. They had to be runaways or the cops would come down on him right away. Sonia had a lot of cute, young friends in just the right circumstances. She was a magnet.

This Lisa had real possibilities. Beautiful body, sweet disposition. He would have to cultivate her. Bring her along as he had so many girls with his no pressure approach. The conquest of a new girl was the supreme pleasure.

He went back downstairs and scanned the area. Nothing missing. Still, there was something about the room that wasn't quite right. The books weren't pushed all the way back in the book case. The Scotch tape, scissors, odds and ends in the kitchen drawers weren't in their usual place. In the basement, he found the CDs in the media center in random order. Some CDs hadn't been fully closed and he always closed them. It didn't look like someone who was looking for money, yet what would a homeless girl be most in need of? On the couch there was a slip of paper where Lisa had been sitting.

It was a receipt from the Columbia University Bookstore for a copy of English Romantic Poetry.

CHAPTER FORTY-FIVE

It was Saturday night, their last gig for the weekend and Rachel couldn't wait to get back to the dorm. They rang the bell of an old colonial in the Bensonhurst section of Brooklyn.

Someone looked through the peephole, then the door opened. Sonia kissed him on the mouth in a way she hadn't greeted the others. After the kiss, they looked at each other only for a moment, but it was enough.

In his open-collar Polo shirt and khaki trousers, Rachel almost didn't recognize him at first, but he had already placed her.

"Rachel, isn't it?"

"You have a good memory, Father. Nice house," said Rachel, not bothering to remove the contempt from her voice..

"How do you two know—"

"Rachel was our guest at Transcendence House—only one night, I recall. I was sorry to see you go."

"I got a lot out of that confession."

"How was your trip?" asked the cleric.

"Evan, we took a cab, not a stage coach. We're staying right?"

"Of course. I'm making dinner right now."

"What's on the menu?"

"I have your favorite."

"Philly cheese—YES. With beef and lamb soup?"

"All of the above. And would you like anything special?" he asked Rachel.

"He makes awesome Philly cheese steaks."

"Sounds good to me," said Rachel.

"Let's get this out of the way, and if one of you would help out, we could eat sooner," said Massey, handing each girl two-hundred dollars. Rachel volunteered for the kitchen duty.

Father Massey put the ketchup and onions on the granite island. "I already thawed out the beef. Just cut the onions and peppers to your liking."

"Could I ask you a personal question, Father?"

"Call me Evan."

"Is this your place or the Church's?"

"Mine. I'm a diocesan priest. We're allowed to own things. Orders like the Franciscans or Dominicans require a vow of poverty. Pass me that knife, if you would."

Rachel stood diagonal to him across the countertop. She watched his hands slicing lettuce, carving cheese swiftly, expertly. Could these same hands that elevate the Host have butchered Olivia?

Volunteering to help him was a bad idea. There had to be a special discomfort in hearing someone's confession, giving penance and blessing, only to later have the process reversed.

"How do you know Sonia? Or did you just come highly recommended?"

"Oh, she and I go back."

"Can't go back that far, Father—she's only sixteen."

"She stayed in Transcendence House a couple of years ago."

"Was she in one of those job placement programs?"

"Yes, she was."

"Did you place her in this job?"

"Sonia has an independent mind. She didn't cotton to structure. You should get into a program of some kind. Doesn't have to be Transcendence House. Pan's ready. Put on the beef."

Rachel's fear gave way to anger. There was no description for the size of this man's ego. Totally blind to his own hypocrisy, he saw himself fit to be counselor, elder, Shepherd of Christ. She couldn't take it anymore.

"Father, the way I understand it, we're not here for a prayer meeting."

The knife stilled in his hand as she wounded him.

"If you want me to leave now, I will," she said.

After a moment, he turned the beef.

"No, I deserved that." He pressed the onions down with a spatula. Steam rose up. "I've made more mistakes than three people make in a lifetime and maybe becoming a priest was one of them. But I've learned from them."

A bead of sweat began to form on the priest's forehead, but it might have been from the pan.

He turned up the fire and shook the heavy iron skillet. Rachel thought of all the implements on this counter alone that could be used as a murder weapon. So it must be in the mind of a monster that also does good. Every thought, however beneficent, was also possessed of a handle, a point, an edge.

"Would you like yours cut in half?" he asked.

"I'll take it just like that."

At least he didn't say grace at dinner.

Afterward, Rachel figured it would be show time, but instead, they watched Titanic. Following the long, sad movie, Sonia retired to the bedroom with her client.

After a settling-in period, Rachel opened the door to the study. There were miles of book cases. There was Joseph Campbell's *The Power of Myth*, a well-thumbed copy of *The Seven Story Mountain* by Thomas Merton and another called *The Infinite Reservoir*, which was the account of his mission in India. *How to Work a Room. Men Are from Mars, Women are from Venus. How to Read a Person Like a Book.* His taste in music ranged from Handel's Messiah to Tomita and Led Zeppelin.

It appeared the priest had a merchandising business selling Transcendence House T-shirts, mugs, copies of his book, a newsletter.

She opened the coffee table doors and sifted through old Reader's Digests, issues of This Old House, and Broadway playbills. She looked under the cushions of the sofa. What was she looking for? A pair of Olivia's panties? A journal where he confessed everything?

A half hour later, footsteps. She grabbed *The Seven Story Mountain*.

The priest stood at the doorway wearing a bathrobe. There was no longer any pretense. Rachel looked at him, waiting for him to speak first.

"I read that once a year," he said.

"You get that much out of it?"

"Oh, yes." He sat down across from Rachel. "It's such a rich book. Like a great musical composition. You can always find more in it every time you look. Do you know what I mean?"

"I think so. I read the Diary of Anne Frank three times."

"Did you? That was one of my favorite books growing up."

"You should read it again."

"There's a new version out. A definitive version where she writes about her budding sexuality, her period, her interest in boys. That was left out in earlier editions. Have you read it?"

"You're quite the conversationalist, Father."

"I have many interests."

"Was I making too much noise down here? I'll be quiet."

"You weren't making any noise at all."

"That was a good dinner. Thanks again. Oh, I should give this back to you." She put the two-hundred on the table. "Seeing as I didn't earn it."

"No, you hang on to that."

Faith, Hope, and Charity—one out of three ain't bad.

"I know I have no credibility in your eyes, but why don't you come back to Transcendence House? I'm sure there's something we can do for you."

"No offense, Father, but you're the one who needs help."

"No one is pure evil, Rachel. Look around you. This is the good side of me, which is just as real as my flaws. You see these pictures of me with mayors and governors and philanthropists. I leave them on the wall to remind myself that there's a better side to my nature."

"Why are you telling me this?"

"I don't want you to hate me. I force no one."

"Pardon my asking, Father, but what *did* your vows include?"

"A promise to befriend. And to strive in the face of hopeless temptation. I knew I couldn't keep their vows, so I made up my own."

"Are you trying to be my friend?"

"Always."

"I can't accept your friendship."

"I guess I'm not used to being with someone who can see straight through me. What do you see, Rachel?"

"My opinion matters?"

"I wouldn't be asking."

She was torn between truth and guile. "I see a very handsome man with a secret. That's usually a good thing, but not this time."

"There's something else you don't see. That no one sees. A lonely man. Do you know what loneliness is, Rachel?"

"I've had moments. But I'm young and I live in the hope of having a boyfriend, a husband, a family. So there's an end to that tunnel."

"I stare into that tunnel every day. You can be the light at the end of it. Rachel, I can love you."

She looked toward the ceiling where Sonia lay in bed.

"With Sonia and me—it's just sex. She knows it and I know it. I also want love." He sat next to her and took her hand. "Do you want love, Rachel?"

"I want truth. I need to know what happened to Olivia. And I think you know, Father."

CHAPTER FORTY-SIX

Massey picked up *The Seven Story Mountain* and opened it. "The search for truth can take us to ugly places," he said as if the truth sat there in his hands. "But if you want truth, then let's begin with yourself." He closed the book and laid it back on the coffee table. "Who are you really? There is no Rachel Barino from Vermont. We follow up on all our kids."

"I don't want my parents notified. I'm never going back. I'm on my own now."

"More reason to have friends who can help."

"And you want to be one of those friends."

"I want you to be my friend. I do need redemption, Rachel. And you can help me. I have to start over."

"With me?"

"If you'll let me."

"I don't know if I'm your type, Father. I'm really eighteen, not sixteen."

"I'm serious."

"So am I. Did you fall in love with Olivia? Anyone would."

"Olivia was well-intentioned. But her work drew her into things she couldn't deal with. The streets took her over."

"Did she know about you?"

"You mean about my imperfections? Yes. She didn't pass judgment."

He was telling the truth, but not the whole truth. After Olivia had caught him with Gabriella at the retreat, Massey had to find a way to assassinate her character in case she went public with what she saw. When Olivia told him about her sister in the brothel and the money needed to free her, Massey gave her Sonia's number. He knew Sonia would take care of the rest.

"I can say this: I've broken all my vows, but I've kept all my promises. In this day and age, that's more than most. Remember your own weakness before you judge me. Remember what you confessed to me."

Rachel had confessed that she'd had an affair with a priest who was then transferred to another parish. She had deliberately picked that sin in order to tempt him into seducing her, exposing himself.

"Did you love the priest you spoke about?"

She wanted to torment him.

"Yes, I loved him."

"How am I different from him?"

"You're younger than he was."

"He was older?" It came out of him involuntarily. And, as in Dr. Sartorius' house, she felt the power she had over this man. But she herself wasn't immune. She couldn't get a date with boys her own age, yet now she had entered into a world where she was the most desirable thing there was. Where men of fame and fortune would risk everything, sacrifice all that they were for her love.

"Where's Olivia?" she asked the priest.

"I had to ask her to leave Transcendence House."

"Why?"

"She had compromised our principles. She was stripping on the side. She was unworthy to counsel our kids."

"But you're worthy?"

"No. I admit it. But I'm fighting against this terrible flaw that I have."

"She stopped stripping. Then what happened?"

"From what I understand, she started selling her body. I just couldn't save her. I'll be lucky if I can save myself. You can help me, Rachel. I need your help. Promise me you'll think about it." He kissed her hand, then left her.

Rachel pretended to go to sleep on the couch. Once all was quiet above, she got up and went back to the library. No PC anywhere. Nothing in the living room or dining room. No iPods or cameras. She looked in the media library, in the TV cabinet. There was nothing—no porn of any kind, no laptop. Just books and photos everywhere.

She went down the stairs to the basement, bracing herself on the rail to put minimum weight on the steps. Every squeak was magnified. In the gym there was a Bowflex Extreme, weights, a treadmill, and a boxing speed bag. Nothing unusual in there.

Back in the living room, Rachel lay on the couch in the dark. Even if he had a PC at the office, he still had to have one at home—who didn't? Was it in the bedroom where Sonia now lay next to him?

Was she wasting her time, abasing herself for nothing? Dammit, this was the one PC she had to get into.

Now that her eyes were adjusting to the dark, she began to perceive a faint green light pulsing every few seconds. As her night vision got better, the light grew brighter. A carbon monoxide alarm? Smoke alarm? She got up and followed the blinking light. It originated from atop the bookshelf. Standing up on a chair, she finally saw what it was. A wireless router. So he did have a PC somewhere in this house.

Rachel took a photo of the router with her cell phone. A Netgear MR814. That was going to be her way in.

"Sorry I can't offer you guys breakfast, but I'm running late," he said the next morning.

Rachel scrambled up and started folding the sheets.

"I'll take care of that, don't bother," said the priest, all business now.

She made it to the bathroom, where she quickly washed her face and used the john. Two minutes later, they were out the door.

"I feel like hell," said Rachel as they walked around the corner.

"You look it. There's a place down the block. We can get some eats."

At the Belgian Deli, Sonia grabbed a table while Rachel stood in line.

"Get me a bacon, egg, and cheese on a roll with an OJ," said Sonia. "Hey, do you have a tampon?"

"In my knapsack."

When Rachel got back with the food, Sonia just stared.

"Something wrong?" asked Rachel.

"You tell me."

"Everything seems okay."

"It should. For you."

Rachel's stomach was pulling down on her throat. Her knapsack contained her Columbia ID and a copy of this semester's bill with her address and telephone number. For a moment, she had forgotten about her dual life.

"Tell me something. Are you homeless?"

"No. I'm not. Sonia—"

"What are you—writing a fucking term paper about me?"

"*No.*"

"I'm sure you'll get an A. I gave you a lot of material. I guess you'll be discussing it in class like a show and tell. You used me. How could you pretend to me that you're on the streets when all the time you live on Long Island? You fucked me worse than any of those men."

"I only did it because of Olivia—she's my sister and I'm looking for her."

"I don't believe you. You're the lowest thing I ever met, lower than I can ever stoop."

"It was killing me—Sonia, don't go. I couldn't take lying to you anymore and I was going to tell you." She walked off. Rachel went after her, took her arm, but Sonia tore it away. Rachel had taken away the little this girl had.

Sonia turned and spoke the words that disemboweled Rachel.

"You used me. And I thought I was keeping you clean by fucking those guys."

CHAPTER FORTY-SEVEN

Rachel took the somber train ride back to the dorm. She called her mother.

"Anything arrive for Olivia?" she asked.

"There's been no mail for a week."

A week without mail? Olivia wouldn't have wanted her parents to intercept the passport, which would have come in an envelope from the State Department. Could she have suspended the mail, so she could go pick it up herself?

"I'm here to pick up the mail for Olivia Wallen," said Rachel, handing her driver's license to the lady at the post office. "I'm her sister."

"Were you her designee?"

"Yes."

The lady went to the back and Rachel tried to think of an excuse if the clerk came back to say Rachel wasn't the designee. Instead, she had the mail in her hand. "Please sign here." Rachel looked at the suspension of mail form. Olivia had written Rachel Wallen in the designee box.

Rachel quickly went through the six-inch pile of mail in her car. And there it was—an envelope from the State Department. She tore it open and there was the passport in the name of Olivia Wallen. She had deliberately worn a T-shirt and no makeup.

Rachel locked her bedroom door and counted all the money she had earned in the last eight days. It took a while to count. $3,222. God.

Expedia.com offered flights from Chiang Mai to New York for $1,697 over the next week.

She selected five flights leaving on different days, which she emailed to Achara along with the Expedia website. That left over fifteen-hundred for the corrupt officials.

One good deed done. Her thoughts now turned to Father Massey's PC. That would have to wait until tonight.

At 10:00 p.m., Rachel pulled her car up to Massey's house. She powered up her laptop and went down the list of available wireless networks in the area. All were secured. Shit. She'd have to crack the encrypted key in order to penetrate the network and that took time.

She pulled the car directly in front of Massey's house and saw the signal strength decrease for three networks and increase for the other three. That narrowed it down to Summit, Network9, and Icarus networks. She put the car back four lengths to get out of sight and began.

First, she started CommView, a network packet sniffer and analyzer which captured packets of wireless information. CommView and Aircrack-ng were open source and downloadable off the web. She selected Summit network and started capturing data packets. When the packet collection completed, she launched Aircrack-ng. This ran a cracking program on the data packets. After breaking the encryption key, Rachel launched Internet Explorer and entered the standard IP address for a Netgear router. The login screen didn't come up, so it wasn't a Netgear.

She disconnected and repeated the process with the other two networks. Only one was a Netgear MRE814. That meant Icarus was Massey's network. She connected to Icarus and brought up the router login screen. The factory ID and password didn't work. She ran John the Ripper password cracker and thirteen minutes later it gave her VICTORY1. She enabled remote management and gave access to "everyone." Now she'd be able to access the router from any PC on the web. It took three hours and twenty minutes. Just past two in the morning, Rachel took off for Columbia. At this hour, there was plenty of street parking.

The next day, she plugged the flash drive into her laptop and checked her emails. Yes! The IP addresses had been mailed to her. She selected Dr. Sartorius' IP address and launched the SubSeven client on her laptop. If his college notebooks were so twisted, he must have something incriminating on his hard drive. As the screen populated, her pulse quickened. She browsed through directory after directory, finding medical and patient records. Billing records. There was no porn.

She searched again. Same thing. There were dual two-hundred Gig hard drives. She performed a "dir" search on all directories, looking for anything with "girls," "fuck," and "sex." Nothing. She repeated this on the other drive. She searched on "jpg," "gpf," and "bmp" extensions. There were only stock Windows images such as flowers and wallpaper. According to the results of this search, there were no photos on this machine. It was risky being in graphic mode as the user might realize there was an ongoing attack, so she marked five large directories for download and started copying data to her own laptop.

The data transfer speed was slow and took three hours to complete. When she opened up the downloaded files, there were still no photos of any kind. The few text files had nothing significant—no perverted notes, no twisted commentary. Was her firewall preventing her from seeing the files? She disabled it and tried again. Same thing.

She penetrated Perlman's machine. There were a lot of docs in Hebrew. Some regular porn and a lot of business stuff. There were lists of girls who worked at Pleasure Palace with their personal information and pictures. Nothing else. She tried connecting to Armand Greyson's PC, but there was no response. This was unbelievable. Was it possible that all this was for nothing? There was no more time to figure this out. She needed Joules' help, but how could she ever explain what she was doing in the homes of these men? She'd die of shame. It was decision time. 3:00 p.m. and Joules would be leaving Cooper Union to get back to the Island within a few minutes.

Rachel lay in her bed with her face buried in her pillow. She had betrayed Sonia and abased herself to no purpose. How could so much effort yield so little result? She couldn't accept it. All she had done had to count for something. She picked up her cell phone.

"It's me. I need your help."

CHAPTER FORTY-EIGHT

L et's start from the beginning," said Joules, tossing his knapsack on the bed. "You're hacking into a bunch of machines because you think one of them might contain something about Olivia?"

"Right."

"How did you decide on these particular targets?"

"Let's just say I was led to them by someone."

"And how did you get their IP addresses?"

"I installed a RAT on their computers."

"As in Remote Administration Tool."

"Right."

"Haven't used that term in a while. You had physical access to these machines?"

"Yes."

"So you were in their homes?"

This was the question she had dreaded. There would be a price to pay for Joules' help. "I was. And I'm convinced there has to be child porn of runaway kids on at least one of these machines, but I can't find it."

"It could have been deleted."

"Don't even say that. Give me another outcome."

"The files could be encrypted."

"Elaborate."

"There are any number of ways to encrypt data—text data and graphic data. Text can be embedded in photographs and photos can be embedded in other photos. It may be that the files are unscrambled before every use. This way, even if the PC is confiscated, incriminating files won't be seen."

"Joules, you have no idea what I did to get near these PCs. The men who own them are evil. I'm convinced one of them knows where my sister is. At least one of them knew the Schrodinger girl who was found dead. I need help."

"How big are the data directories?"

"Combined? Hang on, I wrote them down. Fifteen Gig, twenty Gig—I guess about forty Gig."

"How much room do you have on your hard drive?"

"Um. About one-ninety left. I downloaded some directories and it took like three hours. This could be really time-consuming. Can you—stay over?"

"Let me take a look."

Joules went through the directories that Rachel had downloaded. There was nothing incriminating on any of them.

"It could be child porn, but I'm looking for anything else—a diary, an email—anything that would point to Olivia's whereabouts. I know she was in the homes of these men. I found photos."

"Who were these guys?"

Please don't go there. "Joules. I don't want to get into it too much. It's really unpleasant. I just need you to help me get these files. These men knew her. That much I know."

Joules connected to Dr. Sartorius' PC.

"Bit Torrent."

"Huh?"

"Bit Torrent. It's a program that takes pieces of files downloaded from several peer-to-peer servers and assembles them into a coherent image. None of the contributing machines has a full copy." Joules went into a mind-numbing explanation of the protocol.

"Joules, Joules—I grasp the concept. Can you assemble the files?"

"It looks like they're already assembled. We need the decrypt key, and most people would keep that somewhere on the PC." He found ten password-protected directories. John the Ripper broke the passwords and, sure enough, the decrypt key was in one of them.

Two hours later, he had over twenty images of child porn belonging to Sartorius.

"The PC I really need to get into is Massey's, the priest who runs

178

Transcendence House where Olivia tutored."

"What was the problem accessing it?"

"It wasn't responding. Must be turned off."

"SubSeven will alert you when he comes online. There's a setting for that."

Joules continued downloading the directories. An alert went off. Massey was online.

"Wait, abort this and get into Massey's machine," said Rachel.

"We'll connect in command line mode. Later, we'll take a chance and go in via graphic mode. Meanwhile, we download everything we can."

After downloading dozens of directories, Joules connected in graphic mode.

He scanned the directories for the ones with the most potential. After ten minutes of searching, he clicked on an executable file called fun.exe. Two full minutes passed, then the screen briefly said, *verifying login ID and password*, even though they had entered none.

A menu appeared.

YOUNG ASIAN

PRETEEN

ROMPER ROOM

Joules chose Romper Room.

"Everything's slowed to a crawl. The response time is horrendous all of a sudden," said Joules.

"Why?"

"Not sure. The download speed should be uniformly fast or slow. I see from his Programs menu, he's using photo stacking software. It allows you to layer multiple images onto a single file and the outer layer would be something harmless like a family photo. It'll simplify matters if we can get a hold of the same stacking software to reverse the process. We can probably download a trial version or find a Bit Torrent of a pirated copy. He's also using encryption."

"How can you tell?" she asked.

"File size gives it away. Any kind of encryption adds to the size of a file due to the scrambling algorithm that has to be added. If you see a text file and it's two gig, you know something's wrong. When you consider that you could put Moby Dick in a text file of one and a half megabytes, something which is a thousand or two thousand times bigger can't be a real document. A photo could easily be several gigabytes in size. A video file like an .avi file could be much bigger.

"He's using Arcsoft Photo Studio—that's the photo stacking software. I'll download a demo copy from their website," he said.

"This'll probably go on for a few hours. We'll pick it up tomorrow."

"You better stay—it's like two a.m. Too late to take the train. I have an extra pillow and toothbrush and stuff. If you don't mind sleeping on the floor."

After Joules was settled in for the night, Rachel went down the hall to brush her teeth and change into a sweat suit. When she returned, she couldn't help feeling a sense of accomplishment that she was finally in a position to complain about a man's snoring.

She was wiped out, but there was one more duty to attend to. Achara. She logged onto Yahoo Messenger and waited.

U there? PLEASE BE THERE TONIGHT.

I'm here, replied Rachel. She looked at her watch. 3:05 a.m.

Where have you been??? I thought you forget about me.

Really sorry. I went away to get the money for you. Your passport arrived, wrote Rachel.

O good. Such good news. ☺

And I have the money too.

How much?

$3,222 USD

You so good. Cam?

Still no cam, said Rachel.

Rachel accepted Achara's cam invite.

The girl had visibly aged since she last saw her. The reflection of the computer screen on her face gave her a stark paleness. But there was something Rachel hadn't seen before. A smile.

Where you go?

I had to go far away to get the money, wrote Rachel.

I will make it all up to you. I know I trouble for you.

Don't say that. U r my sister.

OK. We have to hurry. This Friday they move us, Achara wrote.

Give me the address again so I can overnight you the passport.

OK I have.

An address appeared.

Send to that address and they will get to me.

You can trust them? asked Rachel.

She my aunt. She won't betray.

I'll send the money by Western Union tomorrow. You'll have that by

Wednesday, your time. You have a WU nearby?

Yes.

I'll send it through a friend. Her name is Lisa Barino. Write down that name. So the money will come from her, OK?

OK.

You need the entry stamp on the passport to show when you entered Thailand.

Yes. I get.

You know someone who can do this for you?

No, but I bribe at airport.

And you need to show where you stayed for that time.

I say I stayed at aunt's house. u r generous.

I'm your sister. Here is my cell phone number 01-631-555-1756. I sent you an email with different dates to travel and the web site where you can pick flights. Do you know how to use the site?

Yes, I saw flights. When I get money I tell you when I arrive in New York.

OK. I'm going to send you an email with all the information you need here at the airport. They will ask you questions when you arrive. Where you live, why you went to Thailand. OK? Don't worry. We can fool them. But you have to memorize it. I'll go over all that with you next time.

Thanks you. I go now before they miss me. Love you. Bye ☺

Love you too.

Massey hadn't slept. He was waiting for a phone call from a computer expert he had called last night when his firewall alerted him of a penetration. He then noticed that many of his files had been accessed at one in the morning. He had been told to run several commands, take screen shots of the output and send them.

Though he had deleted his incriminating photos, he had put one thing back on his PC that could send him to jail for the rest of his life. It was an icon to login to a child porn site. The priest's mind was short-circuiting. Who had violated him? He expected the police to come bursting through his door at any moment. Massey had envisioned getting caught in several ways, but this wasn't one of them.

The phone rang.

"I tracked down the intruder," said the voice.

"Is there any way of getting their identity?" asked the priest.

"Oh, I have their identity. They were still logged into your machine when I was able to penetrate their PC. The firewall was disabled—pretty careless. I downloaded a bunch of files. I'll encrypt them and send it now. You have the decrypt key, right?"

"Hang on. I haven't used it in a while. I do have it. So it wasn't police?"

"Nope. It was a chick. Looks like a student. I geolocated her IP address to 125th Street and Amsterdam Avenue."

"I owe you one."

Massey was relieved and at the same time intrigued. A few moments later, the email arrived. When decrypted, one file revealed a word document with a student schedule for Columbia University. A picture of the girl appeared. His eye scanned the page until it fell on a name:

RACHEL WALLEN

Massey had just a few hours to do the killing.

CHAPTER FORTY-NINE

A nd what will you be hunting, sir?" asked the kid behind the counter.

"Big fish," answered Massey. "Tarpon down by the Keys. But I want to be prepared in case I run into something bigger."

"Sure. Well, we carry pneumatic and band spear guns, several sizes."

"I'm new at this. What are the advantages of each?"

"Pneumatic guns are compact, not much recoil and have a little more range. But they're noisy and need more maintenance than band guns. Band guns are nearly silent, accurate, and you can increase the power by using more bands—up to three."

"And what are the ranges?"

"Accurate to about fourteen feet. In murky water or below a certain depth, you're not going to see much farther than that."

"Let's go with band. I'll take two."

He paid cash for the weapons, so there would be no record of the purchase. Massey loaded the gear into his trunk, then proceeded to steal two license plates. Next stop was Home Depot. He disguised himself with a mustache, sunglasses, and baseball cap, remembering that police often use the security cameras of stores to prove that a suspect was buying the things they would need to dispose of a body. To camouflage his purchases, he also bought a gallon of white paint, rollers, work gloves, and twenty feet of rope. He was never in this Home Depot and it was at least five miles from his house, so it's unlikely they would ever check there.

Handling the guns with the deer skin work gloves, he loaded each and set up a target of Yellow Books at one end of his basement. Fourteen feet, the kid said. He paced it off, took aim and fired. The recoil was surprising. The spear entered the first Yellow Book and embedded itself about half-way through. He carefully removed it and added a band to the spear gun. This time he missed altogether due to the recoil. Under water you could support the weapon with a single hand because of the buoyancy. On dry land, it was different. He fired again, this time holding the weapon with both hands. It went clear through the first book and stopped about an inch into the next one. That would go well into a human body. Three bands and the spear traveled clear through both Yellow Books. The recoil was substantial. Massey loaded the other gun with three bands and fired several times until he got the feel of the range and could hit the target consistently from twenty feet. It had a lot more range in air than under water and was very quiet. Good. He had considered getting a gun to be on the safe side. He knew enough street people who could arrange that for him, but it would leave a clue, and guns were too easily traced.

He went on Mapquest and prepared the routes he would take. To create an alibi, he signed up for a real estate seminar at the Meadowlands Hilton for the next day and booked a room. This would jive with his recent real estate searches on the Internet when he was researching places to retire abroad.

Massey put on the black turtleneck and black pants that would make him invisible until the last moment. It was remarkably similar to what he might wear as a priest, except for the collar. In his study, he sat for a moment collecting himself. He read a passage from *The Seven Storey Mountain* as he often did before violating the laws of God.

When he was ready to go, he loaded his purchases into a large athletic bag: a large plastic drop cloth and thick rubber gloves, a box of contractor grade plastic garbage bags, and a hacksaw.

CHAPTER FIFTY

The vehicle tooled down the block, stopped, then backed up until it was directly in front of Rachel's home at 114 North Cyrus Street in East Northport. It then proceeded around the block, returned, and parked with the engine off some fifty yards short of the address.

The driver reviewed Rachel's class schedule and personal information. Heavy course load. Biomedical Engineering major. He reviewed her transcripts from Northport High. Straight A's, early admission to Columbia, Intel Award.

He read the essay she had written in her admission application. It was entitled, "The Purpose of My Life." Moving. Even more so, as that purpose would never be fulfilled. He usually spoke at length with his victims before slaughtering them. The more he knew about his prey, the more aroused he got. Unlike Mafia hitmen who killed dispassionately, he made the greatest effort to get close to the doomed, to give them the most hope, so that he could then take away that much more. It was the crushing of desperate hope that he so loved.

This was a quiet neighborhood and there were only three major highways out of Long Island—the Southern State, the Northern State, and the Long Island Expressway. That didn't give him the options he liked. And these cops had absolutely nothing to do with their time, so an abduction or killing would bring out every lawman within thirty miles.

He flipped through the printouts of all the chat sessions he had downloaded from Rachel's PC. She had chat archiving enabled, so he could read word for word what she said to her newly found sister—Achara. Touching story. Of course, Olivia had already told him about Achara in her interrogations. Valiant effort she was making, trying to get her sister out of the whorehouse. And feeling so guilty that she herself fell into whoredom. And this one, Rachel, now posing as Olivia and trying to rescue her. But this kabuki dance had to come to an end now. Those files she had stolen were traceable to him. She had violated him and she would be violated. He had to kill her before she realized what she had taken.

He circled the block again and thought how a home invasion would go. Only the kid and her parents. Father's an accountant. Wouldn't expect much resistance from him. A triple murder would be a big deal in this town. They might find some way to get the Feds involved. No, he needed something cleaner, more surgical.

He got back onto the Northern State toward the city. An hour and twenty minutes later, he was in front of Columbia University on Broadway. Nice looking girls walking around. And brainy. The campus must look nice in the spring with the girls all wearing summer dresses, tube tops, and shorts.

He fired up his laptop, googled Furnald Hall, Columbia University and got:
Layout
Furnald is ten stories high with 187 singles and twenty-four doubles. Each floor contains a separate men's and women's bathroom that the residents must share. In addition, a large lounge is situated on every floor that has a sitting area with a cable television on one end, and a kitchen with two ovens and two sinks on the other end. There is also a spacious main lounge on the first floor.

Using the floor plan, he located her room on the eighth floor. He went over the class schedule again. Assuming she wasn't cutting class, she would be crossing the campus several times a day. Heavy academic load too. He would relieve her of that burden. This wasn't going to be easy either. Not many escape routes out of Manhattan. The car circled the campus several times as the killer contemplated the problem.

Then he came upon the perfect solution.

CHAPTER FIFTY-ONE

It was one of more than ten brothels on the street. Fifteen girls sat in plastic chairs outside their rooms waiting for men to pay 110 Baht—about five dollars—for their bodies. Many of the girls were foreigners from South China, Burma, Nepal, and the Philippines who were enticed here with offers of lucrative jobs as barmaids and domestics. Once here, their passports were taken away, their virginities sold for two to three-hundred dollars and their enslavement began.

Some of the girls were sold by their parents for four-hundred dollars. Others were pawned and handed a bundle of cards. Each time they serviced a customer, a card was removed from the bundle. When the bundle was gone, their freedom could be redeemed. Some had a thousand or two thousand cards in their bundles.

Achara didn't have a bundle. At thirteen, she was adopted by a man who she thought was going to be her father. She was sold to Tong for five-hundred dollars and told to strip and sit in a room for eight hours a day watching porn movies. This was her training. The madam instructed her on special techniques to please men. Her virginity was sold to an Arab. When she refused to have sex, she was dragged into a dark, windowless room and left there without food or water. On the third day, she still refused sex, so Tong knocked her to the ground and slammed her head against the concrete floor until she passed out. When she awoke, she was naked, a rattan cane smeared with pureed red chili peppers shoved into her vagina. She agreed to anything if they would take it out.

As a beautiful fair-skinned girl, she attracted fifteen men a day and was making Tong a lot of money. To pay for the makeup, clothes, and extra rice required to stay attractive, she, like the other girls, borrowed money from the moneylenders at five-hundred percent interest. This money would have to be repaid before she could leave the brothel. Achara was now three-thousand dollars in debt.

At sixteen, she was one of the oldest girls. The customers wanted eleven and twelve-year-olds these days. Still, she serviced eight to ten men a day and did a lot of the chores. Her best job was going to buy beer because it gave her a chance to get out of the brothel for a brief time.

She stood outside her room waiting for them to send her off for beer, so she could pick up the money at Western Union. The WU office wasn't far from the beer distributor, but it was a lot of money and she was worried they would give her a problem.

Tong, the brothel owner, gave her the sign, thrusting his thumb toward his mouth. He was thirty-seven with his black hair slicked back and four rings on each hand like the rap stars in the USA. He loved jewelry, and several gold chains slapped his bare chest when he moved. The shirts were always open all the way to his stomach as though he had a great body, but he didn't. Chain smoking had given him yellow fingers and a permanent stench to his breath, even when he wasn't smoking. The fingernails were meticulously manicured and polished to show the world he didn't work with his hands. The sunglasses, which he wore almost round the clock, covered the wrinkles of his tired eyes. He didn't like people seeing him without his sunglasses, and he would turn his back like some girls are shy about their bodies.

Achara got her bamboo pole that she used to balance the two cases of beer for the one-mile round trip. There were closer places to buy beer, but the warehouse was cheaper.

First, she called to confirm that the money had arrived as her sister had told her to do. It had. For ID, she asked if they would accept a copy of her orphanage discharge paper which had her picture, though it was an old one. The lady said yes.

Achara was lucky she wasn't a foreigner. The foreign girls had all had their passports taken away. The brothel never knew about the orphanage paper. She was going to rip it up last year because she hated it so much, just to cut all ties with her past and begin again. But she kept it.

There, on Nimmanhemin Rd, Soi Fifteen was the Western Union. Her heart began to pound as it had three years ago when she first entered the brothel. If Tong found out about the money, he would kill her for it. Achara passed the entrance and explained that she was there to pick up the money.

"Name?"

She gave it.

The man's brow furrowed when he looked at the screen. "Thirty-two hundred USD?"

"Yes."

"Thirty-two hundred?"

"Yes."

"That's a lot of money." He wasn't making any clerk motions and Achara wished that she had a watch, so she could glance at it now and look important.

"Why so much?"

"Here is my identification."

"That looks like an old photo."

"I called a half hour ago and the lady said this was good identification. That's my money."

"We don't take such ID. And you're underage, I see. You have to be eighteen to redeem money here."

Achara knew he was looking for a bribe or he would have dismissed her already.

"I need my money," she said.

"What can we do?" he said like one who has not a care in the world.

"I'll give you twenty." He smiled and shook his head as he lit a cigarette.

"How much you want?" she asked.

"Five-hundred."

If she had a gun, she would have blown his face off.

"Thirty and I suck your dick." That seemed to make some inroads. "If no, then I tell them to cancel and send it to my brother. I still get my money. You get nothing."

The clerk weighed the options. Thirty was a week's pay plus some free yumyum. He nodded and pointed to the toilet.

"Money first," she said.

The clerk was either anxious to get to the sex or he had trouble keeping numbers in his head. He had to count the money three times. Then Achara counted it three times.

"Receipt?" she said. He printed out the receipt. After everything was deep in her jeans pockets. She said, "Okay, we go."

When she exited the Western Union, her biggest problem was hiding the two huge bulges in her pants. She went to get the beer. Time was short.

At the beverage warehouse, she bought a bundle of incense sticks that were held together by two sturdy rubber bands. In a bathroom Achara secured the two bundles of cash to her ankles by first inserting them in her socks. Now she bought a case each of Singha and Leo and was off to the brothel. Along the way, she stopped at the Internet café and sent a message that she had received the money.

When she returned, Tong was beating Bopha, the Cambodian girl. She had hidden ten bhat from him and he was heaping all his fury on her with a rattan cane—the kind the police stations used.

While Tong got drunk on the Singha, Achara waited for her cousin, Luk, to arrive with the passport. She had called her aunt from the Internet café and was told that the passport had arrived from the USA by overnight delivery. Achara learned over the years to not let apparent good luck make her feel good. The disappointment was too much for her. She would believe it when she held the passport in her hands. For now, she had to hide the money before another client arrived.

Her room consisted of an eight-foot by five-foot area with a pink curtain at the entrance. Inside was a mattress and a small table where she kept her Buddha and her vihara, or spirit house. It was only a small plastic spirit house, not a beautiful one made of teak. According to custom, when people finished building their house, they created a guardian spirit house, then invited the holy deity Pra Prom to reside there. One day, Achara was going to build her own house and only then invite Pra Prom to inhabit the vihara. She could not invite him into a brothel.

She pulled the sheet off the mattress. The stains were so large and dark that the mattress looked like an old map. Another girl had just died on this mattress when they gave it to Achara. That had always disgusted her, and she feared the spirit of the dead girl. She never slept well on it. Six weeks ago, in preparation for using the mattress as a hiding place, she cut several seams and taped them so they would look like repairs. Several searches later, Tong didn't bother un-taping all the seams, having found nothing in the past. She now untaped one of the slits and removed the stuffing. Once she had made enough room, Achara quickly put the money into the opening and refilled it.

Tong was busy drinking now, but Pairat, his assistant, was standing on the porch as always, talking. He was about twenty-two and always wore sunglasses on top of his head. He had an endless supply of friends who came by the brothel in their Vespas, and they also liked to wear their sunglasses on their heads. He enjoyed bossing the girls around and yelling at them even when they weren't doing anything wrong. He yelled at Achara to get outside and sit in front of her room. She put on her white short-shorts and tube top, and sat in the breeze.

Before long, an old man clambered up the steps. She didn't look at him, hoping he would pick the new Burmese girl who was younger, or Lin, the Chinese girl who had beautiful white skin. She didn't want to leave the breeze, but he pointed to her and she had to go with him.

Four men and six hours later and still no Luk. She began to conjure what might have happened. They decided to sell the passport—would a passport be worth anything if it had someone else's picture in it? They got jealous and threw the passport away—this was the worst scenario. Everyone was jealous. Even if what you had was insignificant, someone around you was jealous of it. Once, one of the girls took her plastic Buddha and kept it for days. Achara kept shouting at Pairat to find out who took the statue. He slapped her and she still shouted that she should have her Buddha returned. Finally, he went around to all the girls' rooms searching until it turned up in the quarters of a Chinese girl from a hill tribe.

Achara asked her why she had stolen the statue and the girl replied that she was jealous that Achara believed in God while she herself believed in nothing.

At two in the morning, Luk arrived. She hadn't seen him since he was eleven. Now he was a young man of eighteen and she was suddenly ashamed. She was never ashamed in front of strangers, but this was her blood. He was a cashier in Wal-Mart and respectable. She invited him inside and greeted him with a traditional Thai Wai bow. Smiling, he handed her the passport. She opened it and they both gazed on a face which was hers, but more beautiful than hers. At the top of the first page, it said United States of America and the closeness of those words to her face made her feel that the mythical land was already near. She lit a candle to heat some tea and they sat in glowing silence. Luk said, "You are going to paradise."

U there?

Here. How are you? typed Rachel.

Good.

Did you buy the ticket?

Yes, write this down. Flight 1343 Cathay Pacific Airways arrives at Kennedy Airport day after tomorrow at 2:30 a.m. your time. But don't tell your parents until I arrive.

Don't worry. U r welcomed here.

But keep it secret for now. If they stop me at JFK I can ask for political asylum. But before I arrive, it can be a problem. So don't tell anyone—OK?

KK. Did you read the email I sent with questions and answers for Immigration here?

There was a pause.

Yes.

Let's go over that so you know exactly how to answer, typed Rachel.

No time now. Have to go.

You have everything you need? How will you get away to get to the airport?

I have a plan. But have to go now. I won't be online again. Bye.

Rachel checked her Outlook. She had sent the email with high priority and with "Request a Read Receipt" checked off.

Achara hadn't opened the email.

CHAPTER FIFTY-TWO

McKenna played the Belinda video over and over. It bugged him that the guy filming her was right there in the room with her and there was nothing he could do to see him. No cameraman shadows on the wall. When they erased the girl's body from the video, could they have taken any other valuable evidence with it?

There was nothing to look at except the wall, the girl's head, and the Christmas tree. When the tree came into view, he put it on pause and advanced as slowly as he could. That didn't do much good since the pause feature froze the frame in a blur. Hanging off the tree were the usual lights and made-in-communist-China crap. Gingerbread cookies, nutcracker, globes, clip-on candles, snowflakes. Nothing unusual.

He burned the .avi file onto a DVD and put it in his full-size DVD player. The resolution was better than on his laptop. Now he could slow down the action and there was no blur when he froze it. The first appearance of the tree revealed nothing. The second time it appeared, a silver globe ornament caught his eye. Its spherical reflective surface acted like a wide-angle lens. The cameraman wasn't reflected as there were branches obscuring that angle, but it did reflect something. He sat in his apartment replaying that over and over. The reflected image was of something rectangular on the floor. A vent? A fireplace? A low book case?

He focused on the image within the rectangle. There were figures in black and white. They were distinct, but distorted by the spherical surface, and McKenna couldn't make out what they were. A store logo? McKenna reviewed the notes he had taken when he had questioned Massey both times in his office. There was no mention of a rectangular object on the floor. Also Massey's office walls were off-white, not beige. Of course, that could have been painted over.

The object could have been something transient like a shopping bag with something printed on it. He went back to the start of the video, pausing every few moments. There seemed to be a lighter area on the wall like the outline made by a painting or a photo after it had hung there a long time before being removed.

There was a Picasso in his notes. He didn't know the name of the painting, but it had a horse in it. He googled, *Picasso painting with a horse.*

Guernica. That's what the tree ornament reflected.

CHAPTER FIFTY-THREE

I f traffic on the Belt Parkway held up, Rachel could make it to the terminal by two-thirty a.m. Achara would still have to go through Immigration, so figure two-forty, three a.m. She could probably park right across from the arrivals terminal at this hour.

She had left Joules' house at 10:00 p.m. and gone back to her parents' home. She decided to take a nap for an hour, but overslept. After washing her face and brushing her teeth, she crept out of the house, let the car roll down the driveway, and took off.

Over the last three days, they had downloaded thirty-six gigabytes of data from the computers belonging to Perlman, Sartorius, and Massey. They were never able to connect to Armand Greyson's machine. So far, they had found child porn on Sartorius' and Massey's computers. The kids ranged from about eight to fourteen. Rachel had gone through hundreds of files, but there was nothing pointing to Olivia. No photos, no emails mentioning her, but there was still a lot to go through. At what point should she get Detective McKenna involved? How would she explain how she got access to the computers? Her parents would kill her if they found out. The men with child porn on their machines could be locked up, but what about the others? Unless Sonia testified against them, the law couldn't convict them of statutory rape. Rachel hadn't witnessed what went on in the bedrooms. But none of that would get Olivia back.

Rachel was counting on Joules to help her go through the rest of the files tomorrow. He said he would work on them while at school. What would she do without him? What did he think of her right now, after finding out she was in the homes of all these perverts? He was too discreet to press the matter. But was that out of politeness or indifference? If she had fallen in his estimation, what could she ever do to pick herself up again in his eyes? She hoped he understood that whatever she had done, it was to get her sister back. With Olivia absent, Rachel realized how important Joules was to her, even if he didn't feel the same way.

She wished she had bought a present for Achara. All the niceties of life had dropped away since Olivia's disappearance. What were her parents going to say when they saw this person who was the image of their own daughter, but wasn't their daughter? Would that help or hurt?

They would have to accept her, like it or not. Olivia had, Rachel did, and so would they.

Then there was the matter of telling her that Olivia had vanished and that it was Rachel who had been talking with her these last few days. She would be greeted with one great joy and another terrible blow. She figured they'd stay at her dorm for the night and call the folks in the morning before coming by.

The Belt Parkway West was backed up seemingly for miles, as usual. Where were all these people going at this ungodly hour? After ten minutes of sitting in traffic, Rachel called the airline to confirm the arrival time, something she should have done before leaving. It was on time. That was a relief. Fifteen minutes later, she passed the bottleneck—a fender bender.

Rachel wished she could clone herself to do everything that needed to get done. She wanted to be a full-time student. When this was over and Olivia was back, she would sit and read Byron, Keats, and Shelly late into the night. She could minor in English Lit.

Cars speeded up. The overhead sign said, *TRAFFIC MOVING WELL.* Just twelve days ago it was flashing the Amber Alert for Olivia. Her disappearance had caused only a ripple in the scheme of things. Already she was fading away.

It all depended on the files she downloaded off those perverts' computers. Every instinct told her that one of them knew where Olivia was. There had to be something on one of those PCs that pointed to her fate. She went over the faces of those men one by one. Could one of them have actually abducted Olivia? No doubt some of them had sex with her. But where could she be? Certainly not in any of the homes she had gone to. She had to be found at some point. Rachel didn't want to go there, even in her thoughts, because thoughts were things and she wanted to deny the thought of her sister's death any power.

Joules was on file-decrypting duty tonight and she hoped he could find something by tomorrow. He was her only ally in the world. Everything Rachel had done might come out in court one day. Her parents would die of shame, and Rachel just hoped they would understand why she had done it. But she couldn't think of that now. One of her sisters was coming home.

Rachel entered the airport and looked for Cathay Pacific Airlines on each sign she passed. She had to hit the high beams every time she approached a sign to quickly scan the dozen or so airlines listed on each. She thought she'd missed it when she spotted it. Terminal Seven.

She took the turn for short-term parking and stopped at the booth to get her parking stub. The machine dispensed a ticket which she put behind the sun visor.

There was plenty of parking, as expected, and she pulled up to a light pole a hundred yards from the Arrivals Building. Her watch said 2:15 a.m. She exited the car and walked briskly toward the crossing that led to Arrivals. She felt a bitter-sweet joy at the prospect of actually seeing Achara, of having had a hand in bringing her home. She was so close now.

Rachel hardly noticed the white van that pulled up next to her as she entered the shadow of the overpass. The driver opened the door and shot her with a Taser. Rachel collapsed to the ground convulsing, her body curling up like a burning leaf. In a flash, a man exited the vehicle and tossed the girl into the back seat, then sped away.

CHAPTER FIFTY-FOUR

It was time for her to carry out the plan. If caught, Tong would cut off her nose and ears, and lock her in a room with mirrors. He had done this before and some of the girls committed suicide. Those who didn't kill themselves had to work with a burlap bag over their heads like prisoners condemned to hang and charge only twenty-five baht because they had no faces.

Her sister had explained how to search for a flight on Expedia.com and Travelocity.com. Once she decided on a flight, she would have to go to a travel agent and buy the ticket with cash. Achara had considered doing all that after she escaped, but there would be so little time. The less she had to do, the better were her chances of escaping.

The e-ticket would be waiting for her at the airport, so there would be no chance of Tong finding it. It was almost 2:00 p.m. and time to go fetch beer. Yesterday she had exchanged some dollars, so she would have cab fare to get to the travel agency quickly. It was nine kilometers away, so eighteen round trip, twenty minutes each way through traffic.

Tong appeared at her door and made a drinking motion with his hand. She got up and extended her hand for the money.

The beverage warehouse was in the opposite direction of the travel agency and she had to be seen walking in the direction of the warehouse. She went to the end of the block and took a cab to pick up the beer, then took another cab to the travel agency. She had called the agency the day before and was told she had to bring her passport and any required visa.

She told them she was an American citizen. First there was a silence on the other end. Okay, then just the passport.

In the cab with two cases of beer and dressed like a street urchin, she resolved to act like an American.

She unloaded the cases on the curb and paid the driver, then hauled the beer into the doorway of the agency, so no one would steal them.

"I called yesterday. I'm here to buy my plane ticket to America. I am an American," she announced. She was instructed to sit.

"You speak perfect Thai," said the lady.

"I just received my citizenship and was here to visit poor relatives. Here are two flights I am interested in." She pulled a scrap of paper from her pocket. The lady glanced briefly at it, then looked at her.

Achara felt she wasn't being received like an American.

"I want an e-ticket."

"Passport?"

She slid it across the desk.

The lady looked it over, feeling the paper, inspecting the photo.

"This is completely blank. It has no entry stamp."

Achara had forgotten about that.

"I lost my passport and they gave me a new one."

"You have the police report and the consulate certification of the new passport?"

Achara's mind raced.

"I... I don't have that with me now."

"It's a problem when the passport is not in order."

The pretenses were falling away quickly.

"How can we solve it?"

"Two-hundred."

"Fifty."

"One-fifty."

"Seventy."

She slid the passport back to Achara.

"Eighty-five or I go to another agency. There are many agencies here."

The lady nodded and extended her hand. Achara counted out the money twice and handed it over, then selected a flight.

"Aisle or window?" asked the agent.

"Which is cheaper?"

"It's the same price."

"So what difference does it make?"

"Wait. Let me see something. Neither is available. Very short notice. So you get a middle seat."

"That's fine if the price is the same."

"Sixteen-hundred-twenty-nine USD."

The girl counted out the money three times.

"This is your receipt. The e-ticket will be waiting for you at the airport."

Achara took a cab to the Internet café and, for the second day in a row, there was no sign of her sister. She didn't want to waste money again calling the cell phone number she'd been given. She purchased a card and entered one of the phone booths.

"Hi, this is Rachel. Please leave a message at the beep and I'll get back to you as soon as possible. Thanks."

The girl looked at the number and dialed again. Same message. How could she have given her the wrong number? What would happen if she arrived at the airport and there was no one to pick her up? The police would arrest her and send her to Guantanamo. She resumed her vigil by the PC. A working cam was available today, too.

She looked at the clock. They would notice her gone this long. She wrote an offline message and also sent it as an email.

Dear Sis,

I received everything you sent me. Thanks from the bottom of my heart.

Here is the flight. Singapore Airlines Flight 3244 to New York. Arrives at JFK Airport September 17 at 5:30 p.m. New York time. God bless you.

Achara

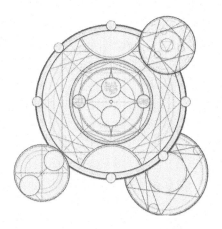

CHAPTER FIFTY-FIVE

Joules unscrambled an image of an Asian girl, about seven years old, having sex with a fat, white guy who was covering his face with a towel. The other pictures were along the same lines. Group sex with three girls, bondage, suspension. There were also .avi files. One was a video of the same man having sex with the girls in the stills. From the sounds the girls made, they were definitely in a foreign country.

Next, he decrypted a text file that was layered in a picture of Van Gogh's Sunflowers. It read like an autopsy. In clinical language, it described the dismemberment of Kirsten Schrodinger, along with photos taken at various stages of the process. There were horrific expressions on the victim's face, so she was still living while this was being done to her. Then he found the video of her killing.

Usually impassive, Joules felt nausea creeping over him, along with the realization that Rachel had been in the home of this monster. He didn't have McKenna's number, but he knew from Rachel that the detective worked out of the 20th precinct. He minimized the SubSeven program to google *NYPD 20th Precinct*. It was then that he noticed the Norton Internet Security red alert. *No, can't be.* But it was. He opened the Norton Security program and saw that Rachel's firewall was disabled. He held on to the last hope that she was using IP anonymizing software, but of course, she wasn't. It was her real IP address, traceable in seconds. He quickly opened Event Viewer Security and confirmed what he had already guessed. Her laptop had been successfully attacked. Joules shook his head at the enormity of Rachel's blunder.

He tried Rachel's cell and left a voicemail. Then he went to her house and was told by her father that she was there last night, but had left sometime later and taken her car. They had tried calling her all morning, but she wasn't answering her dorm number.

His mind, so wired to see patterns and relationships between numbers, couldn't escape the conclusion that Rachel was now in the hands of the man who had butchered Kirsten Schrodinger.

Joules dialed the 20th precinct in Manhattan and asked for Detective McKenna's cell number. He got through and told him what he had found.

"Where's Rachel now?" asked the detective.

"No one knows. I just came back from her house and her parents told me she was there last night and went to bed. She was gone in the morning. I just left a voicemail on her cell. Let me try again."

The detective looked at his watch. Eight o'clock in the morning.

"Still no answer," said Joules.

"Can you send me what you've found?" He gave Joules his email address. The detective stared at the images and only his lower lip reacted.

"How did you get these?"

"I decrypted it off a PC Rachel hacked into."

"Whose PC?"

"The priest. Father Massey. I also realized that Rachel was doing this hack without changing her IP address."

"What does that mean?"

"Whenever you do a hack, you should use IP anonymizing software. That changes your IP address, so that it looks like you're hacking from Poland or Hong Kong or Argentina. If you don't do this, it would take ten seconds to geolocate your PC. Just plug the IP address into ip2location.com and a map with your location comes up. It even has precise latitude and longitude."

"Oh, Christ."

"It gets worse. Rachel was having problems finding the files she was looking for and thought her firewall was the problem. So she disabled it. With her firewall disabled and her IP exposed, she became the target of a counter hack. And it succeeded."

"He hacked into her PC?"

"Right. At that point he knew exactly where she was and who she was."

CHAPTER FIFTY-SIX

The sniper perched on the rooftop of the apartment building had a clear view of the street below and the events that would shortly unfold.

McKenna could see the perimeter unit at both ends of the street consisting of marked police cars to seal off escape and keep bystanders out. The surveillance team made a final pass of the house in the unmarked car and in the distance, the raid team's caravan approached.

Massey's Bensonhurst home was deserted when police broke down the door, but a phone number led them to a realtor and this Richmond Hill house.

In a few moments, the raid team would storm the building. There hadn't been much time to plan this operation, but the SWAT guys were used to working on short notice. Just a few hours earlier, they had received authorization to carry out this mission after evidence had been presented pointing to Massey as the killer of Kirsten Schrodinger. Given the viciousness of the murder, this raid was classified as extremely dangerous despite the absence of any known accomplices.

If the Wallen girl was a hostage, it would change everything. It would mean waiting, negotiating, a siege.

A raid on Transcendence House came up empty a few minutes before. Thank God for that. No one wanted a hostage situation with fifty or sixty kids involved. Another damn Waco incident.

The teams performed a final check of their Browning High Power pistols and H&K MP-5 submachineguns. In their Metro-vests, Nomex hoods and

Bolle goggles, they looked like divers, and McKenna thought that was appropriate. Some of the creatures they went after came from the depths.

The vans stopped two houses away. Instantly the doors flew open with explosive power. Each team of six men took up their positions in the front and rear of the structure. The metal grille door was ripped out with a Ram-it. The device was then reversed and with two men swinging it, slammed into the wooden door, leveling it. In the rear, two men entered through a window assisted by a ladder.

The men poured into the house, quickly securing the living room, kitchen, and dining rooms. The second floor team gave the clear sign for the bedrooms, bathroom, and stairwell. The team on the first floor descended to the basement. Instantly, the Sure-fire lights on their weapons illuminated the darkness.

The place was barren. No furniture, no people. It was like someone had just moved out. Broom clean. The final Code Four was announced and the assault team withdrew.

McKenna, who had been following the assault by radio, moved in with the search team.

There was no sign of a violent struggle, just the echo of their footsteps. There hadn't been enough time for a security leak. Massey must have simply figured he was getting a visit. He'd have no place to run, that was certain. The guy had made the cover of Newsweek, for crying out loud.

Detective McKenna returned upstairs. At least no one had gotten killed here.

But just as he was letting himself relax, he noticed a small smudge of blood on the gray carpeting. There was another a few feet away and by the dining room, there was a third. He signaled his men.

Then McKenna passed a window and saw two of his men lifting black plastic trash bags in front of the house. The bags seemed to have a bad weight to them and McKenna's stomach told him something. When he got outside, the men were already inspecting the contents.

There, in three plastic bags, were the dismembered remains of a body.

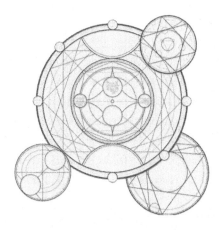

CHAPTER FIFTY-SEVEN

Detective McKenna felt sick at the thought of calling the Wallen parents to tell them he had found their daughter chopped up and distributed among three Hefty garbage bags. He had glanced inside the bags, but they were a dark, bloody mess, and had sent them on their way. Now it was the long wait for confirmation from the lab. There was nothing he could do to make himself forget this for even five minutes. He'd been at this job for twenty-one years and now wished he'd retired last year.

One of the cops had asked why the killer would be so stupid as to leave bags full of body parts in front of the house. McKenna shook his head and answered the question in his own mind. *Not stupid. Arrogant.*

They found Massey's car in the garage of the Richmond Hill house. No trace of anything inside, except for the trunk lined with a plastic drop cloth. The airports had been alerted to detain him if he tried to fly.

They recovered Massey's laptop from the Bensonhurst home and gotten a court order to get into his Yahoo account. Now, he and his men were combing through hundreds of emails for some clue to his whereabouts.

They checked out the realtor and the landlady of the Richmond Hill house. They were clean. Massey had obviously rented the place out to serve as an execution chamber.

He opened Massey's Yahoo Messenger. He had a dozen aliases. Newyorkerboy, Crush007. This guy spent a lot of time online. McKenna printed out the address book contact list. Most of these people had to be kids. What adult sits for hours and chats with other grown men? Christ.

Chat archiving was enabled for all his contacts, so McKenna was able to read the exchanges. The conversations sounded like two thirteen-year-olds talking. Movies they had seen. Parents. School. Lousy teachers. They all started out the same and all ended the same—with sex talk.

Some of the chats referenced photos that were sent. He correlated those dates with the dates in the "sent" folder to find the pictures, but they were all gone. They could be recovered from the Yahoo servers. Nothing ever got erased.

"Check out every person on this list." He gave the paper to Aldo Marchese.

McKenna's cell went off. He held his breath.

"We did a cross check of the art dealer's phone calls and Massey's office number came up," the voice said.

"Okay."

"We went over the things we got out of Greyson's apartment. There were four digital cameras, but the memory sticks were all missing."

"Not in the apartment?" asked McKenna.

"Went over everything four times. Not there."

"Maybe what we got in the email."

So it seemed Massey knew this art dealer who did a Sistine Ceiling with his body in the airport garage. How does the dealer fit in? Did Massey like both kids and men? Or just child porn buddies, swapping pictures and occasionally, kids? Why was Olivia chatting with all those adult men, some in their forties and fifties? Those guys had all checked out clean. Perverts maybe, but not killers.

Where could Rachel have gone in the middle of the night? And why? Her cell phone records didn't indicate she made or received a call at that hour. Meeting a boy? She had a dorm all to herself in Manhattan that she could use anytime, so why leave in the middle of the night? Something occurred to him. Olivia and Rachel shared a room. He found the photo. Yes, there was an alarm clock radio next to Rachel's bed.

"I need someone to find out if Rachel's alarm clock was set to go off in the middle of the night and I need it now," he said on the phone. He kept sifting through the emails. His phone rang.

"Yep, it was set to go off at 12:30 a.m."

So she had an appointment—with who? Not that Joules kid. With Massey? Was she screwing the priest?

His cell went off again. This time it was the lab. This was it.

"McKenna here."

"We've ID'd the body in those bags. It's Evan Massey."

CHAPTER FIFTY-EIGHT

Massey had gotten to the Richmond Hill house early to prepare. All he needed to do now was cock the spear guns. He waited in the bedroom for his prey to enter the house. No one had seen him arrive; in any case, he was disguised. He reviewed the plan once more.

After the killing, he would wrap the body in the plastic drop cloth he had picked up at Home Depot and seal the ends shut with Gorilla Tape. Then he would put the body in the trunk of his car. No one would see that either, thanks to the direct entry from the living room. He'd dump the body in the Meadowlands swamps with diving weights attached and that would be it.

This would delay the discovery by at least a few weeks. And if by chance the body was found, there would be no connection to him. The ID he had used to rent this house was fake, and he doubted the realtor could ever recognize him through the disguise and accent. He would take the Washington job, then, after a few months, resign for personal reasons and retire to Costa Rica, pedophile capital of the Western Hemisphere. There, he could collect the royalties from his book, continue writing, and set up another children's shelter with ample donations from expats. There would be no way to trace anything to him. This screwed up his grand plans, but he had to reinvent himself and adapt, that's all. For money, he had access to all the Transcendence House funds, which he would raid when the time was right. He had set up a generous retirement account for himself which he would tap into in the coming months.

Once he was settled into his new home, he would have the rest of the money wired down to Banco Nacional in San Jose and no one would ever hear from him again. For the past year, he had been looking into real estate in South America, and Costa Rica was the best place on all counts—weather, generous pensionado program, cheap cost of living and, above all, lots of promiscuous kids who don't mind selling themselves for a few bucks. Heaven.

But all that would have to wait. One more task to take care of and it had to be done right.

He had left the front door deliberately unlocked. The target would have to walk through the foyer and make a left to enter the living room. From that angle, all would be invisible from the doorway in case someone happened by.

He checked his watch. Fifteen minutes to go. Massey loaded a bolt into the first spear gun and cocked it. He repeated it for the second. One shot through the center of the body should end it. The second would pierce the throat and silence the victim. At this range, he couldn't miss. The practice in his basement gave him confidence.

Every muscle in his body tensed as he heard footsteps coming up the front stoop. The lights were on out front and he had a view of the street from a dark corner of the kitchen window.

A figure appeared. Alone, as agreed. The figure paused in front of the house and looked both ways. The head tilted toward the address over the front door.

Massey moved into position.

An instant later, the screen door squeaked open. The doorknob turned.

Massey wiped the sweat dripping from his brow.

The screen door closed and the entry door shut behind it.

Massey raised the weapon.

Emerging out of the foyer, the figure came into view, still in shadow.

Massey took aim at the midsection, his finger curled around the trigger. The figure advanced and came into the light.

Massey fired.

The spear bounced off the target's chest and fell to the floor.

Massey grabbed the second spear gun as the figure turned its head toward him. The priest fired, but again the projectile glanced off the torso and hung from the jacket.

"You're careless, Father," said the Webmaster without a hint of fear. "Careless and stupid. Lovely girl you got to masquerade as Cindy. I hope you got into her pants."

Massey had Gabriella send the killer a photo of herself taken when she was thirteen. For the next chat session, she put her hair in pigtails and got on the webcam. The man at the other end was certainly pleased with what he saw. Massey took over as Cindy and invited "Gerard" to the Richmond Hill address, where Cindy's friend was staying alone until her parents returned from Europe. Massey had to kill him before he was caught and brought everyone down with him.

Both Massey and Greyson figured out that the Webmaster was killing the girls, because they had sent them to him. Greyson had sent him Kirsten Schrodinger, and Massey had sent him Belinda Knights. Both had turned up dead. And now Olivia was gone. As members of the Webmaster's child porn site, they had been swapping kids for two years without a hitch. Then they started dying.

It wasn't hard to find his target on the Internet. He knew where this predator lurked.

The man removed a Taser from his jacket and leveled it at the priest. "When I was a boy, I used to go to church every week and kneel in front of the fourteen Stations of the Cross. I did this for years. And look at me. He shot the priest in the abdomen. As Massey convulsed on the floor, the man calmly went on.

"The picture I sent you of that handsome young man was a Trojan horse, letting me inside your PC. Thirteen-year-old girls don't have schedules that include speaking before the Elks and meeting with the First Lady."

Massey's mouth was locked in the open position, but no sound came out as his limbs flailed.

The figure picked up a spear gun.

"Quite a weapon. Three bands—you weren't taking any chances. I used one of these on a man once. But it was underwater where everything is in slow motion."

Massey got tangled in the wires, and the muscles of his face jumped over one another.

The Webmaster removed his jacket, revealing the body armor that covered his chest. He turned off the Taser, then kicked Massey in the face.

"Now I have a question for you. Were you in on the hit the other day?"

The priest rolled on the floor, spasming. A foot came down on his neck to steady him.

"I need an answer. Were you in on it?"

"No," he managed to reply.

"Taking a man's life is a serious thing. As you're about to find out."

He tied the priest's hands behind his back with Flexicuffs, then proceeded to cut his clothes off. Once naked, the interrogation began. The Webmaster pulled a chair up next to the bound man like a confessor.

"I try to get to know all my victims as well as I can in the brief time we have together, but usually they're very young and there isn't much depth to their lives. But you—you are really accomplished. You've lived a fairly long and distinguished life, and I wonder how someone like you ends up trying to commit murder. How a young girl sells her body is easy to understand—youth, money—I get that. But you went through seminary—St. Bartholomew, I believe. In Brooklyn. You became an ordained priest, and still you're willing to kill. You were already a child predator. I don't judge you for it, but make me understand how someone who has come so close to God can turn away and become evil, as you have become. I need to know all your sins."

When there was no answer, he thrust the heel of his shoe into the priest's genitals.

"I'm trying to prepare you to face your Lord. Now confess. Get it all off your chest. I'm your only salvation. Repent."

He confessed his sins to his executioner. Krupal, the girls, everything.

"I downloaded your book off your PC—The Infinite Hypocrisy. Noble work, getting them water for their parched throats. Then, of course, you shoved your cock down their daughters' throats. I would have done the same. We're kindred spirits, you and I."

The killer rolled Massey onto a plastic drop cloth and removed several plastic bags from his coat and a hacksaw. He put a strip of tape across the condemned man's mouth, then cut off his head.

CHAPTER FIFTY-NINE

olice had Dr. Sartorius under surveillance while waiting for a court order to get into his PC based on the evidence Joules had provided. McKenna had checked on the admissibility of all this. The police couldn't hack into anyone's computer without a warrant, but if someone else did the hacking and turned it over to police, it would constitute probable cause.

McKenna recalled how the FBI had arrested Zacarias Moussaoui, the twentieth hijacker, but weren't allowed to get into his PC until after the 9/11 attacks. It would have been worth it to blow the case on Moussaoui to find out about 9/11. McKenna called Joules.

"I need you to bring everything you have on these men down to the precinct. I need all the downloads. A Suffolk County Police car will be there in a few minutes to pick you up."

"No need. I'm at Cooper Union downtown."

"I'll send an unmarked car."

A search of Rachel's dorm had uncovered a camera containing the same photos that were in the email police had received anonymously a few days earlier. So Rachel had sent them. She had stayed overnight in the homeless shelter posing as a runaway. Had she—could she have stayed in the homes of these pedophiles? Could a Columbia kid be that stupid?

Joules placed his laptop on McKenna's desk. Police were already combing through Rachel's computer.

"It's not all decrypted yet, but there's plenty," said Joules.

"Brief our Cyber Crimes guys on everything you found," said McKenna. "They'll need to copy the downloads and delete the child porn from your computer."

McKenna had done a quick background check on Joules. Male friends of missing girls were always persons of interest. He didn't expect what he'd found. The kid had been making contributions to science since he was fourteen, for Christ's sake. Full ride to Cooper Union. Second place nationwide in that Intel contest. *Just don't blow it, kid.*

After Joules was done with Cyber Crimes, he came back.

"She left the house around midnight," said McKenna. "Which is what her alarm clock radio was set to. Any idea who she might be meeting? She just started college, did she mention anything about a boyfriend—you're not her boyfriend, are you?"

"No, on both counts."

"She was in the homes of these men, these pedophiles, wasn't she?"

"She told me she was."

"When did she tell you that?"

"She called me on Monday asking for help in decrypting the files. I asked her how she got the IP addresses of the computers and she told me she'd planted a RAT on each one."

"A rat?"

"Remote Administration Tool. It enables you to hack into the machine later and also downloads basic information you'll need to connect like the external router address and the machine's IP address."

"So to place this RAT on the PC she actually had to be there in the house?"

"You don't have to have physical access—it can be done remotely with a Trojan horse if you can get the target to execute it. But in her case, she was at their homes."

"I don't think she was invited there to install a RAT on their PCs. Any idea why she was there in the first place?"

"She just said that some of these men knew Olivia. She was sure about that."

"Is it possible that she was meeting one of them again—or going to the house of another man?"

"At this point, I'd say anything is possible. She was desperate to find her sister, especially after the Schrodinger girl turned up dead."

"How many separate PCs did you hack into?"

"Three. But some of these guys might not have PCs or maybe she didn't get access to them. So there's no telling how many homes she went to."

"Did she say she was by herself when she did this—going to these homes?"

"She didn't say, and I guess I didn't want to ask."

After Joules left, McKenna sat there trying to figure out Rachel Wallen. *If she was doing this alone, she was putting out for the pedophiles*, thought McKenna. Looks like her sister was hustling too. What the hell was going on with these kids? Giving sex was like giving out lollipops these days. The good-night kiss was now the good-night blow job.

A few minutes later, a voice came over the intercom.

"That Joules kid is back. He needs to talk to you."

"Send him in."

When the boy walked in, he looked at the detective as dispassionately as if he had just figured out another math problem.

"I know who the killer is."

"Let me get this straight," said McKenna. "You're telling me that you connected to Massey's PC and from Massey's machine you connected to a second PC?"

"Right," said Joules.

"Through Massey's machine?"

"Yes."

"So the Schrodinger video was actually on the second machine?"

"Right."

"How do you know this?"

"Just before I accessed the directory that contained the Schrodinger video, the data transfer speed slowed down drastically. I didn't think much of it until I was walking out of here just now. I looked at the properties of an icon on Massey's machine that I clicked on before the response time slowed. It's a login macro that connects to another computer and autofills the ID and password. Everything I captured after that was on another machine. It also explains why some files don't have Massey as the author if you look at the properties of the files."

"And whose PC was it on?"

Joules clicked on an email and highlighted the name at the top.

"This guy."

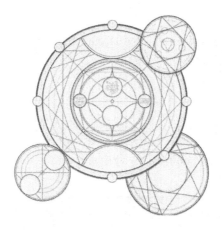

CHAPTER SIXTY

Achara bowed three times before her shrine and said a prayer for safety. She kissed her vihara, wishing she could take this one possession. Now she waited for Tong to tell her to fetch the beer.

When he appeared in the doorway, she extended her hand to receive the money for the last time. He was going to go thirsty today.

Four blocks from the brothel, she flagged down a cab.

"Doi Lo," she said.

Achara could see the driver checking her out in the mirror. She couldn't tell if he knew she was a prostitute or if he was just uneasy about getting his fare from a sixteen-year-old. Either way, she didn't like it. He started to make conversation and she cut him off. The last thing she needed now was to leave any clues. As the familiar part of town receded, she opened the window for some fresh air. Her hand rested on the outline of the passport in her pocket. She took a small number of bills out that she would use to pay the cab. The dollars were secure against her ankles, but the bulges now showed as she sat down. She hadn't thought of that.

The traffic was horrendous as always and it took over an hour to get to Doi Lo.

"Four-hundred baht," said the driver.

"That ride was worth only three-hundred."

"Three-fifty."

"Three-twenty-five." She held out the money.

When she exited the cab, she waited for him to vanish from sight, then flagged down another cab. This way, the first driver wouldn't know her final destination if questioned.

"The airport," she said.

"Picking someone up?"

"Yes."

This would take another forty minutes with traffic, and then she would have to elude Tong for another five hours until the flight left.

When Achara didn't return, Tong summoned all the girls to the front porch. He took out a cane and threatened to beat every girl. No one could tell him anything. Nothing was missing from her room, so she either ran away, or some other pimp had stolen her.

One of the police he employed came up the steps and reported that someone had seen her get into a taxi two blocks away.

He went with the police officer to question the witness.

"What kind of taxi did she get into," asked the pimp.

"New York Style Taxi," answered the old man. Tong threw him a hundred baht.

At the dispatch office of the New York Style Taxi Company, Tong paid the dispatcher another hundred baht to find out who had given a ride to a girl of Achara's description in the last two hours. There was only one driver. He had dropped her off at Doi Lo.

"Show me a map," he demanded. She had taken the taxi north on 108 to Doi Lo. Who did she know in Doi Lo?

Tong called the police captain and told him to send a police car to his location with three men.

Tong rode in the police car with the siren screaming. They cut through all the traffic and got there in twenty-five minutes. This girl was going to be punished in front of the others, so he would never have this problem again. No one was going to make a fool out of him.

"How many taxi companies you have here?" Tong asked a Doi Lo police sergeant when they arrived.

"Five official, but there are a lot of freelancers."

"Get in touch with the dispatcher of every taxi company and find out who drove this girl and where." He handed over a photo of Achara.

A half hour later, the sergeant came back. None of their drivers had taken her.

Tong opened the second pack of cigarettes for the day. She was either here in Doi Lo or had traveled somewhere else. She had no relatives here that he was aware of. From here, she could have traveled to several small towns. He was going to spend a fortune paying off all these police to search for her.

Where did she get the money for the long taxi ride? The customers tip a little, but Tong made sure to get all that money, too. He searched the girls' rooms for any money they could use to escape. She had done a good job of earning his trust—coming straight back with the beer, always had the correct change. It killed him that she had outsmarted him.

"Question the pawn shops near the brothel, she would need money. Also check all the Western Unions in case someone's helping her."

Achara looked at the time on the taxi's dashboard. It was just past one in the afternoon. The flight was for 6:30 p.m. She had to check in by three to go through security. And she had to get her passport stamped with an entry date of two weeks ago. Now she began to dread this part. Would sixteen-hundred dollars be enough to get someone to stamp it? Just a little stamp, but they could get in trouble over this.

Signs for the Chiang Mai Airport began to appear.

"You said Arrivals, right?" said the driver.

"Yes, Arrivals." This was one final precaution in case this driver was questioned. She didn't want him to see which airline she was going to. Once in the airport, she could use the free shuttle buses to get to the Departures terminal.

"Thirty-two hundred USD?" repeated Tong.

"Yes."

"USD?"

"Yes, here is a copy of the receipt." The sergeant handed it to Tong.

Who the hell was sending this sixteen-year-old girl over three-thousand dollars? He looked at the name on the transaction record. Lisa Barino. Who the hell was Lisa Barino? The amount was shocking. It was a year's pay for the average Thai. Who would want her that badly—an American trafficking ring? Achara had started out beautiful, but was looking like shit recently. In the beginning, she commanded four-hundred baht for a screw; now she was down to one-fifty. She'd be down to five baht after he got through with her.

He lit another Lucky Strike and took a deep drag. What would she do with that kind of money? Maybe she had a sick relative who needed an operation? It was enough to get her out of the country, but she had no passport. She wouldn't need one if she was traveling inside the country.

He looked at the map again. They were right next to Route 108, which led straight into Chiang Mai Airport.

CHAPTER SIXTY-ONE

A chara entered the Arrivals Terminal. She had never been in an airport, but she had read about it online. In her email, her sister had told her that it would look strange if she had no luggage for such a long trip, so she would have to purchase a bag of some kind in the airport and take it with her on the plane. Not check in.

At the information counter, she was told which bus to take to the Singapore Airlines terminal. Now time was going faster. Airplanes were taking off all around her.

The shuttle had open windows and the warm breeze caressed Achara's face. There was so much open sky. She wanted it to receive her. All this time her hand hadn't left the passport and e-ticket receipt in her pocket and she could take them out now for the first time without fear. Olivia's face was beautiful. Looking at it now for the first time in daylight, she could see the holographic ghost of an eagle hovering over the face. She needed that eagle to protect her now.

The clock showed 2:10. There was no one standing in line at the Singapore Airlines ticket counter. Achara rushed up to the agent, ready to present her papers.

"I'm leaving on this flight," she held out the paper. "What do I do?"

"Check-in is not for another hour."

"And who stamps my passport?"

"Immigration Police."

"Where can I find them?"

"After you check in, you go past security upstairs, then they stamp your passport."

"Where are the shops? I need to buy a suitcase."

"At the end of this hall, make a left. That leads to the restaurants and shops."

She got onto a moving conveyor and was dazzled by the jewelry stores, the leather goods, and the restaurants. All the names she had seen on TV were here. Chanel, Gucci, Rolex, McDonald's. She got off at a place that sold luggage. In the ladies' room, she took the cash out and put a little in her left pocket, so she could pay without drawing attention.

The prices were so high. She settled on a knapsack for thirty-eight dollars. Now she needed something to put inside it. A chicken sandwich, a chocolate bar, and a bag of peanuts would sustain her for the long journey. In the window of a souvenir shop, she saw the most beautiful vihara. It was made of dark teakwood stained with oil. She went inside and stood before it without touching it.

"You can pick it up," said the sales girl.

Achara looked at her hands, which were dirty, and didn't want to touch something so beautiful.

The sales girl handed it to her. The price was thirty dollars.

She had to make a leap of faith. She had to believe that she could put the vihara in a place she could call home and invite the gods in to reside there. That she would be free.

"How much for the small one?"

"Twenty."

"Twelve."

"Seventeen."

"Fourteen."

"Sixteen. I can't take less than that."

She paid and put the vihara in the bag. After some window shopping, it was time to return to the ticket counter. She got off the conveyor, turned the corner, and stopped short. Tong was talking to an agent at the Singapore Airlines counter.

CHAPTER SIXTY-TWO

A chara turned her back and darted into the ladies' restroom. In a stall, she shut the door and started to sob. She couldn't believe he had tracked her here after all the precautions she took. Was it her destiny to go back to the brothel? Wasn't there anything else for her in this world?

Before, she had time to kill, now time was running out. Check-in for the flight started ten minutes ago. There was a long line now and she would be out in the open. She couldn't stay here. If that flight left without her, she might as well go back to the brothel herself.

She washed her face. It wasn't going to help to look upset or suspicious. She went outside and bought a pair of sunglasses and a large brimmed hat. Tong was gone and Achara got in the line.

"I'm flying to New York." She handed over her passport and e-ticket receipt. The lady drew the passport across the reader, then returned it to Achara. This just checked her name against a database of wanted felons and no-fly passengers. She had to remember that her name was now Olivia Wallen.

"Any bags for check-in?"

"No, just this carry-on."

"The flight leaves at 6:30 from gate forty-seven. Up the escalator to your left."

"This is the ticket?"

"That's your boarding pass."

"Thank you."

The glasses went back on and she went up the escalator. She had never been on an escalator.

At the security checkpoint, she started getting nervous. She handed the first official her passport and boarding pass. He perfunctorily looked at it and waved her on. Next, she took off her shoes and put her bag through the X-ray machine. After passing through the metal-detector, she picked up her knapsack and started walking.

Someone tapped her on the shoulder.

"May I see your passport, miss?" The official leafed through it with practiced speed. "Come this way, please." The girl followed him to the far end of the security area where there were three more guards. *This is no good,* thought Achara. She had to get one of them alone to offer him the bribe. There wasn't enough for all four.

"This passport has no entry stamp," said a female officer.

"I didn't know that."

"When did you enter the country?"

"Two weeks ago."

"You are a US citizen?"

"Yes."

"You're from here. How long have you lived in the USA?"

"Seven years. I just got my citizenship."

"And your name is Olivia Wallen?"

"That's my American name."

"You'll need to correct this before you can fly."

"How can I do that quickly? My flight leaves in less than an hour."

"Where did you enter the country?"

"Chiang Mai Airport."

"Please report to Room 519, 5th Floor, Old Building, Immigration Bureau. Bring a copy of your original flight ticket, boarding pass, or other travel document to show the date of entry and flight number. The officer on duty will make the necessary entry in your passport."

"Where is Old Building?"

"Outside the terminal, all the way down to your left. You really don't have much time."

"I need to talk to the officer on duty about stamping my passport," Achara said to the secretary.

"He's occupied. Take a seat."

"My flight leaves in forty minutes. I really need to speak to him to correct my passport. Can you please tell him this is an emergency?"

"I'm sorry, he's with another person. Please have a seat."

Achara sat down for one minute, then got up and began pacing across the doorway of the office. After fifteen interminable minutes, the man sitting opposite the officer left.

"You need to see me?" He waived her inside.

"I have a serious problem and I hope you can solve it for me," she sat in the low chair. "My flight leaves in less than a half hour and I don't have an entry stamp on my passport."

"You have the ticket or boarding pass you used to enter the country?"

"No, I don't have those with me."

"Can someone get them for you?"

"No, I don't have those."

"You need proof that you entered the country."

"How can we solve it?"

"By getting the boarding pass or plane ticket."

She took the money out of her bag and put it on the desk. "I can give you this."

"What's that?"

"A gift for you if you help me."

"I can't do that."

"I really need your help. I need the entry stamp. Please help me. It's sixteen-hundred dollars."

"I don't work that way. I know everyone else does, but I don't."

"But I need to get to America. Only you can help me."

"I'm sorry. I can't."

"Please, I have a family waiting for me in America."

"I have a family, too."

"That's why it's sixteen-hundred dollars." She tried to control her voice, but it was no use. Passengers were already boarding the plane. Soon the door would close. "It's just a stamp. It's just a stamp."

"It's not just a stamp."

Achara's world was collapsing as she faced the one man in Thailand who could not be bought. She knew from the beginning that it all depended on this moment, that all the planning and all the hope hinged on the corruptibility of a man she had never met.

"I have to get to America."

"Please. I'm sorry. I can't help you." He handed her back the passport. "You should go home now." Those final words descended from the high chair like a death sentence. He was getting up. He walked past her to open the door.

She looked at the name plate on the desk. "Rangsang Wattana, if I don't go to America tonight, then I go back to a brothel." He paused. Her hand reached into the bag again.

"You can have this too." She held out the vihara. He took it in his hand, briefly, then returned it. For a moment, he just stood over her, then he reached out and took back the passport. After stamping it, he put it on top of the money and gave it all back to her.

She fled the Immigration Bureau and caught another taxi to the Departure Terminal. There were only nineteen minutes before takeoff and the door may have already closed.

Again, she went through the security checkpoint. There was a line of people for other flights. She ran to the front and looked for one of the officers who had stopped her before.

"I have it stamped, please let me go ahead. My flight leaves in ten minutes."

He waved her through and she placed her shoes and bag in the scanner. She passed through the metal detector and waited forever for her shoes and bag to advance the five feet. Now to find gate forty-seven.

A voice came over the PA system.

"Yui Ho and Olivia Wallen, please come to gate forty-seven immediately. Your flight is leaving."

She was desperate. There were four directions she could go. She saw a sign for gates twenty-three to fifty-two. Jumping on the conveyor, she ran past all the restaurants full of people sitting leisurely, shopping for souvenirs, the ads of beautiful girls selling Chanel and Omega watches.

"Olivia Wallen, this is your final call. Please come to gate forty-seven immediately. Your flight is leaving."

She saw the sign for gates forty to fifty-two. An immense length of stores, people, and departure gates before her. She ran past Rolex and Longines, Coach and Louis Vuitton. They stopped calling her name. She would have traded all the riches in this place for one more minute of time.

There it was in the distance. Her lungs were bursting. She could see it. She ran past gate forty-four, forty-five, forty-six. Into the waiting lounge of gate forty-seven.

There was no one there.

CHAPTER SIXTY-THREE

Once inside the van, Rachel's hands were bound behind her back and her screams were muffled by Gorilla tape. A hood went over her head. The full magnitude of it all now set in—the simplicity of the trap. She had traced Olivia's steps all the way to death. She wailed at the top of her lungs.

The vehicle stopped at the booth to pay the parking fee, and Rachel desperately kicked the sides of the van to get someone's attention. But the transaction was quick and the car sped off.

Once on the highway, her abductor finally spoke.

"You violated me. And you have to pay. Where we're going, they'll never find you. And I can dispose of a body, so it can never be identified. I'll drill out the pulp in your molars, so they can't DNA it."

She took deep breaths, recapturing her heartbeat, dispelling the miasma of chaos in her mind. There was no hope of escape while the car was moving; with her hands behind her back, she would surely die even if she had a chance to roll out of the car.

Her cell phone was on her belt. If she could get it out of the holster and managed to make two keystrokes, it would dial 911. She couldn't talk, but police could track her with the built-in GPS once they were alerted to a problem. Her wrists pulled at the plastic strap, testing it, but they only dug deeper into her flesh. Groping with her foot for a weapon, she found none.

She tugged at her belt, sliding it around her waist, but the cell phone got stuck at the first loop. Rachel tried to get to the buckle of the thin belt and undo it. She could then pull the belt off her waist and the phone would fall off.

They got onto a highway. It could only be the Belt Parkway. Were they heading east or west? The van didn't stop for any lights. Sliding the belt around her waist to access the buckle was harder than she thought. Getting the buckle past each belt loop was a struggle. Twenty minutes later, Rachel still had three more loops to go. Then she heard the unmistakable steel roadway of the Queensborough Bridge under them. There was no pause for a toll and the metal grid against the tires made a whirring sound. This led to the Fifty-ninth Street entrance to the bridge on the Manhattan side. Then the car would slow as it negotiated the streets and traffic lights.

But that's not what happened. There was no slowing. The car veered sharply right in a U-turn which meant the FDR Drive. North or south? North led to the Bronx and the Hutchinson River Parkway toward New England. South led to lower Manhattan.

There was no stop and go. They were traveling at highway speed for twenty or twenty-five minutes after they hit the Queensborough. And now they stopped. They were still in New York City.

He parked the car and they were silent for ten minutes.

The tape came off and sunglasses went over her eyes. The insides of the lenses were painted black.

"Don't scream. Don't run," said the voice. "I'll split you in half." Rachel felt the flat side of an endless knife travel across her throat. He tore the cell phone from her waist.

The passenger door opened. "Out."

He slung a jacket over her shoulders and took her by the arm.

They ascended the incline, stepping over discarded tires. He opened a metal door and pulled her through, closing it behind them. A crossbar followed and a padlock. Now there was silence. Now they were alone. He pulled off the sunglasses.

"Please…" Rachel fell to her knees crying. She had found what she was looking for. This was the killer she had danced for, whom she had deceived. But the deception was on her.

She begged him to release her and vowed she would never help the police find him. Her tormentor had been uncharacteristically silent since they had exited the car. Could there be people nearby who might help her?

She let out a scream that seemed to come from the throat of the tunnel itself. The sound echoed for several seconds. The man didn't react. They were alone.

Rachel began to pray. *Engage him in conversation. Find a particle of reason in him.*

"Let me go now—I still don't know where I am. I'll never help them find you."

"I'll tell you exactly where you are. You're under the Major Deegan Expressway."

"*No!*"

"This place has quite a history. In 1913, the Interborough Rapid Transit Company blasted a subway tunnel for thirteen blocks from Sedgewick Avenue to meet the city's Jerome Avenue line. This was a busy area when there were baseball games at the Polo Grounds at One hundred and Fifty-Fifth Street. A little before your time. In 1958, the top of the el was cut off and the Major Deegan was built over it. The tunnels were abandoned, but you can still get to them through a portal. The portal we just walked through."

They stood in what seemed like an antechamber, six feet by six. There was another metal door in front of them. He opened this door and led her through to a larger chamber, thirty feet by fourteen. He threw a switch and the light blinded her. Caches of supplies. Walls stacked with canned goods, military meals ready to eat, paper towels, medical kits, water purifiers, mess kits, and ammunition to last out a nuclear winter. This was a bunker. There was an enormous metal "X" bolted to the concrete wall with handcuffs at the end of each limb of the apparatus. There was a hangman's noose screwed into the ceiling, and video lighting and sound equipment focused on a bed. Bloodstains spattered on the walls and floor. Now Rachel understood what was done here. He pulled aside a folding screen.

Sonia and Olivia were tied to a U-bolt in the concrete wall.

CHAPTER SIXTY-FOUR

Detective McKenna rode with Sergeant Nils Swenson and his SWAT team.

"The sheet on this guy is ugly," said McKenna. "Hector Brazos. Assassin for the Mexican cartels—a Zeta. Trained by us no less, but the cartels paid better. The narco bigs wanted the victims tortured and videotaped, not just killed. Real Latin macho shit. They custom-ordered executions of entire families and this guy filled the order."

"Nice."

They had gotten a sheet on Brazos from Mexican authorities. McKenna had seen sadism in his time, but nothing that approached Brazos. Serial killers were nice guys compared to him. A U.N. Peacekeeper in Congo and Bosnia. You've got to be kidding. Accused of rape and killing of three Serbian girls. Never proved. Then he was hired as an independent contractor in Iraq. Uncle Sam was looking for a few good men.

In Mexico, he was put on trial for seventeen counts of mass murder. That is seventeen separate mass murders of families killed at the request of the cartel. Someone had shortchanged a Don, so the guy's two little girls were kidnapped and massacred on tape, then the video was left in the mailbox of the father. The same for the wife, and finally his turn came. There were DVDs of home invasions with masked men raping wives and daughters in front of their fathers, forcing the father to have sex with the kid, then executing them one by one. Never convicted. No wonder the jurors acquitted.

The outer perimeter had already been set up by local police. They would contain the suspect and keep out traffic until the assault team arrived. A hospital had already been put on alert and listening devices had detected sounds from the target location. It started to rain and this would impact visibility.

"We have a sniper position yet?" asked McKenna.

"Two," replied Swenson.

McKenna had no hope that the suspect would surrender, given that he'd already killed multiple people. At most, he would avoid the death penalty. That didn't give the negotiator many bargaining chips.

The two teams closed in from the front and back. Rain came down hard now. One sniper laid across the roof of a parked garbage truck across the street. The other was on the closest flat roof about fifty yards diagonal from the target.

It was an ordinary looking house on Pennsylvania Street. A Cape Cod that no one would look at twice. Reminded him of Adolph Eichmann's house from *The House on Garibaldi Street*. It disguised its resident well.

The signal was given.

They broke down the door and stormed the building. It was vacant. But not unguarded. McKenna looked up at one of the many security cameras and could sense Brazos looking straight at him.

Chapter Sixty-Five

The girls screamed in recognition.

"I'm sorry, Rachel. I'm so sorry," said Sonia.

Olivia was barely recognizable. Her lips were swollen from beatings. She was naked with dried blood on her face and along the inside of her thighs.

In her peripheral vision, Rachel saw him glance back and forth, looking for a reaction that she wasn't about to give him. Breaking bonds was at least as pleasurable to him as breaking bones.

Rachel felt her will slipping away as she was pushed and pulled into position against the wall. Brazos tied Rachel to the U-bolt.

He exited, leaving the door ajar.

Rachel kissed her sister.

"We're going to die," said Olivia.

"Don't talk. Don't talk," said Rachel, looking around.

"This is a dungeon," said Sonia.

"We're underground?" whispered Rachel.

Sonia nodded.

Rachel was amazed that they were all alive. Why hadn't he just killed them at once?

"Mom and Dad?" asked Olivia, softly. Rachel just nodded. She purged herself of sentiment, trying to think of a way out of here.

"What is this place?" she asked.

"A subway station. Abandoned," said her sister.

There was a metal door ten feet away with a sliding bolt and padlock. At the far end of the chamber, another metal door had three sliding bolts and no lock.

There was a power generator with an exhaust tube going through the top of a door. Gas masks, a bio-hazard suit, bottled water, water purifiers, cans of food. Everything needed to survive, but there were no survivors in this place. The floor and walls were stained with blood. Death was prolonged here, not life.

The concrete was cool and now she felt a soft rumbling. A train. She had to find out what was behind those doors. It only made sense that there would be two points of access to this tunnel. Even rodents made sure of that. Joules would think of a way of escaping. He always found a solution. She had to find it too.

She leaned forward and pulled at the bonds with all her strength. It was no use. Footsteps.

Brazos returned and tested the light intensity where the scene would take place. Not good enough. He got another spotlight and fired it up. Better. He thought of all the possibilities with three girls. The cattle prod, the bedsprings, and the whip would play their roles. They could torment each other. At some point, a noose goes around the neck of one girl and another kicks the stool out from under her. But he would leave that privilege to the highest bidder. He liked that hanging idea. It usually took about five minutes to die that way, but it could be extended. The Nazis had a way of prolonging it for seventeen minutes or so, and they made exquisite films of their hangings.

Brazos had made some good movies too. He had studied film at the Universidad de Guadalajara. Admiring the work of Francis Ford Coppola, he dreamed of making a Mexican version of the Godfather. After graduating, he discovered that film degrees didn't bring much income, and Hector Brazos loved money. He joined the military and, after two years, transferred to GAFE, Grupo Aeromovil de Fuerzas Especiales—the Mexican Special Forces.

Shortly after that, he attended the School of the Americas to become a Zeta. There, he was instructed by American, French, and Israeli Special Forces. The training covered rapid deployment, aerial assaults, marksmanship, ambushes, intel collection, counter-surveillance techniques, prisoner rescues, sophisticated communications, and computer training.

But this didn't pay well either, and Brazos knew what he really wanted. He loved watching the young turks in the drug cartels tooling around in their hundred-thousand dollar Mercedes Benzes. And those girls.

He offered his services to a middling *jefe* in the Sinaloa Cartel. His new boss soon had a problem. A competitor had stolen his girl. This was problematic enough in Latin society, but it was emasculating in cartel circles. It had to be addressed—and swiftly.

"I can take care of this," he told his boss.

"How will you do it?" asked Rico.

"You tell me."

"*Tiene que sufrir.*"

"He will suffer. Tell me how you want it done."

"She also must pay."

"Done."

Rico then described in detail how the victims were to die.

"I want absolute proof that it was done this way. You bring me a video tape and you'll have my gratitude."

This was going to be much harder than just taking aim at someone in a parking lot and pulling the trigger. Brazos hoped he hadn't bitten off more than he could chew, or he would end up on a meat hook.

His targets were Geronimo Cartagena and Rico's ex-girlfriend, Pascualita de Bris.

As a still-rising star in the cartel hierarchy, Cartagena didn't always have a security detail with him. Brazos observed him for a week. He knew his target liked big game fishing. He had originally nailed Pascualita on a fishing boat, according to Rico. Twice a month, on Saturdays, he went out for marlin on a chartered boat. The *Santa Clara* had been chartered for this weekend. Brazos went ahead and chartered the *Juaquín* a few slips away. On Friday night, Brazos paid a kid to mangle the *Santa Clara's* engine. Saturday morning, bright and early, Brazos was on the *Juaquín*, ready to shove off.

When Cartagena and his girlfriend arrived, the captain told them the bad news. Vandalism. Would take two days to get the spare parts.

"*Hijo de puta!*" screamed Cartagena, holding a cooler full of beer.

"Your money will be returned of course. Please step into my office."

Brazos was lighting a cigar nearby.

"*Señor, con permiso*," said Brazos, approaching the couple. "I just happened to overhear that your vessel is disabled. You're both welcome to go out on my boat with me, if you don't mind the blue water. I'll be going for marlin."

Cartagena's face was caught between anger and fishing.

Pascualita stroked Cartegena's back. "You see, Geronimo, we can go after all," she said. "That's very gracious, *señor*."

"The pleasure is mine, *señorita*. Please take care of your business. We'll shove off in twenty minutes."

"*Gracias, caballero*." Cartagena extended his hand.

Once on the boat, Cartagena said, "No mate?"

"No, he called in sick today and I couldn't give up a day's fishing. I'll cut the bait, no problem."

"What kind of bait do you use?"

"I have mullet today. I usually go out earlier and catch bonito—nothing beats live bait. But I knew I wouldn't have as much time today, so I bought it frozen from Cicero's."

Cartagena inspected the upright poles and reels like a head of state reviewing a color guard. Alutecnos reels, Shimano rods.

"Nice gear. How many pounds test?"

"Today I have hundred-pound test with five-hundred yards. Sometimes I use eighty test with seven-hundred yards. But I'm not feeling very sportsmanlike today," said the assassin.

"How far out do you go?"

"Usually about twenty miles. A friend radioed the coordinates of a school he saw this morning. We'll head out there. It's a clear day; the schools should be near the surface."

It would be a two-hour ride to the fish, so Pascualita took off her dress and sunned herself on the stern wearing a green Brazilian bikini which left nothing to the imagination. She had a body to die for, and that's exactly what Cartagena was going to do today. Cartagena seemed to enjoy seeing his girlfriend exposing herself in front of a stranger. Brazos pretended to ignore all this.

As they approached the site, Brazos said, "I'll check the fish finder," and went inside the cabin. "There's a school just north," he said, emerging. "I'll maneuver, so the sun's behind them, otherwise they won't see the bait."

Once in position, he said, "Let's set up here. I'm ready for some lunch."

After the poles were baited, they retired to the cabin for a meal.

"After lunch, we'll troll about eight knots up and down this corridor. They should be biting."

Brazos had all the camera equipment set up under a tarp and after a couple of beers and a few lame laughs, he walked over, switched on the camera, and pulled a shotgun from behind the canvas, sticking it in Cartagena's face.

"Drop the gun," he ordered.

Cartagena's jaw dropped, revealing a mouth full of salchicha.

"With two fingers of your left hand. Take it out and drop it. Now kick it over here."

Brazos tossed the gun overboard. "Both of you, on your knees."

He bound the man's hands behind his back.

"Whoever you are, you're going to die a miserable death for this," said Cartagena. "Everyone knows where I am today. They'll wipe out your family. They'll fuck your mother."

"I don't have a family." He kicked Cartagena in the face. "Now you watch your girlfriend and me enjoy ourselves."

Brazos mounted the camera to capture not only his own performance, but the expressions on Cartagena's face. A face that twisted and contorted at the acts it witnessed.

When Brazos was done with Pascualita, he turned his attention to Cartagena. With a bait knife, he cut off his clothes, then took one of those fine marlin rods that he had so admired and shoved it up his ass, no lubrication. The rod bent like he had a two-hundred-pound tuna at the end. Then he pulled it out abruptly, letting the steel guides do their work. Then he relieved himself on the victim's face.

"You, over here," he ordered the girl.

He handed her the bait knife.

"Cut off his cock."

"NO."

He put the shotgun to her head. "Yes."

Twenty miles out to sea, no screams are heard. After raping Pascualita two more times, he shot her in the face. Now it was time for Cartagena. Brazos wrapped a strap wrench around the man's head, then applied torque. It was like taking off an oil filter. Cartagena's head did a three-sixty, then another. His head dangled like a chalk-filled sock. After perforating the bodies to let the gases escape, Brazos tied diving weights to them and dumped them overboard.

Rico loved the video. His honor had been restored. He circulated it to the other drug lords, who were impressed and soon orders were coming in for Brazos to dispose of this guy and that with proof of death videos. The fees far exceeded those of a regular hit since it required that he capture a man who was usually well protected. But Brazos had been trained well and he made a fortune using his cinema skills acquired at the university.

In the end, the assignments just got too difficult. Brazos had to hire his own squad of assassins to mow down the bodyguards, so he could do his film work with the intended target.

One day while bidding on a rappelling harness on eBay, it occurred to him that if the victims were easy to get to, this would be a great moneymaker. He knew there was a market for snuff films, but how would he contact the clientele and collect the money for anything he sold them? By then, he was making good money running his child porn site with porn from Thailand, the Philippines, and South America. He had over five-hundred subscribers worldwide. Then it came to him.

He created a special site offering his services to an elite clientele. Mega-rich customers in Japan, the Middle East, and Russia who bid hundreds of thousands to see unspeakable depravity. And Hector Brazos was here to provide it for them.

Today's special was a three-girl package that would command a fortune.

CHAPTER SIXTY-SIX

Gentlemen, the bidding will be extended because we have a unique item for sale. As you can see, there are now three lovely girls. The blonde is called Sonia, just a common street prostitute, but the brunette is the adoptive sister of Olivia. Her name is Rachel. You can read about her in the New York newspapers if you have doubts. You have the pleasure of her company and the chance to bid for her death. I'm offering all three as a package.

"Rachel and Sonia, please remove your clothes. Shoes and socks too. Yes, stand there and turn around. Lovely girls aren't they? You'll be able to interview each girl as usual, just send in your questions. You can sit, ladies. We'll start with questions from Client Number One.

"And the first question is, how old are you, Rachel? Eighteen. Next, are you still a virgin? Answer is yes. What are your pastimes? Reading and exercise. Commendable. That's how she maintains that firm body. No, don't get dressed. I said don't get dressed." He grabbed Rachel by the hair and said something out of earshot of the clients. "And what do you read? What books do you read?" He slapped her across the face.

Rachel named a few authors. "That sounds familiar. You have the same taste as your sister. Client number Two would like to know if you have a boyfriend. Answer is no. And would you like a boyfriend? Answer is no. Of course we need to know why. She says she just doesn't. Here, speak into the microphone, Rachel. They're having trouble hearing you. And you have such a lovely voice."

They went over the Intel Award and the men were impressed. "We have a budding research scientist here," said Brazos. "A potential Nobel Prize winner. This is quality. And you are currently in school? And what school do you attend? Columbia University. One of our great institutions here. And what do you study at Columbia? I asked you, what do you study?" He grabbed her by the hair. "Biomedical Engineering. I should tell you a side story, gentlemen. Rachel came to my home with Sonia pretending to be a stripper, but was actually looking for her sister. And now they've been reunited."

After Rachel's interview, it was Sonia's turn. Brazos explored the story of her abusive Uncle Lemuel in great depth and the men listening found it endlessly fascinating as they probed with great detail the sessions of abuse and her final revenge. One man clapped. She was praised for her resourcefulness and the brilliance of the retribution. They asked to describe her uncle's face after the chainsaw ripped it apart. They wanted to know her feelings when she was told she was HIV positive. The ultimate reality show.

"This concludes the interviews, distinguished guests. Now that you're all well acquainted with our victims, the bidding will start at one-hundred-thousand dollars. Due to time constraints surrounding these girls, we'll skip the preliminary rounds we've had in the past and go directly to execution. Please place your bids."

One-ten.

One-twenty.

One-fifty.

One-eighty.

Two-twenty.

Two-fifty.

There was a pause.

"Gentlemen, remember the uniqueness of this situation. Three girls, and two are sisters. Think of the possibilities. They're endless. Let me make a few humble suggestions." Brazos described a few scenarios and the bidding resumed.

Two-eighty-five.

Three-ten.

"The winner will have a unique record. Think of the difficulty of obtaining what you will have in your hands, like a rare gem, a work of art. And you'll be the author of its beauty. Can you look at Michelangelo's David and say you had a hand in its creation? The Last Supper? Here, you will be the artist. I'm only the hand of the artist."

Three-forty.

Three-sixty.

"I have three-sixty. Do I hear three-eighty? Three-eighty. Do I hear four-hundred? Three-eighty going once. Three-eighty going twice. Sold for three-hundred-eighty thousand dollars to Client Number Two. Gentlemen, thank you all for participating. You'll be notified of our next session. Congratulations to you, sir. A fine purchase. I'm sending you the account information you'll need to make the payment. It will be a live event, and I will also provide you with the exclusive download of the scene in accordance with your specifications. Again, think of me as the hand of the artist."

CHAPTER SIXTY-SEVEN

The Cyber Crimes Unit found the chat session with Achara containing her flight number. That led police to Rachel's car in the Terminal Seven parking lot. There was no sign of a struggle. Her parking stub was in the sun visor, time-stamped at 2:14 a.m. the previous night.

"I need the time of entry and exit of every vehicle in this lot between midnight and four a.m.," McKenna told the duty manager. "Also, I want to know if any cars that came in during that window are still here."

The detective walked the path between Rachel's car and the terminal. There was nothing on the ground, no blood, no weapon.

The duty manager came back.

"Forty-two vehicles arrived during that window. Only one is still here. This one."

"Any security cameras trained on the parking lot?" he asked.

"Sorry, no."

Great.

McKenna went to the Cathay Pacific desk and flashed his badge. "Was there was a Flight 1343 arriving at 2:30 a.m. last night?"

"Yes, originating in Chiang Mai, Thailand," said the girl.

"Can you look up if there was an Olivia Wallen on the flight?"

She scanned the screen. "No, sorry. No such passenger."

"What about—" He took out the paper. "Achara. I guess that's her first name. I don't have a last name."

She paged down a screen quickly.

"There were three. Yes, three Acharas. It's a fairly common name."

"Is there a way to find out if any of them had an American passport?"

"Customs would be able to assist you there."

"Thanks."

At Customs, he inquired about the three Acharas that arrived last night.

"Could I get their ages?"

"Eighty-one, eighteen, and twenty."

"Any issues with any of them? They all entered without a problem?"

"No issues."

"I need to see the surveillance tape for that flight."

McKenna went through it twice. There was no one resembling Olivia, that is, Achara. So she wasn't on that flight.

The detective came back out to the parking lot. This was where Rachel disappeared. There was no doubt in McKenna's mind that she was abducted. She had to walk toward the underpass to get to the terminal. It would have been dark there, even with the lighting. It didn't look like a crime of opportunity—no mugger sits in a parking lot in an airport at two in the morning waiting for a mark. It had to be someone who followed her or knew where she was going to be. It could only be the killer.

Ninety percent of all kidnap victims are dead within twenty-four hours. He looked at his watch. 3:32 p.m. She was taken over twelve hours ago. McKenna knew he probably had less than ten hours if he was going to find her alive.

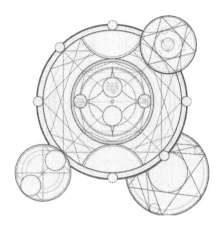

CHAPTER SIXTY-EIGHT

B
razos received the email he was waiting for. After decrypting it, he read it through twice and was impressed with the imagination of Client Number Two. This would be a first for Brazos. He logged into his offshore bank account and confirmed that the money was there.

Now he had to go out and purchase the things he needed.

"He's been gone a while," whispered Rachel. "How long does he usually leave for?"

"He buys things," said Olivia. "He bought things to butcher that poor girl. Before my eyes."

"Kirsten Schrodinger?"

Olivia nodded, unable to speak.

"Don't think about that. You getting your medicine?"

Olivia nodded. "You know about Achara?"

"I got the passport to her. And money. I went to the airport to pick her up and he was waiting for me. I don't know how he knew. I told no one."

"So…"

"I don't know what happened to her. I sent her all the information she needed to get past Immigration. She's got the address of the house. How did he know I'd be at the airport? Something or somebody tipped him off."

"He asked me Achara's Yahoo Messenger password," said Olivia. "I didn't think much of it. He asked me about every detail of my life."

"Her YM password?" repeated Rachel. Then it all became clear to her. Rachel smacked the back of her head against the wall, furious at herself. "Oh God, he was chatting with me, posing as Achara. Son of a bitch. And I fell for it. I hacked into a bunch of PCs, looking for you, but his wasn't one of them. I should have brought Joules in from the beginning. I did it on my own. Left a trace or something."

"Oh my God. He hacked into my laptop. Joules was using his laptop, too. If he traced Joules…" Her thoughts stopped at the edge of the precipice. The image of Joules coming through that door with his hands tied behind him was too much. Anguish gave way to fury.

"Look, we're all tied to the same thing. Let's try to loosen it. All together lean forward. Put all your weight behind it." They struggled like this for many minutes and became immediately exhausted. The U-bolt was immovable.

"The ropes just get tighter," said Sonia. "It's cutting off my blood."

"What's behind those doors?" asked Rachel.

"That one's a storage closet or something. I don't know what that other door leads to," answered Olivia.

"If it's an old subway station, then that could be the tracks."

"Whatever it is, there's no one there. We've screamed enough to know."

Brazos checked on them when he returned, then got to work. He made several trips back and forth from his car unloading the items he had bought.

A plastic drop cloth, a nylon towing strap, thick rubber gloves, a propane torch, a pick, quick drying cement, several D-clamps, and a fence post. Next he hauled in a hundred pounds of river rocks. Then, two Macy's bags.

What followed was the equivalent of prisoners, condemned to hang, watching their gallows being erected. But Brazos wasn't going to hang them.

Brazos swung a pickaxe at the concrete floor until he had made a foot-deep hole. After picking out the debris, he put in the fence post and emptied a bag of Quikcrete and a gallon of water into the hole. Next he fired several anchors into the concrete ceiling and inserted steel hooks through them. From the hooks, he hung ropes. He tested the ropes with his own weight. Over the next two hours, he built the set of their executions, arranging the cameras to take in all the action.

The client requested that the girls dress up in school girl outfits, then Rachel would be put on trial for espionage. There was a script for this.

After the jury of her peers found her guilty, she would be condemned to a series of tortures which included the pear of anguish, a medieval instrument recommended by Brazos which was inserted into body cavities. As a handle was turned, the spoon-shaped lobes opened, causing excruciating pain. She would then be given a choice between this and rape. She would of course choose rape. Brazos would do the honors in all of her openings. Finally, the victim would be impaled through the anus on the sharpened fence post. This had to be done carefully or death would come quickly. If done properly, the victim could last several days. While impaled, the other girls would stone her.

Sonia and Olivia were to undergo the full panoply of medieval torments. Finally, all were to be dismembered alive.

Brazos approached with a knife in his hand. The girls started screaming for mercy. With one slice, he cut their bonds.

"Put those on," he commanded, pointing to the school uniforms. They undressed in silence while Brazos shined lights on them and took readings.

"That's no damn good. It has to be ten inches above the knee." He disappeared behind one of the steel doors which was the storage room and returned with two scissors, thread, and a tape measure.

"Ten inches above the knee and hurry it up." He tossed scissors, needles, and thread on the bed.

"I need my medicine," said Olivia. "I can't move without it."

Brazos again entered the storage room and returned seconds later with insulin and a hypodermic needle. He tossed it on the bed.

They cut the dresses while he positioned three video cameras on tripods. Brazos inspected them. "Good."

While Brazos was looking, Rachel put the scissors and thread on the edge of the bed.

"Turn around. Nice. He reached into a Macy's bag and pulled out shoe boxes. Put these on with the white socks." Brazos grabbed the scissors and measuring tape, and started toward the storage room. As soon as he entered the room, the door slammed shut behind him. "Lock it!" Rachel screamed to her sister.

Brazos threw himself against the door but it wouldn't budge. That voice had come from below, so she had to be on the floor, wedging herself between the door and the wall. It was the only way she could possibly hold it shut.

He could see Olivia through the crack, pushing against the door, trying to lock the slide bolt, but he was throwing off the alignment. Then she dropped to the floor too and braced her legs against the door. The tool box was just out of Brazos' reach. If he abandoned the door, they would lock it. Keeping one hand on the door, he stretched for the toolbox. It crashed to the ground. He stuck a screwdriver through the small crack between the door and the frame. Now it would be impossible to lock. He had had enough of this game. He quickly removed a sawed-off twelve-gauge shotgun from a canvas case. The shells were right above him. With ten rounds of double-O buckshot loaded, he pointed the weapon at the door knob.

The explosion sheared the hardware off its mounting screws and sent it crashing into the wall behind the girls. A second and third shot came, each time sending its shattering force through the door and into the girls' bodies. The slugs didn't penetrate the steel of the heavy door, but the impact against the girls' feet was like bastinado.

"The tripods," Rachel yelled. "Tighten them against the door."

Olivia unscrewed the cameras and braced the tripods between the door and the wall. This was repeated with the second and third tripods. The shotgun blasts were deafening. Rachel motioned for Olivia to push the point of the screwdriver in with a camera. She slammed the camera into the screwdriver and it fell inside the storage room. The door shut and she slapped the sliding bolt into its bracket.

"Retighten the tripods."

The girls sprang to their feet.

They backtracked to where they had entered the dungeon. The steel door was locked from the inside with two huge padlocks and chances were that Brazos had the keys.

"Forget it. The other door," yelled Rachel.

They threw off the crossbar and pulled open the door. There was total blackness in front of them.

They stood in a subway platform that hadn't been used in decades. They felt their way to the end. A dead end.

"Watch it here," said Rachel. "It's the track."

"There's nowhere to go," said her sister.

"We go down."

Rachel climbed down the sheer wall of the platform onto the derelict track. "Come on."

Another shotgun blast. In the tunnel, the report was transformed into a fusillade. Rachel hoped that in a few moments their eyes would adjust to the dark, enabling them to run.

Brazos put the shotgun away and wheeled an oxy-acetylene torch into position.

It took twenty minutes to slice through the steel door. He opened a small leather case and removed a pair of AN/PVC-5 night vision goggles. The night-vision system consisted of a self-contained image intensifier. Forty feet into the tunnel there was no light.

He cut several feet of nylon rope, which he fastened to his belt and then slipped a thirty-eight revolver into his waist. He'd try not to use it—slaughtering them in the subway tunnels wasn't profitable.

Brazos wasn't worried about them getting very far. When he moved to New York years ago, he toyed with the idea of burrowing into a bank vault via the city's maze of abandoned subway tunnels, some of them going back to the Civil War when the cars were pulled by mules. He had embarked on a study of the abandoned tunnel systems, some of which weren't even in the official records because they were privately funded by entrepreneurs. He collected every map, scoured every website and now knew the location of every abandoned subway tunnel in the five boroughs. This one was part of the IRT line that serviced the old Polo Grounds. The defunct tunnel ended two levels below an active subway station.

With a few simple modifications, it became the perfect dungeon for Brazos' executions. The tunnel was pitch black with lots of broken glass and rubble. And they had no shoes.

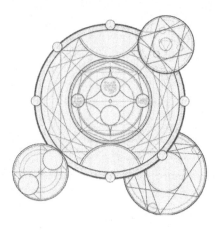

CHAPTER SIXTY-NINE

They were blind, lost, and barefoot.

"Give me your hand," Rachel told her sister.

"This is just a fucking tomb," said Sonia.

Searing pain shot up Rachel's spine as something pierced her foot. It was a hypodermic needle. Her hand felt around and there were dozens of them on the ground along with used condoms.

As they entered deeper into the tunnel, an overpowering stench engulfed them. Suddenly Rachel's foot pressed down on something soft. A dead rat. Her back spasmed at the realization and only a greater fear enabled her to stifle a scream. Her hands groped ahead of her, flailing as though drowning in the thickness of odor.

"What is it? What?" asked Olivia.

Rachel didn't want to open her mouth to speak.

"Don't scream. Dead rat."

The slightest hint of moving air brushed Rachel's face and she wet her parched lips to get a bearing on it.

They walked for over twenty minutes, hands flailing before them in the total darkness. Travel was slow as every step had to be tested for something sharp that might stop them altogether. Rachel understood now why POWs and discalced nuns had to surrender their shoes—few things humbled a person as much. A sliver of glass or a sharp pebble had the power to stop a man. It made you give respect to small things you had always crushed underfoot.

Where did this tunnel lead? Was there a connection with the outside world or was it just a long dead end?

"You've got to believe me when I tell you I never knew anything about him," said Sonia. "I never knew who he was."

"Let's just try to get out of this. Do you know anything about this tunnel that would be worth sharing?" said Rachel.

"Nothing."

"Can you see me at all?"

"No."

Rats swarmed around their feet. Sonia inhaled to deliver a scream, but Rachel found the other girl's face and clamped a hand over her mouth.

Everywhere she stepped, there was a tail, a soft body, the chatter of fleeing things no higher than an ankle. The smell, the fear from behind, from below, sent Rachel reeling into a wall, vomiting on her insteps.

Let this lead somewhere, anywhere, thought Rachel. The air seemed to be getting more stagnant, not fresher. Eventually he would catch up to them, even if all he had was a flashlight.

"I can't take this stench," said Sonia, bending over. Soon after, Rachel heard the sound and smell of vomiting.

Olivia leaned on her sister. "I'm getting really weak."

"You've got to go on, you hear me? I didn't come this far to find you, so you'd die, so you just hang on and keep going."

It was getting hotter, which meant they were descending. They reached a mound of concrete rubble, a dead end. Their hands probed the surrounding walls for an opening. There was none.

"Boost me up," said Rachel. Sonia made a sling with her hands as Rachel tried to get a purchase on the loose mortar. Sonia stepped back as chunks of cement rolled toward her feet.

Rachel felt movement in the air, not quite a breeze, but definitely the boundary of something. She pulled away some mortar.

She cleared enough debris to fit her body through the opening, then began to climb down the other side. A small landslide sent her to the ground.

"Rach! Rach!" whispered Olivia.

She had landed on a sharp chunk of concrete.

"Come on," said Rachel, still trying to get up. "Olivia first. Help her." With one girl pushing and the other pulling, Olivia made it through the opening. Sonia followed and Rachel grabbed her waist to slow the descent.

Rachel felt the walls, which were now smooth tile, the kind used in bathrooms.

This portion of the tunnel was still abandoned, but it appeared to be built more recently. Rachel could hear dozens of rats scurrying. Something hairy and sharp fell on Rachel's face. She screamed and covered her head while flailing with the other arm. They had disturbed the hundreds of bats that lived down here. Their bare feet sank in two inches of bat guano.

"Bats leave their roost every night. That means there has to be a way out of here," said Rachel.

The scream didn't go unheard by their pursuer. It was difficult to judge distance in this world, but it wasn't far away. This had to be brought to a close soon. Brazos proceeded swiftly in the darkness. Still, they had gone farther than he had thought they would in the allotted time. Many had wept down here and these girls would be no different. The lassos were ready. In the dark, it would be easy to flick it over their heads. It had been a long time since he was this far in the tunnels. He was getting near the end of the old tunnel. Where were they? There was no place to hide.

He got to the rubble where there had been a collapse. There was enough room at the top of the pile for someone to fit through.

Now he was angry. Once past this, there were ways of getting to the surface. There were even some homeless people who might be witnesses. He would have to kill them right here as soon as he found them. Brazos quickly scrambled up the mountain of concrete, enlarged the opening and lowered himself to the other side.

"I can hear him," said Sonia.

"Keep moving," said Rachel. There was more debris on the ground. They stepped on glass and bottle caps, human excrement.

They made it to another station platform and climbed out of the tracks. They felt around in the dark, finding a stairway blocked by a gate and padlock. They lunged at it.

Suddenly, they were caught in the beam of a flashlight.

The figure didn't react to their screams that echoed in the tunnel for several seconds. Rachel smelled him before she saw him. The beam reflected off a wall and dimly illuminated the man. He was large with an Old Testament beard and rags that hung shapelessly from his frame.

"Please help us," said Sonia. "There's someone after us." He seemed to have forgotten language; he just stood there in disbelief that three school girls would wander into this world.

"Which way is out of here?" demanded Sonia.

They walked around the stranger without taking their eyes off him. When they got to the end of the station, they climbed back down onto the tracks.

"Stay off the third rail. If you see a train come, duck into one of these," said Sonia, putting Olivia's hand into a maintenance recess.

Rachel fell, hitting her head against a railroad tie. Her chest heaved. She staggered up and hopped on one foot. A broken bottle lay at her feet.

The laceration was deep and blood oozed out. "Oh shit, this is bad." She ripped a piece of her skirt off and wrapped it around her foot. "Keep moving."

A gunshot rang out with deafening echoes.

"Oh my God," said Sonia.

The only way out was to get to the next station and hope that there was an unsealed exit. Rachel wished for a train to come now, but no one was going to come here to rescue them.

"Run! Run! Dammit," screamed Rachel, pulling her sister by the arm, running her hand along the wall to guide them in the dark.

The heat was intense, their mouths parched. This was a city beneath the streets, another plane of existence within New York. The three girls held hands as they stumbled ahead. The next station was at least four blocks away. The pain of their ravaged feet gave way to terror. She could feel a curvature to the wall. This was a turn. *Please let this lead to somewhere.* As they rounded the curve, Rachel turned around and the flashlight was gone. This was their chance to lose him if they could get to the next station.

"Faster." Olivia tripped over a tie and the others held her up. They were now almost dragging her. Rachel looked behind her. The flashlight was back and closer than ever.

"Look, there's light ahead," said Sonia. It was true. The faintest glow appeared in the distance. Rachel could start to see tracks several feet in front of her if she kept her eyes moving.

Brazos turned the homeless man's face with his foot, now that he had extracted the information he needed. There was a sheer ray of light filtering down from two levels above.

How he'd love to work them over with a knife, but there was no camera to record it. It was too far to drag all three back to his lair. He would have to end it here. What a waste.

Over the next two minutes, he cut the distance in half. Brazos was just a few hundred feet behind them. He'd been careless to let things get out of his control. Now he'd have to retake control, but give up a major payday. He reloaded, then closed in on them.

They were bent over panting, and when Rachel stood up erect, he was facing them. He leveled his pistol at Rachel. From a hundred feet it was an easy shot.

Sonia dove to her left, pushing Rachel to the ground. The shot rang out and the three girls fell. When Rachel scrambled to her feet, Sonia didn't move. There was a spout of blood coming out of her temple and Rachel kneeled, screaming, cupping her hand over the mortal wound.

Rachel and Olivia staggered through the low light. He pulled the trigger again and again, emptying the gun. That was all right because he knew what was ahead.

The sisters reached the platform and ran to the end. The tunnel had been sealed here.

There was no way out.

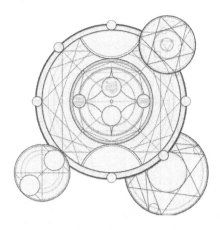

CHAPTER SEVENTY

Brazos started to put the weapon in his belt, then he changed course and slipped it into the small of his back as though he would soon be using the front of his body.

They stood ten feet apart. He threw Rachel to the ground and straddled her. Olivia jumped on him and he slammed his elbow into her stomach, crumpling her.

One hand was around Rachel's throat and the other was up her skirt. He ripped off her underwear. She thought of her parents, of Joules. All the things she didn't accomplish in her life. They would read about her in the papers. When she managed to bite his wrist, he slammed the heel of his hand across the side of her head, making her see lights.

"I want you to have a pretty face while I fuck you, then I'm going to turn it into pulp."

He probed her with his hand, once again gathering information. Then he pinned her to the ground with one arm while he pulled his pants down around his knees. After prying her legs open, he lowered himself onto her crotch. As he was trying to force himself into her body, she hooked her arm around his neck as she would a lover. With the other hand, she plunged the dull point of a discarded hypodermic needle into his carotid artery.

He struggled, breaking the needle. Olivia jumped on him from behind and sent the hypodermic that Brazos had given her into his neck. His fist slammed into the side of Rachel's face. He threw Olivia to the ground again, breaking the needle. The entire insulin vial that Olivia had sewn into the hem of her skirt was emptied, but was it coursing through Brazos' veins?

Rachel clamped one of his fingers in her teeth. The more violently he pulled the hand away, the harder she bit. She could hear her molars penetrating the skin, then cutting through the thin muscles.

A shot to Rachel's stomach made her curl up in fetal position. Had they injected him with enough insulin to disable him, and would it take effect before he killed them?

The onset time of Lispro insulin was four minutes. But it was normally administered intramuscularly in a dosage of one-hundred units. This quantity, injected intravenously into a person without insulin deficiency, was lethal. There was no telling how long before it would take effect, but they had to survive until then.

The killer stood over her. "What was that?" he said in a measured tone that had reserves of force behind it. When she didn't respond, he reached down and picked her up with one arm. "*What the fuck did you shoot into me?*"

As long as she didn't answer, he might let her live, thought Rachel. He slapped her across the face with the back of his hand.

"*Run!*" she yelled to her sister.

Fists came down on Rachel like cinderblocks and she curled up into a ball. *Make his heart pump as fast as possible.* When he tried to grab her throat, she clamped his knuckle in her mouth. A hammerhand came down on her head and she let go. She rolled over and staggered to her feet. She ran a few yards toward her sister, then he tackled her.

Brazos assumed it was insulin that they had shot into him. But what if it was something else? He felt no ill effects. He decided to haul them back to his lair and make his money with their deaths. The truth would come out then. The cattle prod never failed in bringing out the truth. Brazos grabbed Rachel by the hair and pulled her along in a forced march. The other one was stumbling up ahead ready to drop.

He grabbed Olivia under his right arm and dragged them back toward the death chamber.

They walked a hundred yards, but Rachel couldn't feel his pace or his grip weakening. She had used one of the needles she had found on the ground and now wondered if she had plunged the dull point deep enough into Brazos' neck. There was no telling if Olivia was able to empty hers in the right spot in her condition. He had Rachel by the waist and she picked up her feet as he dragged her, making him expend more energy. His grip was vise-like, even with a load of over two hundred pounds. At some point the drug would wear off. There were hundreds of yards of track before them. She glanced at her sister. She was only semi-conscious, both from the blows and from lack of insulin, which she hadn't taken in order to have this weapon of last resort.

They passed Sonia's dead body. No one would ever know she was here.

Rachel could see a broken Coke bottle coming closer. She extended her hand at the last moment, reaching for it, but it was too far. Another bottle. This time she was able to grab it on the fly.

He stopped, adjusted both girls under his arms, and continued. Then he stopped again. It began to happen with greater frequency. In the last five minutes, they covered half the ground than in the previous five.

Then she felt it. She had felt it a few moments before, but thought it might be her imagination. Now there was no doubt. Ever so slightly, his grip had let up. She dared not make her move yet. Rachel wanted to be absolutely certain he was incapacitated. The last thing she needed was for his adrenaline to kick in, reviving him.

Brazos laid both girls on the ground with his arms still around them and he kneeled. His breathing was halting, irregular. His hands were sweaty. Rested, he rose again with his burden. He let them fall to the ground and dragged them by their wrists through the broken glass and concrete. Rachel had hidden the bottle with her body and he grabbed the extended arm, her right arm. Now she briefly looked up for the first time to see his face. The look was blank like an automaton. Anger seemed to have left him, replaced by a primitive instinct like that of a plant turning itself toward the light.

Rachel's wrist slipped out of his hand. He went to regrip it.

Now.

Rachel sprang up and slammed the bottle into his head, breaking it, then she stabbed at the hand that held her. His hand didn't withdraw; he seemed confused. She ripped her arm away, freeing herself. He stepped back, feebly reached out to grab her and released Olivia in the process. Unable to gauge his state, Rachel grabbed her sister and ran. He took a few steps in pursuit, then fell, rose and fell again.

He got up and began to close the gap in awkward, staggered strides. He was slowing, but Rachel had the added burden of Olivia, who was now nearly dead weight. The last few hours had sapped her of any reserves of energy and running for her life didn't change that. Then, she tripped over a railroad tie, falling. Brazos seemed to be recovering. He closed the distance quickly. He caught them.

He was gasping for air when he threw Rachel up against the track wall. He then leaned on her to rest, sweat dripping down on her from his chin. Ninety-five degrees in the tunnel. But this was more than thirty yards worth of perspiration. He was more than winded.

It begins with sweating, a racing heartbeat, and subtle shaking. As he pressed on her now with his chest against her back, she could feel all of these. Then there was the tell-tale sign. He yawned. As soon as he pulled his weight off her, she tried to run again, but her strength had left her. Brazos threw a punch that missed.

Now the insulin descended with crushing force. His knees bent and he yawned again and again. He drew the gun and aimed it at her head. When he pulled the trigger, he seemed to recall that he had run out of bullets some time ago. He swatted at Rachel with the weapon, but she ducked. He swung the pistol again, striking the concrete wall. Rachel suddenly rose and thrust her knee into his groin. They both fell and she bit his hand again. He released her, only to grab her with the other, then rolled on top of her.

"*Run!*" Rachel screamed. "Olivia—get out of here!"

He started to get up and she wrapped her arms around his neck like a yoke, pulling him down.

"*Get on the platform and run!*"

Olivia backed away, still facing Brazos. He got up again, this time with Rachel clinging to his neck.

"Go!"

Olivia stumbled down the tunnel toward the station, turning back every few seconds to look at her sister. Brazos was on his feet again, fading fast into the darkness as he dragged Rachel back to the execution chamber.

Olivia needed insulin or she would die within two hours. She was exhausted, but told herself not to lie down or she would never wake up.

Her feet were a bloody mess and walking was agony. Even worse—where was she going? The homeless man they had passed. He would know how to get out. She sat down on the tracks, took off her skirt and ripped it in two, then wrapped the rags around her feet.

Using the tunnel wall to balance herself, she made it back to the station platform and looked for the homeless man. She struggled to climb onto the platform. He was lying on the blanket with the flashlight on. It took a few more seconds to see why he wasn't moving. Nausea made her lean against the wall.

Olivia grabbed her stomach; the abdominal pain made her buckle over. She urinated in this position and before she took her weight off the wall, she did so again. Stress hormones had blocked the assimilation of her last injection and her blood sugar was critically high. Within half an hour, she would be unconscious. She picked up the flashlight.

There was the sound of water, but she couldn't locate it. Was it raining outside and dripping in? That might mean an opening to the outside. As she walked, she became aware of a definite downward grade. She was going deeper into this. There was a pile of something ahead. Clothes. It was a campsite with some spare possessions and the stench of urine. She put on a stinking sweatshirt.

Then she thought she heard a baby crying. Yes, there was no doubt.

"Hello!" she yelled. "Hello!" The crying stopped and she couldn't get a bearing on it.

"If there's someone there, please answer me. *Hello!*"

It was getting harder to steer around the used condoms and needles on the ground. It would be the supreme irony to get out of this alive only to die of AIDS later. But it meant that this place was inhabited.

"*Somebody answer me!*"

She heard the crying again and she tried to run toward it. This time, she got the direction. Olivia approached a doorless utility closet. In it was a woman of about thirty-five holding a hatchet. Behind her was a six-month-old child on a pad.

Before Olivia could say anything, the woman rushed to the edge of the doorframe brandishing the weapon. Olivia fell to the ground.

"I just need the way out. How do I get out of—"

The woman spoke only Spanish and cared not at all for company. The area smelled like airplane glue and her eyes were bloodshot. There was no one behind those eyes. Olivia lifted her hand up to placate the woman, then slowly got up and backed away.

In this echoing landscape, the screams of the child sounded like the steel brakes of a train. Olivia would have to find other help. She stumbled away without direction as lost here as she would be in the middle of the ocean. Then, she vomited.

Thirst was taking her over. Ketoacidosis was setting in. When insulin levels in the body go very low, the body can't burn glucose—the system's first choice for fuel. It then begins to burn fat, producing high levels of ketones and acidity in the blood. When this was combined with dehydration, death followed shortly afterward.

Olivia stepped onto the steel steps and held herself up by the handrails. Slowly, she descended. When she got to the bottom, she spotted a puddle in the distance. The pain from her feet was finding its way to her brain now without the anesthetic benefit of adrenaline. There were empty wooden skids on the wet ground. This was a storage area at one time. As she limped through the puddle, her feet created clouds of blood.

She stopped at a doorway. There was a breeze blowing on her bloody face. A broken door leading to another staircase. She could hear what sounded like traffic above, faint.

Olivia climbed three flights of steps and arrived at another abandoned station. More light came from above. The air was more breathable and cooler. She moved faster now toward the turnstile. It was broken and led to another staircase. She ascended the endless flight of steel steps on all fours, relieving the weight from her feet. There were street sounds and they were getting louder. She had to make it to the top. She got on her back and grabbed the handrail, thrusting with her feet and pulling herself up hand over hand. Her grip slipped and she dropped straight down on the edges of the steel treads. Her eyes closed for a moment and she instantly felt herself drifting into sleep, into death. Olivia shook her head and took a deep breath, then, summoning all her strength, flung herself at the handrail and began to climb. Now there was a lot of light. Freedom was approaching. A gate came into view. She righted herself and parted her hair away from her face. There was a padlocked gate at street level.

The pain in her shredded feet now forgotten, Olivia got up and yelled until she got someone's attention.

"Call 911! Get me out of here!"

CHAPTER SEVENTY-ONE

There was a two-hour stopover in Vancouver, then the twenty-hour flight to New York continued. Achara had spent the last eighteen hours memorizing the data sheet that her sister had sent her. It was two full pages of information to get her past Immigration once she arrived. She was now Olivia Wallen, American.

These last few hours had been the happiest in her life. She had been shattered when she got to the departure gate and found no one. She ran down the boarding ramp and screamed at the flight attendant who was closing the cabin door. Achara expected one more obstacle, but when she showed her boarding pass, she was simply told, "Fourteen C, to your left."

Those were the most wondrous words she had ever heard. There really was a seat for her.

"We will be arriving in fifteen minutes at John F. Kennedy International Airport. The local time is 5:15 p.m."

Now the old fear came back.

She looked down at the faint outline of land below.

This was America. For the twentieth time, she checked her data sheet and passport. Now she had another document—the declaration form. What would they ask her? Would they detain her? Would they send her back because she had an accent? Or would she go to Guantanamo? She preferred Guantanamo to Thailand.

The plane touched ground and maneuvered to the hangar. Achara told herself to act normal. There were many Asians on this flight and she would blend in with them. She followed everyone up the ramp and then she saw the signs for Immigration. There was a ladies' room and she ducked into it. Her hands were moist, her breathing irregular. She washed her face and arms and combed her hair with her fingers.

Out came the data sheet again. Going over every point, she got to the instructions about what to do once the plane landed.

Get on the line for U.S. Citizens at the immigration area. The officer will say hello. Say hello and smile. Answer all questions calmly and be friendly. Here are some questions they may ask:

How long were you in Thailand? Tell them.

What was the purpose of your trip? Visiting relatives.

Where did you stay in Thailand? Give a relative's address.

Do you have anything to declare? This means did you bring anything illegal into the country.

Where were you born? Thailand.

They may test you with a few questions such as:

Who was the sixteenth president of the United States? Abraham Lincoln.

How long have you lived in the United States? Seven years.

What are the 2 baseball teams in New York? The Yankees and the Mets. You are a Yankee fan. And you hate the Boston Red Sox.

What high school did you attend? Northport High.

What is your home address? 114 North Cyrus Street, East Northport New York 11731

What is your home phone number? 631-555-1756. That's my cell phone in case they call.

As a last resort, the instructions read: *If they don't believe you and detain you, say to them "I request political asylum." Once you say that, they can't deport you right away. They have to give you a date to appear before a judge. By then, we will be able to help you. So stay calm.*

One more review of the bio and she went out the door to face the immigration officers.

The line went quickly. Most of the passengers who were called up stayed no more than one minute in front of the officer. That made her feel better. Her breathing was acting up again and she took long draws of air. She just needed to act normally for one minute and she was done.

The officer motioned her to step up. She handed him her passport which he swiped through the reader. He said, "How are you today?"

"Very good, thank you." She smiled.

"What were you doing in Thailand?"

"Visiting relatives."

"What part of Thailand did you visit?"

"Chiang Mai."

"How long were you there?"

"Two week."

"How long have you lived in the US?"

"Seven years."

"You go to school?"

"Northport High School."

He was typing something on a keyboard.

"Do you have anything to declare?"

"No."

"Please step over here, miss." He hadn't told the others to do this.

A female agent came over and said, "I need to inspect your bag, Ma'am."

Achara handed it over.

Half a chocolate bar and the vihara spilled out. The agent felt the sides of the knapsack for hidden pockets.

"This is all you brought with you all the way from Thailand?"

"My bag was rob at the airport." Her face was no longer calm. They knew something was wrong.

"And how old are you?"

"Sixteen." She was getting ready to request asylum, but couldn't remember the words.

"Who will be waiting for you at the airport?"

"My sister, I hope." She was trying to remember the exact words for requesting asylum as though it needed the preciseness of an incantation to succeed.

And just like that, the officer handed back her bag and passport.

"Thank you," said the officer. "Welcome home."

CHAPTER SEVENTY-TWO

McKenna and the swat team entered the tunnel from the One Hundred and Forty-seventh Street side. Even he hadn't been this deep in the bowels of the city. With the map given to them by the Transit Authority guy, the team descended three levels and got to the abandoned tracks that Olivia had described: dead rats; bats on the ceilings, dropping shit on top of them, covering the ground with it. They had passed a couple of homeless people one level up. Christ, how can anyone live down here?

Olivia said Sonia had been shot through the head. On the unlikely chance she was still alive, a medical team was waiting on the surface. She should be a few hundred yards from this spot. The air reeked of urine and dead rodents. They all donned their night vision goggles as the light died off. The medical folks said Brazos couldn't have gone far with that amount of insulin injected into him if he was even alive. McKenna wasn't taking any chances. The six men walked along the walls in full body armor, staggered, so one high-power bullet wouldn't take out multiple targets. There was something lying on the tracks up ahead. McKenna could make out the shape of a girl. Sonia lay face down. He rushed to her and turned her over. She was dead. *Damn.* They picked up their pace. With any luck, Brazos would be lying on the tracks just as dead.

Swenson pointed to drag marks on the ground and footprints. The line of dragging feet ended. This is where Rachel had struggled with Brazos and Olivia escaped. There was the Coke bottle Rachel used.

No killer.

"Okay, boys, he's alive. Watch out for anything that looks like booby traps. He's trained."

The team advanced block by block toward the collapsed end of the tunnel leading to the hideout below the Major Deegan Expressway. When they got there, they stopped.

It was the perfect place for an ambush. Only one man at a time could pass through the opening. It wasn't a good place for a concussion grenade, either, as the whole tunnel complex could come crashing down. One man got up and shone a flashlight through the opening. He gave the all clear and lowered himself. The others followed. When they were all on the other side, they advanced toward the execution chamber.

On the ground there were more rats, hypodermic needles, and condoms, but no sign of the animal they were searching for. The door of the chamber was closed. One man tried the handle. Locked. Only Brazos could have done that. The safeties came off. The tunnel was much sturdier here and closer to the surface. One officer attached detonation cord to the handle. The explosion rocked dust and loose mortar from the ceiling and the men poured into the hideout. The lights were out, but the night vision goggles revealed a warren of chambers. A storage room full of rice and canned goods. Another with ammo, grenades, tear gas, a shotgun. Enough to make a stand. There was a metal X on the wall. A table with restraints. When all the rooms were secured, they found a light switch connected to a series of car batteries. Bloodstains everywhere. It was a slaughterhouse. Video and lighting equipment to record it all.

Damn prick got away. But no sign of Rachel, either, and that meant she was probably still alive. It would have been too easy to just find him lying on the tracks nice and dead for pickup and delivery. This bastard was going to put McKenna to a lot of trouble, and he wanted to be the guy to put the bullet through Brazos' heart, if he had one.

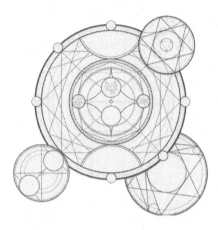

CHAPTER SEVENTY-THREE

A t Lincoln Hospital, Olivia was recovering from surgery. Her feet had required ninety-seven stitches.

McKenna knocked at the open door. Her parents were by her bed. He hated delivering bad news to parents.

"Detective, come in," said Ed Wallen. "Anything?"

"I'm afraid the tunnels were a dead end. He was gone. But Rachel was gone, too, so she seems valuable enough to him to keep her alive. I'd like to ask Olivia a few more questions, if you don't mind." Ed Wallen gave him his seat.

"How are you doing, kid?"

"I'll live."

"I saw Joules outside."

"He's still working on those files."

"He's got a job with the department when he graduates. I just don't think we can afford him." He took out his pad and pen. "Feel up to a few more questions?"

She nodded.

"During the time you spent in the tunnel, did Brazos ever give any indication that he had another hideout? Or maybe more than one house where he lived?"

"Nothing like that."

"Did he ever mention another person? Someone he might be working with?"

"No. There were just those men on the other side of the camera. The foreigners that he called Client Number One, Two, Three."

"How do you know they were foreigners?"

"He said at one point, 'The skin is like pearl as you like it in the East.' In the West, they like tanned skin. And it's true that in the East they compare white skin to pearl."

"You said he would leave periodically and come back. Any idea where he went when he left the tunnels?"

"I know he owned a bar in Long Beach. I just figured he worked his job and came back on his off hours."

McKenna started thinking about what he'd like to do to Clients One through Three when Joules appeared in the doorway.

"Detective, I need to show you something."

He motioned him inside.

Joules put the laptop on the nightstand and brought up Rachel's email.

There was a message with the subject "Flight."

"This is from Achara. She says she's arriving on Singapore flight 3244 at 5:30 p.m. today. That's thirty-five minutes ago. The original flight was Cathay Pacific."

"She wasn't on the Cathay Pacific flight," said McKenna. "We saw the later email with the new flight."

Joules opened Yahoo Messenger and entered Achara's ID and password, which he had broken.

There was one offline message from Rachel.

I'll be waiting for you, baby.

"This is time-stamped 10:14 p.m. two nights ago," said Joules. "Rachel was already missing for nearly ten hours." He looked at McKenna.

"Rachel didn't write that."

Chapter Seventy-Four

McKenna made a call to JFK Airport security telling them to detain a girl carrying a passport with the name Olivia Wallen. After a long wait, his face fell.

"She went through Immigration ten minutes ago."

A disheveled man with a bouquet of flowers and a placard saying, *OLIVIA WALLEN*, waited at the arrivals area. The plane was on time, and that was good because he didn't have much to spare. Just standing was an effort.

He observed as the passengers of flight 3244 exited the door. There were some nice looking Singaporean and Thai girls. Assuming she made it through Immigration, she would be coming out just about now.

When Achara appeared, he made his way through the crowd and flashed a smile as she made eye contact with him. He handed over the bouquet and said, "Welcome, Achara. I'm Robert, a friend of Olivia. She sent me to take you home."

Her face lit up and she embraced Robert.

"Thank you, thank you. My journey is over. Where is Olivia?"

"She's home waiting for you with her family. They have a big reception for you. Big celebration."

As they walked out of the terminal, Robert kept up the conversation.

"It's a long trip, eh? You must be very tired."

"No. Not tired. Happy. Very happy. But you look tired."

"I worked late last night. Did you have dinner on the plane?"

"They serve chicken. Very good."

"I think you'll like the food in America. You like pizza?"

"Never have."

"Oh, you'll like it. It's my favorite food. I eat pizza four times a week."

"Olivia house far?"

"About an hour from here. There was a lot of traffic from that direction, so they asked me to pick you up. I live in Manhattan and there's no traffic from there at this time. Easier for me and I can get you home faster."

"Oh. So nice."

"Well you look just like your sister—just as beautiful."

"No. Only flowers are beautiful. But I happy."

They took a cab to the JFK long-term parking lot, about two miles away on Lefferts Boulevard. When they stepped into the parking lot, there were few people in sight. An elevator took them to the fourth floor. Now there was no one and their footsteps echoed against the cold concrete walls.

"My car is just over here. Almost there."

Achara smelled the roses.

He opened the back of the van and threw Achara's knapsack into it. Then he slammed his fist into her stomach, crumpling her. He tossed her into the back and stuck a gun in her face.

"Make any sound and I'll kill you and your sister. I have her, too."

CHAPTER SEVENTY-FIVE

That's her," said the female Customs officer when McKenna flashed a photo of the girl.

"We need to see any security cams that would have a view of the arrivals area."

In the security office, the officer entered the time of the flight's arrival.

"This is when they just started exiting the door," said the officer.

"Is there a view of the people in the waiting area?"

"Sure."

Multiple screens showed a three-sixty view of the passengers exiting the door.

McKenna's eyes darted between five monitors. The guy had to identify himself to her in some way. Everyone was waving at someone. Hugging, family reunions.

"These views are all synchronized, right?"

"Right."

Then she appeared. Achara walked out the door and scanned the crowd. On another screen, a man stepped forward and held up a sign with *OLIVIA WALLEN* on it. He smiled at her and she smiled back. Then she stepped from one screen into the next as though entering another realm. He gave her a bouquet of roses and they embraced. A death embrace. Then they walked out toward the taxi stand.

"Get hold of the dispatcher. I want to know who was taking fares at that moment and where they went."

Ten minutes later, the answer came back. "Car 876 took two people fitting that description to the long-term parking lot on Lefferts Boulevard. The girl was carrying roses."

"You have cameras in long-term parking?"

"That's a private parking lot, but they have surveillance."

"Is that self-park or valet?"

"Self-park."

"Why the hell would he go to long-term parking?" asked Marchese. "He must know they have cameras there."

"He was already here to get Rachel. Doesn't want to take a chance someone recognizes him or the car out in the open—my guess."

"I need to see the surveillance video for the last hour," he told the security guard at the parking lot.

"Which level? There are six."

Shit. This was going to be much harder.

"All of them."

To make matters worse, these cameras were analog, not digital, so the tapes had to be wound back, then fast forwarded. There were long stretches where they were just looking at cars sitting there. The detective looked at his watch. It took over fifty minutes before they got a hit. They were on the fourth floor, Achara carrying a bouquet, holding them to her nose. Brazos yapped away, flashing a smile, pointing to his car. The girl had no clue. He opened the back of the van and put her bag in it, then turned and slammed a fist into her stomach. She crumpled. He caught her before she hit the ground and threw her in the back. A gun appeared and he pointed it into the van, his face now tied into a grimace. He shut the doors and walked around confidently. That confidence was what got McKenna. He'd break him of that confidence.

"Can you zoom in on that plate?" They could see only four of the numbers, but the vehicle make and year would complete it. McKenna called it in and it came back. The van was registered to a Simon Zarazuela. It was reported stolen two months ago.

"Put out an APB for a white Econoline van, plate number ZYP189, and an Amber Alert. Use Olivia's picture for the alert and make sure the media knows that this is Olivia's twin sister to make it more newsworthy. I need a chopper out there immediately. He's got about a two-hour head start. He won't go for any of the bridges or tunnels. He'll figure they've already been alerted. He'll stay in Queens, Brooklyn, or the Island."

"He could have made it to the Queensborough, that's only a twenty minute ride," said Marchese.

"He'd have to take the Van Wyck. If he made the bridge in twenty minutes, that's a new world record. That would put him in Manhattan, not the fastest driving. From there, he could go for the Lincoln Tunnel or the Holland. Outbound, there's no toll, but I just checked—there's a thirty-minute delay and this is rush hour. Everyone on the other side has already been alerted. He's got to know that. I say he stays local."

Achara tore up the floor of the van and pulled at some tools to fix flats. There was a jack and a tire iron. She couldn't pull the jack out, so she freed the tire iron and rammed it through the rear light. She screamed through it, but no one heard her through the din of traffic. Achara knew a lot of girls who were kidnapped like this. A girl at the brothel told her what to do if it ever happened to her. She destroyed the other bulb. Now when it got dark, the police might pull him over for no lights. It was broad daylight. What time did it get dark in America?

She swung the tire iron at the handle. It didn't budge and the noise was deafening in the steel chamber. Some light now streamed in and she could see a little. She looked around for anything else she could use to escape. There wasn't much. Jumper cables, a can of tire sealant. Then something moved on the other side of the cargo space. She caught a glimpse of it in the sliver of light that came through the broken signal. Now it made a noise.

She lifted the tire iron with one hand and advanced on her knees toward the sound. Her left hand felt in front of her. Then it touched a blanket with a body under it. She tore off the cover and a girl rolled over on her side. She'd been beaten badly.

"Achara," whispered the other girl. "I'm Rachel. Olivia's sister."

A helicopter flew overhead, but kept going. The noise coming from the back of the van was going to be a problem. He should have brought a tranquilizer, but he still wasn't thinking straight from the insulin.

Brazos had just managed to make it to his hideout in time to drink three cans of warm soda. This had kept him from passing out and his senses began to return. His hands still trembled and he felt weak, not even half his normal strength.

The helicopter made another pass. The white van might as well be sending up flares. Brazos looked at his Garmin GPS. He had to make this van disappear from view in a hurry.

He swung onto the ramp for the Verrazano Bridge. At Exit Seventeen, he veered onto the ramp for SR-27 West toward North Conduit Avenue. In seventeen minutes, he was in East New York.

The van continued up Van Sinderen Avenue and pulled into the entrance of Greenlawn Cemetery. There was a Popeye's Chicken and Biscuits and a Burger King across the street. After finding a deserted spot, he parked the van with the back toward the dead.

As soon as he opened the rear door a tire iron came at him so fast he barely had enough time to block it. He pulled Achara and her makeshift weapon out in one motion and slammed his fist into her face. She slumped to the ground and he kicked her in the ribs. Then he grabbed Rachel's ankle and pulled her out with one yank.

"Up! You make noise, I kill you and your sister."

He put painted sunglasses on them. The GPS glowed in front of him and he quickly found his next target.

The abandoned East New York station tunnel ran a half mile, four tracks wide and hadn't seen service since 1924. It was only two-hundred yards away. They made their way to the tunnel entrance and he dropped them down the side of the retaining wall. They proceeded into the maw of the abandoned shaft. It ran about three-thousand feet and was originally sealed off, but junkies and homeless people had broken through. They marched on until there was no more light from the street.

Navigating with a flashlight, they stumbled over needles, condoms, mortar, dead rats. It was getting dark outside fast and the night belonged to him. The GPS said they were about half way through this tunnel.

No one could hear their screams in here, but he had to make sure. He forced rocks into their mouths, then ripped off a piece of Gorilla tape and sealed their lips. More tape bound their hands and feet.

He thought about raping them, but he wanted to conserve his strength, and he wasn't feeling very horny after the bout with insulin.

They would stay here until dark, then move on to the final objective.

CHAPTER SEVENTY-SIX

Still no sign of the van," said Marchese.

Three hours had passed since the killer had picked up Achara. Three hours, enough time to put someone through a wood chipper. *How can God allow men like Brazos to exist*, McKenna mulled to himself. Nothing meaningful had come back from the FBI—no aliases, no other addresses in the U.S., no jobs. The guy had a phony social security number, stolen off a dead kid in Jersey. Was he heading for the Mexican border? Canada? Brazil, which had no extradition treaty with the U.S.?

A break finally came at 9:20.

"McKenna here."

"A tow truck operator was called to haul away a white van from the grounds of Greenlawn Cemetery in Brooklyn after closing time. It belongs to Brazos."

"And inside?"

"A kid's knapsack with some kind of bird house and a half-eaten candy bar. No sign of blood, but there was plenty of struggle. The rear headlights were busted from the inside."

"On my way."

Cops combed the grounds of the Greenlawn Cemetery with the K-9 units. McKenna scanned a Google Earth map of the area on his laptop. There was a subway El, a baseball diamond, a couple of fast food places, gas stations.

"He had to walk out of here or steal a car."

"There're no reports of stolen cars in the area for the last two and a half hours, which must be a record for Brooklyn," said Marchese.

"He had at least one hostage with him," said McKenna. "Unless he already killed her and left her somewhere, so he could travel light." And was Rachel with him too? Or had he disposed of her already? Where can you hide around here? He turned to the Google map again. It kept zooming in and out.

"Damn thing has a mind of its own." He oriented himself again on the screen. He clicked on every icon and the name of the location popped up. Reyes Deli Grocery, Shell Fuel, Popeye's Chicken and Biscuits, Bushwick Walking Tour, C-Town Super Market, Subway, Quality Inn, Tunnel Approach.

"What's this—Tunnel Approach?" He clicked on it and a photo expanded. It was a gloomy looking entrance to some kind of passageway. He right-clicked on it for directions. It was just a few hundred yards away.

The dogs picked up Rachel's scent as soon as they entered the tunnel. McKenna was relieved for a second, then he thought of what they might find.

"Where's the exit to this," said McKenna.

"It's about a half mile south, but it's been sealed up for years. No trains come through," replied Marchese. "I grew up here."

The SWAT team entered with night vision goggles. It was already dark outside, and inside the tunnel it was pitch black. McKenna wore body armor and carried an AR-15, and was praying for a chance to use it. Deep down, he didn't want this to end in an arrest and trial.

The scent was getting stronger, judging from the dogs. On the ground there was the usual detritus. He didn't want to see a body added to this trash.

His GPS said they were about half way into this tunnel. Fifteen-hundred feet and it may as well be the center of the Earth. The dogs stopped.

"The scent ends here," said one of the handlers.

The handlers led the dogs further ahead, but they came back. They alerted strongly on one spot on the ground where the garbage had been cleared away.

"She was right there for sure," said the handler. No sign of a struggle.

Back outside, McKenna demanded a report of all the cars stolen within the last four hours for a one-mile radius. When the report arrived, there were six cars.

"APB on all these. I wouldn't expect all of them to be on the road anymore with all the chop shops in the area. But he'll be on the road."

Brazos left the girls in the tunnel tied up while he stole a car. After parking the Nissan Maxima in the Popeye's lot, he went back for them. Checking the streets, he sprang out with the girls in tow. He held them tightly by the hand as he walked them blind up the street to the waiting car.

"Stay down or you're both dead."

After Brazos dragged Rachel back to the execution chamber, she thought her life was over. He had downed three sodas to counter the effects of the insulin, then sat for ten minutes, ordering her to lie down on the floor. Then two hands picked her up and threw her against the wall. He ordered her to put her street clothes on, then he beat her till she passed out.

When she had awoken in the van, she was sorry to see Achara, but relieved that Joules wasn't there too. That meant he was safe.

Where was he taking them? Did he have another hideout? Why didn't he just escape alone without the baggage of two girls in tow? She checked her pockets. Empty.

CHAPTER SEVENTY-SEVEN

On Bushwick Avenue, a lone cruiser flashed its lights five cars behind Brazos. He slammed down on the accelerator and made a right onto Grand Street, then a left at Vandervoort. Brazos zigzagged around several blocks, then landed back on Vandervoort. A right onto Division Street and a quick left at Porter Avenue. He had lost the cruiser, but a radio call had no doubt gone out. Brazos mounted his GPS on the dash and punched in his next destination. Rain was coming down hard.

Ten minutes later, he spotted a police helicopter overhead. He was still too far from his target to abandon the car. Just keep within the speed limit and follow the digital voice that now guided him. A spotlight dropped down on Brazos' car like a net. The chopper was directly over him. He punched in an alternative objective and changed course. Two minutes later, Brazos pulled into a dump off of Schenck Avenue. Lots of abandoned cars. Good. With a map of the ground in his head, he stopped the car and pulled out the girls.

He marched them in the dark two hundred yards to a stand of trees and took a pry bar out of his backpack. It took a few minutes of rooting around, but he found it. He levered up the manhole cover and pointed to the hole in the ground.

McKenna popped the trunk on the Nissan Maxima. Nothing.

"Seal off the area," said McKenna. "He's got the water on one side; I don't think he's swimming to Rockaway."

The dogs picked up the scent right away. They scratched at the manhole cover.

McKenna turned to the K-9 unit. "These manholes are six or eight hundred feet apart. Be there if he comes up for air."

McKenna made sure the safety on the AR-15 was on and descended the ladder. It was an eighty-four inch storm drain and that meant they would travel faster without having to slouch. But so would Brazos. When the six-man team had descended, they put on night-vision goggles.

"Figure they have a thirty minute head start," said McKenna. "Double time." They jogged through the concrete tunnel, keeping their feet on either side of the stream running down the center. Water from the rain came in from multiple inlets and was pooling. How fast could Brazos travel with two girls? Were they hurt? That would slow him down more.

He scanned the walls of this tomb. It wasn't the first time humans were here. The walls were covered in graffiti. *Joey and Louise fucked here 1992.* Spiders all over. Whenever a car ran over a manhole cover, it sounded like thunder. What were they going to find at the end of this shit hole?

Brazos had Rachel by the wrist and Rachel had Achara's hand as they were dragged through the cavern. Brazos wore night vision goggles and he was going at a blistering pace. They were ankle-deep in water and the tunnel grade went steeply downward. A storm raged above and water poured into the chamber. Brazos looked at the Tritium dial of his watch. The water was rising and it wasn't just from the storm. If it got too high before he reached the end of the tunnel, he'd have to make an escape through one of the manholes. Hopefully, it would cooperate and open. After a few hundred yards more, the water was up to his shins. Brazos had to get to the end quickly to make his next objective. Suddenly he stopped and cupped his hand over Rachel's mouth. Sound carried in this place. Cops were on his trail. Maybe a thousand yards. He should have lost them, but that damn chopper had spotted him. This chase had gone on long enough. He had to get the job done and get out. Next stop, the execution chamber.

The water had slowed McKenna and his team. The storm outside had abated, but the water kept rising. Half-way up his shins now. Could Brazos still be in the tunnel? How fast could two girls move in this?

McKenna couldn't help noticing the ease with which he fell into the role of hunter once again. It was like the chase reflex in big cats. Here he was again going through the bowels of the earth in pursuit of evil. He had lain awake at night thinking of this freakazoid and McKenna felt violated that Brazos could intrude on his sleep, follow him into the toilet, and walk with him to the store.

He grasped the synthetic stock of the weapon with his wet hands. It was hot as hell down here and getting hotter as they descended. The smell in the tunnel was more briny. He scooped up a handful of water and put it to his nose. Seawater. "Hold it. Anyone know what this tunnel drains into?"

"We're heading south and south is Jamaica Bay," said Sergeant Escobar.

"That's what I thought. High tide is coming in."

"Where are you taking us?" asked Rachel.

"Where you'll never be found," replied Brazos.

The water was up to Rachel's knees and she could feel the steep incline. How much deeper into this were they going? They would all drown.

Brazos' GPS lit up every three or four minutes like a lightening bug in the dark. In those moments of illumination, Brazos' countenance took on a green tinge and with the night-goggles, he appeared insect-like.

When was this ordeal going to end? How was it going to end? Did Olivia make it out? What a twist of fate that Olivia was replaced by her twin sister who had escaped one hell hole to arrive at another in the land of milk and honey. She could feel Achara starting to fade. At first, she was clinging to Rachel's elbow, but now Rachel's arms were taught between her and this killer.

Suddenly there was a faint light ahead. Yes, she could see it. The ground was steeper than ever; the water was now up to her thighs. They had reached the end.

"In," he commanded. The sky was above them and in front was the ocean. Rachel grabbed Achara's waist and they plunged into the cold water. "Keep your mouths shut from here on."

Brazos pulled them to shore. But the freedom of the open air wasn't going to last. The GPS snapped on and that meant they were going somewhere specific. There was nothing improvised here, Brazos knew what he was doing. Her destiny was in that little box.

Rachel was right. Within ten minutes, Brazos led them to a half-buried freight container. There was a rusted opening on its side and Brazos pushed them through it. A flashlight hurt Rachel's eyes, then revealed an entrance to what Rachel dreaded most—another tunnel.

"This thing's filling up," said the sergeant. "We've got to make a decision." The water was up to their thighs and rising. "There's a manhole cover up ahead. There won't be another one for hundreds of yards and the water may be over our heads before that."

McKenna wanted to go on, but he couldn't be reckless with their lives.

"Okay, let's try the manhole cover."

One man went up the ladder and struggled for five minutes. McKenna looked at his watch. Five minutes lost.

"This won't budge," said the guy above.

"There's another one three hundred yards back, but no guarantee that'll open either," said McKenna. "Let's go on for ten more minutes. If we don't reach the end, we abort." All agreed.

McKenna set a blistering pace. Five minutes later, the water was up to their waists and still rising. This tore him up. He wished he was alone, so he didn't have to be responsible for six guys drowning. If they had to abort now, could they even make it out before the water was over their heads? Now the water was chest-deep and he felt for bodies under his feet. No way a couple of five-foot-three girls made it through this.

"Hold it," said McKenna. The rain outside had stopped and there was only a trickling of water entering the tunnel. "Anyone see a light ahead or is it me?"

"Yeah, look at the water up ahead. It's lighter," said the sergeant.

"It might be the tunnel outfall, but it's totally submerged. Give me that rope." McKenna tied it around his waist. "Pay it out as I go. If I pull on it twice, reel me in. If I pull on it three times, I want one man to follow at a time."

McKenna put his goggles back in their waterproof case and took a deep breath. He'd have to swim underwater, find the exit, then take a chance and follow it to the surface.

He dove in with the Maglite flashlight. The seawater stung his eyes. Visibility, two feet. More tunnel, shit. But more light too. If the rope snagged on anything, he was dead. McKenna committed himself and kicked hard, thrusting forward. His lungs were bursting. More tunnel. He could barely see now. Forward. It was time to tug the rope twice or he'd die here. A few more feet and he'd tug. The light brightened just enough to tempt him to go on. His diaphragm was spasming as he kicked toward the light and broke the surface in Jamaica Bay.

He quickly tugged the rope three times before they decided to pull him back on their own. His feet touched the bottom and he made his way to shore quickly to provide resistance to the rope as the next man came up. The others would make it through in half the time with the rope to pull on.

He anchored himself against the shoreline and pulled the rope taught. Then, as if big-game fishing, he felt a huge tug at the end of the line. He counted the seconds and prayed for no screwups.

Santos surfaced first. Escobar was last. But no time to rest. Brazos' lead was extended.

They radioed for the K-9 unit and within ten minutes, they were back on Brazos' trail. The dogs alerted on Rachel's scent, not Brazos', so she was still alive. The trail led them to a half-buried shipping container. There was an opening on the side.

"That hole goes into the ground," said the sergeant. He lowered himself in and popped out three minutes later. "It's an old subway tunnel. We'll take the dogs. Bend those edges, so they don't get cut."

"Get with the MTA and see if they can email us a map of this tunnel," McKenna said into the radio.

He and the six-man SWAT team went in first, followed by the K-9 unit. The night-vision goggles went back on.

"Brazos didn't just find this tunnel by accident. He knows where he's going and this place could be booby-trapped," said McKenna. "Proceed accordingly."

It was part of the old Jamaica line from the look of it. How many of these places did Brazos have? The last one was a slaughterhouse. Was this some kind of a sick pied-a-terre? There were stairs leading to a lower level. McKenna's guess was that's where they went and the dogs agreed.

There was a fishing line running across the bottom of the stairs from railing to railing. McKenna signaled. One guy would have to stay behind and disarm it. After carrying the dogs over the tripwire, they got back on the trail which led to the edge of the platform.

"They're on the tracks. Watch out for the third rail. It could still be live," said McKenna.

A shot rang out, dropping Santos. The others scrambled to the maintenance recesses. They called in the 10-13. Santos was shot through the shoulder. "Get that damn thing disarmed before anyone else arrives," ordered McKenna.

The team advanced from one maintenance recess to the next. Santos was dropped in total darkness, which meant Brazos had night vision. One man down, two disarming a booby trap, and two carrying Santos back up—that was a bad exchange. That left McKenna, the sergeant, and two dog teams to go after Brazos.

This place was as near to total darkness as you can get, so the night vision goggles were just working off the built-in infrared and had a visibility of only a few feet. Brazos had to be using thermal goggles in order to see at that range.

His phone vibrated. McKenna jerked in reaction, then answered it. It was the email. Yeah, the old Jamaica line. Map, where's the map? See attachment. He counted the seconds while it downloaded. And there it was. Two levels. Bottom level extended between Canarsie and South Jamaica. They were heading east toward Jamaica. There was a platform about four hundred yards ahead. He glanced at the sergeant who was looking at the same email. The men signaled each other in the brief glow of the cell phone screens. Another shot rang out, missing. They couldn't return fire without the hostages in sight. They would just have to take it.

Brazos pulled Rachel and Achara up the platform and descended onto the tracks on the other side. Several hundred yards later, he pushed them into a utility room and shut the door. He snapped on a lantern to reveal another cache of supplies—shelves of ammo, a bullet-proof vest, tools, rope. Rachel glanced at the bulge in Achara's pant leg. It was still there. She hoped those rubber bands held; it was their last hope.

"Against the wall," he said. He put on the vest, then fired up a laptop. A dark image appeared on the screen with moving figures. As they advanced toward a red line on the screen, Brazos took out his cell phone. He hit a speed dial number and a huge explosion echoed through the tunnel. The figures were gone.

McKenna and Sergeant Escobar were a hundred feet away from the epicenter of the blast and were still blown back several yards. The dogs and the handlers took the worst of it. One dog and his handler died. At this point, McKenna didn't care what happened to him—he had to kill Brazos. His night-vision goggles didn't work.

"Your goggles okay?" he asked the other man.

"Yeah, still working."

"Good, give them to me. You head back. That's an order. Take the dog."

McKenna stumbled over the debris with only himself to worry about. His balance was wobbly and his ears would be ringing for a week. Was the explosion triggered by a tripwire? Motion detectors? There was no point in slowing down now. At the platform, he leapt up and scanned the area. Nothing. Then, on the ground, he saw a twenty dollar bill. It was wet, but looked like it had come right out of a teller's tray. Even smelled fresh. McKenna looked up and down the tracks. Ahead on the west-bound tracks there was another bill. It was fresh too. What did this mean? Was Brazos chumming the water? Did the girls have money on them? In Rachel's emails to Achara they talked about money to get over here.

His heart pounded at the thought that he was getting closer to his quarry. Now his attention was divided between the ground and any motion ahead. There was another bill on the floor and McKenna started counting the number of paces between bills. Just under two hundred, which for a small girl would be about two hundred even. He got to some kind of storage room. It was padlocked. He knocked. No answer. The tunnel grade was rising and there was much more light coming in from the upper level. The visibility was several hundred feet. The bills appeared with greater frequency, about every hundred feet. They *had* to be alive. McKenna increased his pace, not bothering to pick up the bills along the way. The tunnel bent to the right and when he made that turn, he saw three figures about two hundred yards up ahead. He knelt to take the shot.

McKenna let the crosshairs rest on Brazos' torso. The target moved and the crosshairs followed. McKenna focused on the beating of his heart.

Systolic, diastolic. The best shots are fired in the space between heartbeats. He waited. His finger tightened around the trigger.

He fired. He missed. Brazos responded by emptying a clip in his direction. Dammit, he should have taken the shot from the prone position. Now Brazos lined the girls up behind him as human shields. McKenna saw them mount the platform ahead and vanish from sight.

He was still stunned from the explosion and got vertigo when he rose to his feet. He closed the distance to the platform quickly, then slowed as this would be the perfect place for an ambush. As McKenna approached the platform, he hugged the wall, pointing his weapon at torso level. Advancing one step at a time, he could hear no shuffling up ahead, nothing. He listened for hard breathing. Brazos may be in good shape, but those girls weren't trained to hike like this. He ducked into a maintenance recess which gave good cover from the platform line of sight.

Above, he saw rusted truss work supporting the ceiling. About fifty feet diagonal to him was a package that looked out of place and out of time. McKenna scrambled to another recess that was on the opposite side from where he was.

An explosion ripped through the cavern, bringing down tons of concrete, collapsing the old truss work and sealing off the tunnel.

Brazos opened another utility room, this one much bigger than the last. When the lights came on, the place looked like the set of a cheap porn movie. A filthy mattress, chains on the walls, an axe, hacksaw, propane torch, ropes, leather masks. And video equipment. Brazos snapped on a spotlight, which blinded the girls after a night of darkness. He seemed agitated as if he was about to rush something that's normally prolonged. Rachel had briefly seen the figure on the laptop screen when Brazos set off the bomb. There had been only one person pursuing them and now he was gone. Her hopes were dashed. Achara shook and clung to her waist. Brazos lined up some implements on a table: propane torch, hand cuffs, gag, rope, and an axe. Rachel shivered along with Achara. This was the end.

He pointed several video cameras at them to record their terror.

"Take off your clothes."

Rachel stood between Brazos and Achara with her back to the killer and started to undress. She told Achara to do the same. Achara removed her shirt and bra, then undid her belt. Rachel aligned herself with Achara's left leg, keeping in mind Brazos' position behind her. When Achara pulled down her pants, Rachel dove forward and ripped the can of tire sealant off her calf. She pivoted, pointing the nozzle at Brazos' face, and shot the flammable green slime into his eyes. Brazos' hands came up, but Rachel lunged forward, keeping the spray going, and grabbed the propane torch with her right hand. She ignited the stream, turning the can into a flamethrower, engulfing Brazos in a column of fire.

Brazos slammed into the walls screaming, igniting the mattress. Rachel emptied the can on him, then went for the door, pulling Achara with her. The video cameras would record the flesh melting off Brazos' bones. It was an execution worthy of one of his own online murders.

EPILOGUE

Rachel finished putting on makeup and pulled on the new black jeans she had bought at TJ Maxx. She had to sit down for the next step. Her feet were still healing a month after getting forty-seven stitches, but she was determined to wear the new black high heels. Just in case she couldn't take it later, she packed her tennis shoes in her knapsack.

The strains of Bach's unaccompanied cello suite flowed in from the parlor. Olivia had deferred enrollment at Harvard for a semester and was spending the time home-schooling her new sister. For her part, Achara had started teaching Rachel and Olivia the rudiments of Thai.

Life had slowed down after Achara's arrival, and that was good. It gave Rachel a chance to reflect on her own passions and priorities. Chemistry was dropped and replaced with Romantic Poetry: Keats, Shelly, and Byron. It was one credit less, but so much more fulfilling.

She had read a great line from Byron last night:

Who would be free, themselves must strike the blow.

Not a bad motto to live your life by. She could lose herself in the music of the verses, in the power of words that she suspected was almost as great as the power of love. She hoped that if she ever fell in love, that it wouldn't eclipse the poetry, but she wasn't sure that it wouldn't.

After the ordeal, Rachel had embraced Joules in a spontaneous moment and her lips fell on his cheek in the hope that he would kiss her. He patted her on the back, which body language experts say is a bad sign. Her hopes were dashed.

The shoes were on and she stood up like a new-born colt. She took a few tentative steps up and down the room. Now she tried doing it with grace. That took a little more acting.

A final check of her email before leaving. She and Detective McKenna had kept in touch. He said he was going to retire this year. The maintenance recess had saved him, but his hearing was gone in one ear. His last update stated that they had arrested two-hundred and fifty-nine subscribers to Brazos' child porn site. But there was little hope of getting to the twisted souls who paid fortunes to see the slaughter of young girls. Rachel had tried to imagine what they looked like, those men. But they probably had ordinary faces and went home to their families every night.

She had become paranoid about her laptop being raided again, so Joules had come over and installed a fortress of security measures. As he was explaining what each component did, she became lost in his voice and couldn't help thinking that his heart had all these measures installed, too, so no one could get to it.

"But for every measure, there's a countermeasure," he said. She made special note of that. She had expected him to bolt as soon as the software was installed and duly explained, but he lingered. He wore jeans, sneakers, a sweatshirt, and that bushel of blond hair. They were in her bedroom and her parents were out. She wondered for a nano-second how he would react if she closed the door, but she might lose him forever. How she wished that he would step into that other world where he would be jocular, sensual, and free of whatever held him back. She knew she was attractive and God only knew how she was awed by his brilliant mind, his detachment which ascetics struggle for in mountain caves and that face that grew more chiseled and handsome with every year. She had remembered his predilection for lemonade from when they were children and had made some in advance. She excused herself and fetched two tall glasses. She feared he would leave after finishing it, but the discussion extended into the afternoon.

Rachel closed her email and gave herself a mental command to banish all negative thoughts, at least for tonight.

She stood at the parlor entrance listening to Olivia on cello. The Bach prelude was lonely, dark, and so beautiful, the more so as it came from someone who had been immersed in ugliness. Achara sat opposite her, wearing dog paw slippers and her favorite clothes—flannel pajamas.

"How's your student doing?" Rachel asked Olivia.

"Brilliant." In the corner of the room was the vihara with three candles burning, which meant that Pra Prom now resided there as well.

"What are you dolled up for?" asked Olivia.

"Joules is taking me to Cooper Union tonight. Michio Kaku is giving a lecture. He's a physicist."

"Lecture on what?"

"The Heisenberg Uncertainty Principle—it's not dinner at the Stork Club, but I'll take it."

Olivia smiled. "Uncertainty Principle, eh? Sounds like a sure thing to me, kid."

ACKNOWLEDGEMENTS

I would like to express my gratitude to the many people who saw me through this book.

In particular, Diane O'Connell, a great writing coach, and most especially, my wonderful agent, Stacey Donaghy, the hardest working agent on the planet.

It's been a long, great journey.

ABOUT THE AUTHOR

Gustavo Florentin was born in Queens, New York and received a bachelor's degree in electrical engineering from the Polytechnic University of New York. He spent a decade in the defense industry working on the F-14 Fighter jet and classified electronics projects.

After the fall of the Soviet Union, many thought America wouldn't need weapons anymore, so while others waited for the peace dividend, he moved on to the financial sector where he is currently a network engineer. His passions include violin, travel to exotic places and exploring worldwide conspiracies. He lives in New Jersey where he is working on his third novel.

His thriller, In the Talons of the Condor, won the following awards:

- WUACADEMIA—Prix d'Or Best Novel

- The Verb First Chapter Contest--First Prize

- Mount Arrowsmith Best Novel 4th place

- The Writing Show—Second Prize Best First Chapter of a Novel.

- Second Place—16th Annual International Latino Book Awards

THANK YOU FOR READING

Please visit http://curiosityquills.com/reader-survey to
share your reading experience with the author of this book!

Charming, by Krystal Wade

Sixteen-year-old Haley Tremaine had it all: top-notch school, fantastic family, and a bright future. All of that changed when an accident tore her family apart. Now, an alcoholic father, a bitter younger sister, and a cold headstone bearing her mother's name are all she has left.

Chris Charming has it all: a powerful CEO father, a prestigious school, a fortune at his fingertips. But none of that matters when he lands a reputation as a troublemaker. Struggling to follow in his father's footsteps, he reaches out to the one person he believes truly sees him: Haley.

And someone's determined to bring the two together, even if it means murder.

Blow Up the Roses, by Randy Attwood

How much pain, horror and anguish can one culd'sac endure? Why is so much murder, mystery and sexual brutality condensed among the few duplex homes built so close together on the Elm Street culd'sac?

The answers lie within the language of flowers; and the language of flowers can be brutally frank. They can also save your life.

Blow up the Roses is, in part, a plea of warning that we protect those we love from those we cannot understand and that we understand better those we love.

Murder, Madness & Love by Yolanda Renée

Detective Steven Quaid is the Anchorage Police Department's top investigator. When he's called in to protect a beautiful widow from a stalker, he's not entirely sure she isn't behind the scheme herself. Before long, Sarah has him wound up tighter than barbed wire.

But one of the police department's best and brightest detectives may just be in over his head, especially when the facts start pointing to a conclusion he isn't willing to face. With a killer on the loose and a climbing body count, Steven can't afford to hedge his bets—or his life.

Is Sarah a victim or a very skilled manipulator?

Negative Space, by Mike Robinson

Los Angeles-based surrealist painter Max Higgins collects photos of missing people and incorporates them into his canvases. The practice stems, in part, from the disappearance of his father. Then, someone recognizes a face in one of his paintings, sweeping Max into an excursion involving a paranormal investigator and a young, troubled woman who may be his half-sister. Together, they seek the truth of Max's father, a journey that proves to be as surreal as anything from Max's paintbrush.

Family Cursemas, by Rod Kierkegaard, Jr.

When the wealthy Goodman family assembles for its gloomy annual holiday reunion in their divorced mother's crumbling mansion, Holly Singletary is pressed into service to help cater the Christmas Eve dinner. When "the storm of the century" hits, the attendees have more than a blackout to worry about. Someone—or something—is killing off the Goodman family one by one.

Only Holly can solve the mystery of the murderer's identity before her first-grade sweetheart becomes the final victim…

The Strong Brain, by Nathan L. Yocum

Simon Craig is many things… psychic, alcoholic, drug addict, unlicensed private detective, frequenter of nut houses and rehabs in equal measure. The voices in Simon's head reveal everything, whether he wants them to know or not.

When a crooked detective hires Simon to retrieve the runaway daughter of local crime lord, all seems routine. That is until a psychic maniac takes notice and wages a battle of wills against the unruly Mr. Craig.

Who will survive when powerful psychics clash?

CPSIA information can be obtained at www.ICGtesting.com
Printed in the USA
BVOW08s1502120815

413077BV00004B/57/P